The Case of the Screaming Skull

Witch Haven Cozy Mystery - book 10

K.E. O'Connor

K.E. O'Connor Books

Preface

The Witch Haven series has been created so you spend time with four amazing witches:

Books 1-3 tell Indigo's story: Spells and Spooks, Hexes and Haunts, Curses and Corpses

Books 4-6 tell Luna's story: Muffins and Moonlight, Cupcakes and Cauldrons, Pancakes and Potions

Books 7-9 tell Odessa's story: Hauntings and High Jinx, Hauntings and Havoc, Hauntings and Hoaxes

Books 10-12 tell Storm's story: The Case of the Screaming Skull, The Case of the Poisoned Pumpkin, The Case of the Cursed Candy

And there are two bonus origin stories to enjoy: **Fire Fang** and **Silvaria**

Chapter 1

"It stinks like unwashed armpits and despair around here." I stepped over a pile of what looked like rotting cabbages left on the chipped, pothole strewn road.

Fire Fang took a sniff of the mound of oozing grossness. He whined and backed away on his enormous hellhound paws, his long nails clipping against the ground.

"I feel sorry for you, buddy. It can't be fun having such a sensitive nose and being surrounded by this."

We were in Bog Valley. It was as grim as the name suggested. Fog swirled around us, a constant damp unwelcome cape of nastiness, drenching my clothes and sticking my hair to my face.

When we'd left Witch Haven yesterday, it had been cold, but nothing like this foggy, smoke-ridden nightmare of negativity. The toxic swirl of vibrations that choked Bog Valley had worked deep into my bones until they felt full of ice. Crunchy, jagged ice. Not the fun kind that goes into a slushie.

With my hands stuffed deep in the pockets of my thick coat, I continued along the trash strewn road. We'd been here for three hours and hadn't seen another soul. Don't get me wrong. There were other things here, but from the vibe I got, they were inhuman and unfriendly. They chittered static laughter, grumbled threats in the depths of their throats from the shadows, and scraped claws against brick.

I stopped as something concealed in a nearby lump of darkness shuffled its feet. Or maybe it was a tail.

Fire Fang growled softly and lifted his nose, inhaling deeply. His coal-black eyes, rimmed with red, narrowed. He headed fearlessly to the source of the noise.

The lumpen shadow faded as we neared, leaving behind a waft of decay and a faint laugh. Bog Valley sucked.

We continued along the road, passing abandoned stores with blocked up windows and doors hanging open like gaping mouths. 'Come inside,' they whispered, 'and we'll drag out your deepest fears and sell them to you for double their value.'

Bog Valley was the place you visited when hope was lost. Everything was tinged with gray, and it only accepted those who'd given up on life and planned to live out their days surrounded by destruction and madness.

"Why would Eden visit this place?" I said, more to myself than Fire Fang. It was the question that ran through my mind ever since I'd received the last concrete lead on where my younger sister had disappeared. "She has so much to live for. Something has dragged her here against her will."

Fire Fang nudged me with his enormous head, a move he made when he wanted my attention. On all paws, he was a giant of a hellhound, coming up past my hip, and I wasn't short. But he swelled to twice that size when angry. It was awesomely impressive. My temporary, furry lodger came with interesting abilities no hellhound should have.

"You got something?" I whispered.

He nudged me again, but didn't lead me in any direction. Maybe the funky vibe was freaking him out.

Someone could have brought Eden here to trade her. She hadn't been fully in her witch powers when taken, so her magic could have become twisted. She may even be using dark spells without realizing it was wrong. Dark magic was powerful, and a pliable dark witch was something many would pay a lot of money for.

Her persistent missing status lodged in my gut like a blunt, twisted blade. It sat there, turning now and again to stir up the pain. The one job my parents had expected of me was to keep Eden safe. And I'd messed that up.

Fire Fang whined softly. He was often quick to pick up on my mood shifts. And when I slipped into an Eden funk, he was ready for it, offering head bumps and a warm body to hug when no one was looking.

The unsatisfactory open ending about who took Eden from her bed and left no clues behind always slid my mood into sour patch when I dwelled on it. And I was an epic dweller. But no matter how long it took, I wouldn't give up looking for her.

A rank sulfuric stink slammed into my face. It was no surprise to smell demons in Bog Valley. It must be on their top ten destination list to visit. The despair and hopelessness would give them an energy boost. Misery loved company.

Whichever demon had belched in my face wasn't brave enough to show itself, and the scent faded.

I pulled out my wallet and flipped it open to look at the faded, crumpled picture I kept with me. Eden and I looked alike, with the same pale skin, blue eyes, and dark hair, but I always thought she was way cuter and smiled more than me. That wasn't hard.

Fire Fang loped over to a burned out, abandoned hotdog cart and nosed around it.

I tucked away the photo and followed him. "There won't be anything edible in there. You're wasting your time."

He kept nosing about, while I stood still for a moment, absorbing the atmosphere and attempting to get a fix on Eden's location. I didn't want this to be another wild ghost chase, but my hope faded like an over-watered orchid, black traces of rot creeping up the delicate stem of my optimism.

I wasn't giving up. There'd been two separate sightings of her in this area.

Eden had always been the good child and our parents' favorite. Did I mind that? You bet I did. It stank worse than that demon burp. My dad said Eden had read the 'How To Be a Good Baby Book' when she was in the womb, because she did everything she should. She fed when she was supposed to, slept through the night almost straight away, and hit the markers of when to smile, say her first word, and take a first step. Eden was the golden child.

And for a time, I'd hated her. It hadn't helped our parents spoiled her. They let her pursue every hobby and interest and bought her all the expensive equipment to go along with those hobbies. But as we'd gotten older, we'd become friends. Rather than shoving her away, I'd protected her.

My parents told me I had to keep my little sister safe. And I tried. But one night, one horrible, dark, scary night, Eden was lost to us. It was etched into my brain. The silence, the empty bed, the empty look in my parents' eyes as they were forced to admit their special daughter was gone.

One night changed everything. My parents withered. Eden's disappearance destroyed them, and they were dead within the year. Hearts broken, lives shattered, love gone.

Fire Fang wagged his tail and pulled his head out of the hotdog cart. I wrinkled my nose when I saw he was chewing something.

"You'd better not get sick on the way home. I'm only renting that car, and I don't want to lose the deposit because I got hellhound puke on the seats. That smell does not come out."

He swallowed whatever gross thing he was eating. His wagging tail froze, and his eyes glowed as his hackles raised. It was a sign we weren't alone. What dark and unfriendly thing was skulking out of the shadows?

I crouched and turned slowly on my heels, seeking the source of Fire Fang's grumbling attention.

Purple glowing eyes peered at me from an alleyway. They blinked once, twice, three times before vanishing.

It was the first sign of life I'd seen since we'd gotten here, and I wasn't letting it go. I marched to the alleyway, flicking on my torch, and peered along it.

"Hey, witch. Check your twelve o'clock."

My head lifted at the sound of the voice above me. The demon was small, maybe three-foot tall. Gray and green scales covered its body, and it used its claws to cling to the brickwork.

Fire Fang slid to my side, his tail brushing my arm in a sign of support. His claws glistened in the light as smoke floated from his nostrils.

The demon skittered farther away. "Don't set your hound on me. I come in peace. I'm just a messenger."

"What message have you got for me?"

"I can only tell you if you're the right witch. State your purpose."

Demons. Always so nosy. "I'm looking for someone."

"A friend? A date? This isn't the place to visit unless you're looking for trouble." The demon's small, forked tongue flickered from between sharp teeth.

"I'm not afraid of trouble. I'm looking for a girl. Well, a young woman. She looks like me, just a few years younger."

A chittering sound of excitement echoed from the demon. "Another witch?"

I nodded. "Someone would have brought her here. She wouldn't be here willingly."

"You'd be surprised. More magic users arrive at Bog Valley than you'd expect. Magic doesn't bring a happy ending to all."

"I'm not looking for happy. I just want Eden."

"Eden." The demon stretched out the name. "Perhaps the one you seek came here herself."

"Eden would never come to a dump like this."

The demon hissed. "It's my home. A pretty dump. A place for fun."

"Not my kind of fun. And not Eden's. Have you seen anyone who looks like me in Bog Valley?"

"I must touch your heart."

Fire Fang was instantly in front of me, his teeth bared as he snapped at the demon.

The demon slithered higher up the bricks and hissed a warning. "Not to eat. Never eat a witch's heart. To know of your true intentions, I must touch."

"You're a Shuro demon."

"I am. It's how we know intent and whether we have an enemy before us. What kind of witch are you? Black, white, a muddy gray?"

"One you don't want to mess with."

"Your name, witch, or I won't help. Remember, I bring a message. Perhaps about your missing witch."

This demon couldn't do me harm if I gave it my name. Demons loved to gather knowledge, and this was a small trade if it gave me anything useful about Eden.

"I'm Storm Winter."

"And the witch you seek is family? A sister?"

I nodded.

It scratched its claws over its scales as if scoring that information into the tough skin. "And now your heart. To know your truth. Then I will give you the information."

My pulse increased, not from fear of being touched by this demon, but because it knew where my sister was.

I beckoned the demon closer. "Any odd moves, and Fire Fang eats you. Then he spits out your bones and burns them. He'll keep the ash and use it in spells. Twisted ones that have your essence screaming for mercy. Got it?"

The demon hissed at Fire Fang, who was still growling. "Got it."

I rested a hand on Fire Fang's enormous, coarse-furred head, and his growling subsided.

The demon inched nearer, flexing the three claws on the ends of its fingers. It stretched out a bony, scaled arm and rested its hand over my heart.

A flood of jagged heat hit me, but it was gone just as quickly.

"Yes," the demon hissed. "You speak the truth. You seek those who are missing. You are a protector. A powerful one."

"Tell me about Eden. You've seen her here, haven't you?"

"Such impatience. You've been searching for many years. A few more minutes will do you no harm."

"They'll do you harm," I growled out. "Have you seen Eden Winter, or are you wasting my time? If it's the last option, you'll hate the outcome."

"She is here. I will take you to her last known location."

"What do you want in return?" Demons did nothing for free. It was easier to pay them off or give them some gross little treat they coveted. Or food. Many demons adored junk food.

"Payment. In silver."

It was a typical demon request. Their favorite currency was usually silver. Some hoarded it. Others made it into weapons. Some just kept it as trinkets.

I reached into the pouch strapped to my utility belt and pulled out a single silver coin, which I held so the light from my torch glinted off it. "You'll get this when you take me to where you last saw Eden."

Teeth clacked together in a gruesome applause. "Hurry, hurry! She's not far. This way. Follow, follow!" The demon scuttled along the brickwork and around the corner, out of sight.

Fire Fang blocked my way and growled. He swung his head from side to side.

"Relax. Following demons is never risk free, but we need to check this out. No lead can be ignored."

Fire Fang's growl turned into a whimper. He stuck one huge paw on my chest and pinned me to the wall.

I let out a sigh and forced his paw off my chest. "I get it. It's cold, we're hungry, and I've dragged you on dozens of futile searches. But this could be the one."

He growled again, and a series of odd sounding grunts came out of his nose.

"I wish I could understand you. We really need to get you talking."

Fire Fang grunted again before following me out of the alleyway in the direction the demon had scuttled. Fire Fang was an incredible hellhound, but he wasn't mine. He was a foster until I found him a home. That meant we had a communication barrier. When a familiar bonded with a witch, they forged a link to enable them to talk to each other. Despite trying dozens of spells to open a channel without forming a permanent bond, nothing got Fire Fang talking. That meant I was left deciphering his growls, grunts, and grumbles.

"Hurry, hurry," came the hissy whispered voice of the demon in the distance.

I picked up the pace, despite tiredness making my feet feel like I'd slid them into leaded boots. But as I always told my friends, I'd sleep when I was dead. Why should I get an easy ride when Eden was missing?

Fire Fang's growling grew worse, as did the grunting and nudges with his head. And those nudges weren't gentle. He was a beast of a dog and played rough.

"Quit distracting me. We'll know soon enough if this demon is telling the truth. If it isn't, you'll get to have your fun."

"Always truth. Always right," came the demon's voice overhead. "This way. Keep going. Almost there. Almost to Eden. Almost back to happy."

The road curved around, and as it straightened out, I came face-to-face with six demons lined up in front of me.

I was more tired than I'd realized, or losing my edge, to get caught out like this.

The attack came at once. I dodged a shower of demon goo, knowing if that stuff got on my skin, it would be like bathing in acid. Acid that made you stink like ripe diapers.

Fire Fang flew fearlessly through the air and brought down two demons.

That left me with four, and they were nothing like the treacherous scaled jerk who'd lied to me and brought me into their path. These guys were over seven feet tall, fangs dripping with something gross and slimy, and their jagged teeth on display.

"I have not got time for this." I swiped my hand in a large triangle shape and cut through it with a jagged W. Lightning blasted from the sky and slammed into two demons. One turned to dust, while the other howled and collapsed to the ground, engulfed in fire.

I set my sights on the final two demons, a smirk crossing my face. "What will it be? More lightning, or shall I conjure a tornado to whip your scaled behinds?"

A howl of distress cut into my heart, and my gaze shot to Fire Fang. More demons had arrived. They were hoisting him in the air by his legs as he was muzzled. How did they get him down so quickly?

More of my lightning magic slammed into the pack of snarling, slashing demons. They bounced away, and Fire Fang was free.

But my distraction cost me. A blast of pain slammed into my right arm and knocked me down. Something hot and stinging slapped against my skin, and my vision blurred as the burn of demon goo took hold.

Another pained howl came from Fire Fang. By the time I'd cleared the goo from my eyes, a dozen salivating scaled nightmares had surrounded us.

Magic flickered on my palms, and thunder rumbled across the sky. I wasn't going down without taking as many of these jerks with me as I could. If I had to pin them with my teeth and tear them apart piece by piece, they were going to die horribly.

"Whatever you do, don't look. Keep your eyes closed."

I had no idea who'd just shouted or what they were planning, but since I couldn't see clearly anyway, I shut my eyes for a second.

An ear-piercing scream filled the night. The sound made my brain shake.

Everything went dark.

Chapter 2

A hot, heavy presence that smelled of damp fur and spicy sweat was the first thing I noticed as I regained consciousness.

A familiar rumbling growl reassured me it was Fire Fang sitting on top of me and not some demon.

I dug my fingers into his fur, scratching against his warm skin to let him know I was awake. He shifted a few inches so I could squirm upright, but that was as far as he was moving.

As I filtered sounds and smells into my consciousness, I realized it wasn't just me moving. Whatever I was in was cruising along smoothly, the suspension feeling like the gentle sway of a ship.

"I'd offer to help, but I value my limbs. And that creature protecting you would shred me apart if I made a wrong move." I couldn't see who was speaking, thanks to Fire Fang blocking my view, but the voice was male, low, calm, and had a thread of amusement running through it.

I peered around Fire Fang. Sitting on the other side of the car, well, I say car, but from the size of the thing, I had to be inside a limousine, was a distinguished-looking man. He wore a smart suit and polished shoes. From the lines on his face, I aged him in his mid-sixties. But he was a well-preserved guy. When our eyes met, he remained still, his gaze appraising me almost clinically.

I nudged Fire Fang to my left a few inches, so I could see the guy without leaning and get one leg free. "Who are you? And where are we?"

"You could say I'm your savior. You were having trouble with those demons back there."

"We were handling it."

"The shroud of demon goo you wear suggests otherwise. That's got to sting. I have water in the car if you want to wash it off." The guy still sounded amused, and his voice was also familiar.

"Have we met before?"

"No, but I've been trying to reach you for days. You're a difficult witch to connect with."

"I don't like people bothering me."

"Apparently not. I visited your business, but it was only when I asked around in Witch Haven that I learned where you were. What unpleasantness brought you to Bog Valley?"

"The kind of unpleasantness that's none of your business. You still haven't told me who you are." I held out a hand for the water. As my senses clicked into place, I realized how badly my skin was burning.

He leaned forward but stopped as Fire Fang growled a threat, rumbling it deep in his chest so it vibrated through the floor of the limousine.

"Move slowly and throw the bottle," I said. "That way, you might not get bitten."

The guy followed my orders and tossed me a large bottle and a soft towel. "You have an effective beast working with you."

"Fire Fang protects the people he likes, so you'd better watch yourself." I poured water into the towel and scrubbed it over my face and arms until the stinging lessened. "What's your deal? It sounds like you've been stalking me."

"Not stalking, but I've left you a dozen messages. You haven't replied to a single one. That called for direct action. I don't like to be told no or ignored."

I pointed a finger at him. "I knew I recognized your voice. Lucian something or other, isn't it?"

"Lucian Barkridge, at your service. Although I'm hoping you'll be at mine."

I sat back in the seat as I glugged down water and then poured some for Fire Fang to drink, leaving a puddle on the floor of the limousine. "You're hassling me because I won't take a job?"

"I need the best to work for me. You're the best in the business. Your detective work is unparalleled, if unethical."

"I'm flattered, but I'm also busy, so it's still a no. What screamed before I passed out?"

"If you'll allow me to explain the job, you'll understand everything." Lucian rested a hand on a box beside him. A white and black ring on his little finger glinted in the interior lights of the car.

"I'm listening, but I'm still not taking the work. I don't need the hassle. You'd be hassle."

His lips pursed for a second before his face fell back into impassive calm. "In the messages I left, I explained an old friend had been murdered."

I ticked back through my memories. "Delano, wasn't it?"

"Delano Discord. You do listen to your messages."

"All of them. I just don't respond to most of them."

"Why not?"

"Because I have other priorities." My gaze shifted to the tinted window. "You can drop us off here."

"Allow me five minutes."

"You have one. Then we're getting out whether or not you want us to."

"Delano was my oldest friend. I worked for him for years."

I gestured for him to continue.

"I'm the family legal adviser."

"And a witch stalker," I said.

"Delano paid me well. It meant I go above and beyond the typical duties of legal advice to ensure he thrived, as did his business and his family. It was a successful partnership. I've lost a true friend." A shiver of emotion crossed Lucian's face. Then it was gone.

The designer clothes he wore revealed just how richly he'd been rewarded for being a yes-man to Delano. "That still doesn't explain what screamed."

"I can't risk showing it to you. But inside this box is the murder weapon that killed my friend."

Despite my determination not to take this case, I leaned forward, squashing Fire Fang, who still guarded me like the last burger on the barbecue.

Lucian tapped the box. "It's a screaming skull. And it carries a curse. Whoever sees the skull when it screams has seven days to live. Once the time is up, they stop breathing."

I stared at the box. I'd heard about cursed objects, but never a skull. "You took a risk back there. If Fire Fang or me saw the skull when you let her rip, that would have been a death sentence."

Fire Fang grumbled his disapproval.

"I had no choice. I was following you, with a plan to persuade you to investigate who killed Delano. Before I approached you, you got ambushed. I'm a warlock, so I have magic, but I don't use it every day. It was take the risk and let the skull out or watch you die. The skull scared off the demons."

"We wouldn't have been killed by those demons. I was playing with them."

Fire Fang whined and tilted his head as he looked at me.

"You keep quiet." My attention returned to the box. "I know the name Delano Discord or, more accurately, I know of his family. They're new magic, aren't they?"

"They have several hundred years of magical ancestry behind them. They made their money recently and then formed powerful alliances to strengthen their position in our community."

I nodded along as Lucian spoke. "I'm not interested in his history."

"So why ask about the Discord legacy?"

"Someone as high-profile as that being killed would have come to the attention of the Magic Council. Why don't you work with them to solve who murdered Delano?"

"They're involved, but their methods are slow, and they have too many rules to follow. The first two deaths—"

"First two deaths? Who else has died because of this skull?"

Lucian rubbed his hands together slowly, as if shedding a film of skin from his palms. "It took time to realize the connection with the skull, the screaming, and then the deaths."

That sounded like an excuse. "Who died?"

"Two servants who worked for Delano were exposed to the skull. Of course, they didn't die straightaway, and this skull has a habit of disappearing, so we missed the connection."

"Someone tested the skull on Delano's servants before they used it on him?" I said.

"It's hard to know, but it seems that way. Perhaps whoever wanted to kill Delano made a mistake. They placed the skull in a location where they thought he would be, but someone else discovered it. When the first servant died, Sam, we thought it was bad luck. He was old and on his way to retirement. But then Suzanne died. She was young and healthy. Then we made a connection to the scream and the skull seen by them both."

"Why have you got the skull if it's so dangerous?"

"It safe in this box. There's a protective ward around it. I planned to store it somewhere before it vanished again."

"Why are you able to carry it around? Have you got a connection to it?"

"Yes, but not the one you think."

"How do you know what I'm thinking?"

A humorless smile appeared on his face. "That I killed my best friend."

"You got me. Did you?"

"No. My connection is unfortunate. I trapped the skull after it screamed at Delano."

"You're that powerful, you can control a cursed skull?"

"Not powerful. Lucky. We'd discussed the deaths of the servants and the appearance of the skull several times, but Delano was uncertain there was a link. I was convinced the skull was the reason the deaths had occurred."

"How did you get this lucky break?"

"I'd been researching binding spells to capture the skull if it should appear again. I was at the house the night the skull screamed at Delano. The second I heard it, I raced toward the noise with a spell primed."

"Was that selfless or stupid? If you'd seen the skull while it was screaming, you'd also be dead."

He didn't flinch. "I'm not stupid. By the time I saw it, it had stopped screaming, so I lunged. I grabbed it and contained it in magic until we could get it in this box."

"And then you kept it?"

"As evidence. And to assist you."

"I'm not working for you."

Lucian's gaze remained steady. "By then, it was too late. My oldest friend had been cursed."

"That's bad news. I still can't help."

"We did everything we could. We contacted every mystic or powerful magic user to see if they could undo the curse, but nothing worked. Delano died. And his killer is still free." Lucian spoke as if he hadn't heard me. Was it arrogance or him being thick-headed? I'd yet to decide.

"Some cases never get solved."

"This isn't one of them. I must find his murderer."

"Then keep looking for someone who'll help you. Just don't look in my direction."

"I must know who did this. I need to honor my friend. He helped me so much. And he left behind a family. They're devastated by his loss."

"While I appreciate that, I'm not taking the job. I've got a full caseload and my own things to deal with. There's no room for more drama."

"This isn't drama. A man lost his life."

"Three people died. Or don't the servants count?"

"They do. Of course." His gaze didn't flicker. Everything about Lucian was consistent and measured. Typical legal type. "How much?"

"How much what?"

"Money is not a limiting factor for this family. They'll pay whatever you ask, so long as you find out what happened to Delano."

"How does a billion sound?"

"You're being ridiculous. Although that would be possible."

I hesitated for a second before shaking my head. "I don't need your money, and I don't want this case. A cursed skull is a danger I don't need near me. And you shouldn't have it sitting in a box beside you like a gift for a nephew. Unless you hate that nephew."

"If not money, there must be things you need. A new apartment, perhaps?"

"The one I have is perfect."

"Then experiences. The family has homes all over the world. You could travel, stay in luxury, or make use of the best hotels. Everything would be paid for. You just have to ask."

"That's not of interest either. Besides, few places accept a hellhound as a travelling companion. And we go everywhere together." I rested a hand on Fire Fang's back.

"Anything is possible when you have influence over people," Lucian said. "There must be something. Everyone I spoke to recommended you. I need you to work this case."

"Of course they did. I'm great at what I do."

"I need the best working on this. You are the best."

"You have the skull contained. Hand it to the Magic Council and let them deal with things. Eventually, they'll figure out who did it."

"That's not good enough."

"It'll have to be."

Lucian sat forward in his seat. "I saved you from those demons. You owe me."

"I didn't ask for that save, although I appreciate it. The answer is still no."

His forehead crinkled for a second before smoothing out. "Is there nothing I can offer to convince you to take this job?"

"There isn't. This has been a waste of your time. And mine. Now, take me back to Bog Valley. I need to pick up my car. It's been a long, gross day. I'm tired and my patience just snapped."

With a grim-set expression on his face, Lucian tapped the partition separating us from the driver. "Back to Bog Valley."

The limousine turned smoothly.

I shifted in my seat until I could get out from under Fire Fang. "I can give you a list of contacts, people who'll consider the job. They're good. Almost as good as I am. I send them work I turn down."

Lucian's nod was curt. "We have to know who controls this skull and why they used it to kill Delano."

"Sure. And I'm sorry about your friend. It's not fun to lose someone you care about."

"But not sorry enough to figure out who killed him?"

"Afraid not."

The rest of the journey continued in silence. I kept glancing at the box containing the skull. I was curious about it, and if I hadn't been busy tracking leads on Eden and dealing with existing clients, I may have taken the job. But I knew when to draw the line. If you took on too many complications, something broke. And I was broken enough.

The limousine rolled to a stop. I slid across the seat and opened the door.

Lucian handed me a small card with his contact details on. "If you change your mind, get in touch. As I said, money is no object. Anything you want, it's yours."

I tucked the card into my back pocket. "I hope you get this figured out."

Fire Fang climbed out, but not before doing a full body shake, sending demon goo and fur flying.

I stood with him by the side of the road as the limousine left before turning and looking at the dank, foggy expanse of Bog Valley looming behind us. The lead on Eden had led me nowhere. All I'd gotten from this day was burned skin, dirty clothes, and a near miss with a cursed skull.

"Come on, Fire Fang. Let's go home and eat our body weights in potato chips."

Chapter 3

"Is she still out there?" I lifted my head from the couch, where I'd been lounging since I got back from Bog Valley, ruminating over the wasted hours and trying to convince myself I didn't still stink of demon.

Fire Fang had loped to the window and was peering out.

"Careful! If she sees you, she'll howl again." I picked up the bottle of skin soothing lotion and dabbed more onto the sore spots where the demon goo had burned me. I could use a healing spell, but I was exhausted, and my magic well depleted. Weather magic took its toll.

Fire Fang made a show of peeking over the edge of the windowsill and ducking back quickly.

"Well? Is the cat still there?" When we'd gotten back, the annoying stray who haunted my life had appeared and howled and yowled, even after I'd tossed out kitty treats.

He nodded as he headed back to the couch and flopped beside it.

"She'll have to leave soon. I need to go grocery shopping and don't want her jumping out and trying to get inside. I'm starving, and the cupboards are bare. We need our freedom to go find food."

Fire Fang looked pointedly at his empty food bowl that sat on the floor in the kitchen of my open-plan apartment.

"The last time I went for food, that cat got in. I don't know how she does it. She's full of annoying magic tricks."

Fire Fang's head shot up, and he growled. It was a happy growl, if that made sense. I'd gotten used to his almost permanent state of growling, but the growls had different tones. This one emerged when there was someone coming to the door he didn't hate.

I set down the bottle of lotion and headed to the door. Pulling it open, I found Odessa Grimsbane, Luna Brimstone, and Indigo Ash standing outside, carrying brown paper bags.

Odessa lowered the hand she had raised to knock, her smile sunny. "I should have known your early warning system would tell you we were here. We brought dinner."

"Great. Did we have a night in planned?"

"No! But you've been missing, so we're forcing you to be sociable. I got the dessert." Luna waved a bag in front of my face.

"You're a mind reader. I was just wondering what to eat."

"Empty cupboards again?"

"Kind of."

Indigo marched in, and the others followed. "Too distracted to food shop?"

"I've just been—"

"Busy." Luna finished the sentence for me. "You're always busy. What is it this time? Lost dog? Cheating husband? Someone stolen the family jewels?"

"All the above if you want to look through my caseload." I followed the delicious scent of garlic bread into the kitchen, my stomach growling in appreciation at the food it was soon to receive.

"You need a proper break," Odessa said. "I'll forget what you look like if you don't spend more time with us."

"Soon. I'll get a break soon." When I didn't have Eden to find and twelve cases to wrap up.

I peeked into the box Indigo had pulled out of a bag, and a huge cheese covered pizza greeted me. I went to take a piece, but Odessa slapped my hand away.

"Get plates. We also need something to drink. And napkins."

"Isn't that what pizza boxes are for? You're supposed to eat out of them." I tried to grab a slice but got another slap.

"Plates, napkins, drinks." Odessa tilted her head. "And don't tell me you're eating off paper plates again."

"I have plates. A couple, at least. They're not clean, though." I'd meant to run the dishwasher days ago, but it had slipped my mind.

Luna groaned. "How many years have you lived here?"

"A few. I have the essentials." I glanced at the cardboard box that doubled as a side table beside my couch. It did the job and had cost me nothing.

"Out you come, you four." Luna opened a huge purse she'd slung over her shoulder. Three furry cats' heads poked out. Nugget, Tuffin, and Earl, my friends' familiars, hopped out and stretched.

A small black spider, Hilda, scurried out next.

"You spoil them," Indigo said.

"I love them." Luna grinned as she set down her purse. "But they are heavy. Nugget has a little gut."

"I heard that," Nugget said. "And it's not a gut. I'm on a bulk. Underneath, I'm all lean muscle."

"Where's Russell?" I asked.

"Open the window," Indigo said. "He flew because he didn't want to get squashed by the fluffies."

"Or eaten," Luna said.

Fire Fang obliged and opened the window for the beautiful crow, who appeared a second later. He was still growling, but wagged his tail as the familiars strutted around the apartment like they owned the place. He kept sniffing them, getting a boop on the nose as a reminder not to get too close and not to shove his muzzle where it didn't belong.

Once the food and drinks were sorted and we'd settled around my pallet table, Indigo pulled out a vial from her pocket and placed it down. "Not only did we bring food, but we also have a spell."

"What's it for?" I said.

"We're hoping it'll get Fire Fang talking," Luna said.

"You think? I'd almost given up on making that happen. We've tried so many things, and all he ever does is grunt and growl."

"He turned green once," Indigo said.

"Don't remind him of that. He looked like a hairy cucumber."

"There's always another spell to try," Odessa said. "And this one is promising. I traced its origins back to the original witch who made it. She's legit."

I glanced at Fire Fang. Nugget rode on his back as he trotted around the living room. Tuffin was drinking from his water bowl, and Earl was wriggling his behind as he planned an attack on Fire Fang the next time he got close enough.

"It would be good to know what's on his mind. I know he understands every word I say, but I've yet to decipher his growls. Well, I've got a handle on the basics, but he's smart."

"You should form a familiar bond with him. That would solve the problem," Odessa said.

"He's not mine. I don't do long-term commitment. If I form a bond with Fire Fang, then..." I sank my teeth into more pizza.

"You're admitting you like him and want to keep him," Indigo said. "There's nothing wrong with that. Having familiars is great."

"You're spoilt for choice with yours," Luna said.

Indigo had three familiars, Nugget, Hilda, and Russell, which was unusual, unless you were an extremely powerful witch. And Indigo was one of the strongest I'd ever met. That was when she didn't doubt her power.

"Familiars need looking after," I said.

"You can do that. Fire Fang is in amazing condition," Luna said. "You know what you're doing."

I was still cautious about committing to Fire Fang. My continual search for Eden meant I was often away for weeks, and I sometimes forgot to feed myself and change clothes when things got intense. If I couldn't remember the basics for myself, it was unfair to inflict that on Fire Fang.

"He has no plans to stay for long. We both know the deal." I pretended not to notice the looks of exasperation passing among my friends. I wasn't changing how I ran my life. Not for anyone.

"Deals can be altered. We can try the spell after we've finished eating," Luna said.

"Sounds good," I said, knowing the deal wasn't budging but not in the mood for an argument.

There was silence as we all ate and paid no attention to the unfinished debate.

Luna scooped up some pizza. "How's everything with work?"

"Busy. How about you?"

"I've been focused on finalizing my honeymoon venue."

"Sounds like torture," I muttered.

She chuckled. "I've had worse jobs."

"I'm still working on the house," Indigo said. "It's almost done. Once the workers clear out and the new paint smell has gone, I'll invite you over for a grand unveiling."

"Just us?" I didn't do huge parties.

Indigo tilted her head from side to side. "I was thinking about an open door policy. I know some locals are still wary of me, so I figured they'd like something fun and informal. It will give them a chance to get to know me."

"They're not wary of you," Odessa said. "They've mostly forgotten you went dark and tried to kill them."

"Thanks for the reminder." Indigo set down her pizza slice. "I figured people might come if there was free food and drink. They'll see the house is different and there's nothing scary about me."

"There's a lot scary about you," I said. "Don't worry about what anyone else thinks of you."

"You're only a tiny bit scary." Luna flapped her hand at me. "Ignore them. A party is a great idea. I'll help with some food from Uncle Albert's bakery."

"I can bake muffins," Odessa said.

"Let me guess, they'll be pumpkin flavored?" I said.

"Of course. Everyone loves pumpkins. Especially mine."

"How's it going at the farm?" Indigo said.

"It's perfect." A dreamy look flickered across Odessa's face. "My scarecrows have never been so happy. And we're busy. I've barely stopped since I married Sol."

My friends chatted about their idyllic love lives, while I stuffed down more pizza. I was happy for them. They'd all had their trials but had come out the other side stronger and crazy in love with their perfect guys. It was Hallmark movie sweet.

"How's your dating life?" Indigo said to me.

"Bordering on dead in the water like a gutted merman. Guys don't like to hang around for long."

"Because you shove them out the door when you're bored," Luna said. "You've dated some great guys. One of them must have been good enough for you."

"I don't remember any of them being great. Anyway, I'm too busy for dating." Relationships were complicated. Guys didn't like straight talk, and if a guy annoyed me, I told him so. I'd not yet met an ego who could put up with that. So it was easier to be single. That way, I could wear what I liked, eat what I liked, have marathons of my favorite horror movies, and not worry if I hadn't had a bath for a few days.

"This cute guy came into the bakery the other day," Odessa said. "I got his name and checked he was single."

"You're bored with Sol?" I asked.

"No! Not for me, for you. I could introduce you. He's been coming in every morning to get a bagel and coffee. He's new to the area, so he needs a friend to show him around."

"I'll pass."

"He's your type. Shaggy dark hair, stubble, a bit of an attitude, but when you get to know him, he's all charm."

"I'll still pass. Any more cheese feast pizza left?"

Indigo shoved the box my way. "Dating for fun is a good idea. It'll take your mind off things."

"What things do I not need to be thinking about?"

"Eden. And from the state of your clothing, I'm guessing your visit to Bog Valley didn't go well. No new information?"

I looked down and realized I'd forgotten to change. There were dried blobs of demon goo spattering my shirt and several holes where the goo had eaten through the fabric.

"It was a waste of time. I got ambushed by demons. It was a setup."

"Is that why your skin is blotchy? You were burned?" Odessa touched a pink spot on my arm.

"A little. It'll fade."

"I've got a healing spell to help. You shouldn't be in pain." Odessa was out of her seat and kneeling beside me.

I didn't mind blotchy skin, but I wouldn't mind the stinging going away. "Thanks. I'll take the spell. I'd have done it myself, but my magic needs a recharge, and I got distracted by the stray cat that keeps hanging around. She's still annoying me."

"We saw her when we arrived, but she ran off. You'll adopt her, eventually. Just like you have Fire Fang." Odessa wiped her fingers on a napkin. She held her hands a few inches over my face, moving them slowly up and down.

"No to both options. That cat is a nuisance, and so is Fire Fang."

Fire Fang growled as he strutted past the table, all the cats now riding him. Earl had gone for a showy sidesaddle move, which he looked in danger of losing control of at any second.

"You love them both. You just don't like to admit it."

I had some feelings for Fire Fang. As for the cat, we weren't friendly.

After a few minutes, my stinging skin eased.

"That feels much better," I said.

"You look less blotchy." Odessa inspected my face before kissing my cheek. "Perfection. Although you smell bad. I wish you wouldn't go on these searches alone. I worry about you sneaking about in gross places like Bog Valley."

"I'm never on my own. I have Fire Fang. He took down two demons on his own."

"How many were there?" Luna said.

"Six. To start with." I raised a hand as the protests began. "But I'm alive. We got out. There's nothing to worry about. How about we try this speech spell?" I scooped up the vial, eager to distract my friends. They always worried, but I could take care of myself.

"Bog Valley isn't a place to go on your own," Indigo said.

"I have a giant, mean, hellhound mutant. He's the perfect backup. I couldn't ask for better. And he's almost indestructible."

"Even so, check in with Olympus before you go on another suicide mission. He can assist."

"I'm not asking the Magic Council for backup." I snorted a laugh. The Magic Council kept tabs on all magic users, but their methods were slow, their reaction times slug-like, and they did everything by the book. That wasn't how I operated.

"At least call one of us," Luna said. "We'd have come with you."

"I had everything under control."

Odessa stuck a finger through a hole in my clothes. "It looks like it."

"Let's do this spell," I said. "Fire Fang, get over here."

He jumped up so fast, Nugget flipped onto the floor with a dissatisfied howl, landing on her paws, Earl and Tuffin dropping behind her.

Fire Fang loped over and sniffed the vial.

"Do you want to give it a go?" I asked.

He grunted several times, but since he didn't back away, I took that as a yes.

I looked at my friends. "I just get him to drink it in one go?"

"That's about it," Luna said. "It may not work right away, though. And you'll have to monitor him for a few hours in case of side effects."

"What side effects are we talking about?" I unplugged the vial and a small hiss of smoke drifted out, followed by the scent of clove and something mossy.

"Fire Fang could get tired or hyperactive, and he may be thirsty. It won't be anything terrible."

"Are you ready?" I held up the vial for Fire Fang.

He opened his mouth, tilting his head back, so it was easy for me to tip the contents in.

We stared at him as he swallowed and licked his lips, the furry familiars included.

Fire Fang growled at the unwanted attention.

"Say something," I said.

Another growl came out.

"Give him time," Odessa said.

"He may need a booster spell," Luna said. "We could lay hands on Fire Fang and pour gentle magic through him. An activation spell should do it."

"You okay with that?" I said to Fire Fang. He went twitchy if too many people got close. This hound had strict personal boundaries, unless it was just me.

He grumbled a few times but flopped on the floor, spreading out his legs so there was plenty of him to touch. Not that it was a challenge, given his size.

"Familiars, you get involved too," Indigo said. "All paws and hands needed."

Tuffin, Nugget, and Earl stood on Fire Fang's back. We formed a circle, and each rested a hand on him. A gentle pulse of warm magic flowed out of us and into Fire Fang, sending sparkles from the tip of his nose to the end of his tail.

After a few minutes, we eased back the magic. The cats hopped off Fire Fang as he shuddered. He lurched one more time, trying to get to his feet, then coughed and closed his eyes. A slimy furball flew out of his mouth and splattered onto the wooden floor.

"Is the spell supposed to make that happen?" I edged away from the furball.

"I... I don't think so. Maybe Fire Fang needed to get his airway clear before he can talk." Odessa eyed the soggy lump of fur, her nose wrinkling.

Fire Fang's eyes remained closed.

"He is still breathing, isn't he?" Luna said.

I shot forward and rested a hand on his side, relief running through me as his chest slowly rose and fell. "He's good. Let's give him a minute."

The minute turned to five, then ten. Fire Fang remained asleep.

"Why don't we have dessert? Give him time to get used to the spell. It was powerful magic." Odessa stood and headed to the table, where a box of raspberry and dark chocolate brownies waited to be opened.

I cleaned up the gross furball, washed my hands, and joined everyone at the table. I kept an eye on Fire Fang as I ate a large piece of brownie topped with pumpkin infused cream.

"It will be great to have Fire Fang talking," Luna said.

"Sure, but I don't want our magic to cause him pain. Maybe Fire Fang doesn't want to talk. We should give up trying to find his voice," I said.

"He's always trying to communicate with you. And if he didn't want the spell, he didn't have to drink it," Indigo said.

"I should focus on what's important and figure out a permanent home for him. Fire Fang needs a place with stability, where his food bowl is brimming over, and he has a backyard to romp around in and terrorize squirrels."

"He does fine here. You feed him," Luna said.

"Not always hound food. He sometimes gets pizza."

"Does he complain?"

I shook my head. But being stuck in this tiny apartment wasn't doing him any good. Some days, it didn't do me much good, either.

Luna touched my arm. "Don't worry. He'll be fine. We all know how tough Fire Fang is. A little speech spell won't knock him off his paws for long."

"I know. I was just thinking about his future."

"His future is with you," Indigo said. "Everyone can see that."

"It shouldn't be with me."

"No one else would help this flea bag. You're stuck with him, whether or not you want him." Nugget leaped onto Indigo's lap and investigated her dessert bowl.

"Fire Fang belongs to no one but himself. And he can leave any time he likes," I said. "I can't figure out why he sticks around."

"Because he loves you. He chooses you," Indigo said. "And even though you won't admit it, you've chosen him, too. And why not? As you said, he's an amazing sidekick. Imagine the power you'd have if you formed a familiar bond with him. You'd be unstoppable."

"I'm already unstoppable."

Indigo rolled her eyes. "Then you'd be twice as unstoppable."

"Even though that's not possible, I agree," Odessa said. "Keep Fire Fang."

"And if you insist on going to places like Bog Valley, you need all the help you can get," Luna said.

"What the goblin nobble is going on?"

I jerked upright as an unfamiliar, deep male voice rumbled through the apartment. I looked at Fire Fang. He had his eyes open, looking shaky as his tongue swiped across his nose. "Was that you?"

Fire Fang coughed, and his gaze swept to meet mine. "Who else would it be? Didn't you crazy buttoned witches give me a speech spell?"

"It worked!" Odessa said. "I knew we'd find the right combination."

"Did anyone else hear him say goblin nobble and crazy buttoned witches?" Indigo said.

"He must be adjusting to a new speech pattern." I rose from my seat, kind of stunned. My hellhound talked!

"No, I goblin nobble didn't. My speech is fine."

"He just said it again," Indigo said.

"What do you mean, Fire Fang?" Odessa approached him on her hands and knees.

"Exactly what I say. Goblin nobble."

"I know what's going on." Nugget hopped onto the couch and ran a paw over one ear.

"Care to share, fuzz muffin?" Fire Fang growled.

"Say a cuss word, Fire Fang. Something rude. Something that would even make Storm blush."

"Nothing embarrasses her."

"Try it. I'm testing a theory."

"Chicken armpits. Fuzzy granules. Flowery pie." Fire Fang growled at the end of his sentence.

A laugh burst out of Odessa's lips before she clasped a hand over her mouth. "Oops! That might be my fault."

"Oops? Did you do something to the speech spell?" I said to her.

"Just a tiny thing, and I wasn't sure it would work. I figured Fire Fang may be rough around the edges when he finally found his voice."

"Because he spends so much time with Storm?" Earl said.

Odessa chuckled. "No! That never crossed my mind. But when Storm got him, he had some... kinks to work through. So I added a secret ingredient. Every time Fire Fang swears, it comes out as a nonsense word or something inoffensive."

"I have a cursing hellhound?" I grinned at Fire Fang, who didn't look happy with Odessa's revelation.

"Chicken armpits. Let me cuss. What's wrong with you, button witch?" Fire Fang prowled toward Odessa, and she backed away on her hands and knees.

Tuffin jumped on her shoulders and hissed a warning at Fire Fang. "Touch my witch, and I'll shred you to pieces."

"Everyone calm down. Not being able to cuss is a good thing," Indigo said. "Fire Fang, you don't want to offend a little old lady when you're out for a walk, do you?"

"He'd only swear at the people who annoy him," I said.

"So that's everyone if he's been learning from you," Luna said. "Forget the cussing hiccup. Fire Fang can talk! That's amazing. So what if he can't get his cuss words out? You'll know exactly what's going on in his head. You can share everything."

"I guess it's not so terrible," I muttered.

"We already share everything. Storm doesn't shut the bathroom door when she uses the toilet," Fire Fang said.

"Hey! Don't share that!"

"A hellhound who can't cuss. You'll be the laughingstock of the familiar community," Tuffin said. "Wait until everyone hears about this."

"You try, fuzz bucket." Fire Fang lunged at Tuffin. She leaped off Odessa's shoulders, and they chased each other around the room. After a few seconds,

Nugget and Earl joined in, too. Russell and Hilda watched the chase, wisely staying out of the way.

We retreated to the table to avoid being crashed into by a bundle of overexcited familiars. Having a talking hellhound could take some getting used to, but I was cautiously excited to try.

Just as I was selecting a second brownie, there was a knock at the door.

"I'll get it. I'm closest." Odessa hopped up from her seat.

"Whatever they're selling, I'm not interested," I said.

"Unless it's more pizza," Luna said. "Then we're interested."

"Okay. Unless it's that."

Odessa opened the door. "Huh! Storm, did you order a skull?"

Chapter 4

The smile slipped from my face. Icy fingers of horror wrapped around my stomach and squeezed until I thought I'd be sick. "Get away from the door! Don't look at that skull."

Odessa glanced back at me and then turned to peer at the skull.

"Storm, what's going on?" Indigo was also ignoring my advice as she leaned sideways to look at the skull.

The air vibrated, and a hot wave of energy hit me. "Everyone close their eyes." I blasted Odessa away from the doorway with a spell, sped to the door, and kicked the skull into the hallway. Then I threw myself on top of it.

A scream ricocheted through my body like a dozen bullets. It shook my bones and made me black out for a few seconds, but not before I got the door shut, so this screaming nightmare wouldn't affect anyone else.

The scream stopped, and after half a minute, I inched open one eye and looked at the skull.

"If you hurt my friends, I'll ruin you. There'll be so many pieces of bone scattered around, no one will be able to put you back together." I rolled back, so I rested against the wall and set the skull to one side. I could hear my friends on the other side of the door and the scraping of claws on wood.

That had been too close for comfort.

I shrugged off my shirt and wrapped it around the skull. I felt it buck. This thing was alive. It continued to wriggle and slipped out of my shirt, thudding to the floor.

The skull screamed. Just for half a second, but that was all it took. I'd been looking at it.

My foot lashed out, and I kicked the skull. Maybe the scream hadn't lasted long enough. I would be okay. I wasn't cursed.

With a tight stomach and shaking knees, I stood, keeping bent over as I sucked in deep breaths. I felt fine. No curse pains or headaches. It was good. I was good. Everything was good.

Footsteps approached along the hallway, and I turned my head, still in shock over what had happened. A pair of shiny designer shoes registered, and I peered up to see Lucian looking down at me.

"I knew there was one way I could persuade you to take this case."

Anger blew through me like a category five hurricane. I scooped up the skull and slung it as hard as I could at Lucian. Before it could smash into his head, the skull disappeared.

No skull to use as a weapon? Fine by me. I'd use fists and magic. "You sneaky, deceitful warlock. You planted the skull outside my apartment door."

Lucian looked around as if seeking the skull, not concerned by my anger. "You left me no choice. I'll do whatever it takes to find out what happened to Delano."

"I already told you I'm not available to help." A rumble of thunder spiraled along the corridor.

"Are you sure? If you don't find out who killed Delano, you'll never know who cursed the skull. And if you can't find the origin of the curse and destroy it, you'll be dead, too."

I grabbed him by his stiff shirt collar and shoved him against the wall. "You're the only dead thing around here."

"I protect my friends. I'm sure you'd do the same for yours. And you needed motivating."

Lucian's lack of fear annoyed me, so I shook him a few times and rumbled more thunder overhead. "I'm motivated to destroy you. You didn't have to do this. You could have found someone else. I'm not the only witch who can solve a murder."

"You're the only witch I want. Your track record proves you're the best. And now, you have seven days to prove just how good you are."

The apartment door slammed open. Fire Fang was first out but was quickly followed by my friends and their familiars.

Fire Fang raced to my side and snarled at Lucian.

"Ease up," I said to him. "And keep this calm. No one else needs to be involved." My pointed look went to the startled faces of my oldest friends. Witches who put up with my stubborn head and sharp tongue. They were my rocks, and I'd die to protect them.

Fire Fang kept snarling, but he backed off a few inches, sensing this was a tricky situation.

"What's going on?" Odessa said. "Why did you whack me with a spell?"

"And where did that scream come from?" Indigo was eyeballing Lucian. "Does this guy have something to do with it?"

I glared at Lucian and let him go, a silent warning in my eyes for him not to make any stupid moves or say anything that would sign his death warrant. It seemed he understood, because he didn't make a peep, simply smiled and straightened his shirt.

"Sorry about hitting you, Odessa, but I didn't like the look of that skull. It's never good news when a skull turns up on your doorstep unannounced." I stepped away from Lucian, but made sure I was close enough to grab him.

Odessa rubbed her arm. "I'll live. But what's going on?"

"And where did the skull go?" Indigo said.

"It was the skull that screamed?" Luna said. "I've still got chills from the noise."

I shrugged and tried to look nonchalant, even though my heart pounded with shock at the mess I was in. Odessa had been a second from being cursed. That was too close. Too much of a risk.

"Storm! What's going on?" Indigo approached Lucian. "Shall I call Olympus?"

"This isn't Magic Council business. This is... a new client." I patted Lucian's shoulder.

"Why did he bring a screaming skull here?"

"Ladies, I'm—"

"Just leaving. And he had nothing to do with the skull. It must be some dumb kids messing around. Lucian, you know the way out," I said.

His face remained impassive. "Of course. I'll be in touch about working together."

"Me, too. Really soon." I gave him a not so gentle shove, and he walked away.

"I'll follow him," Fire Fang said.

"No need." I turned back to the others. They shared identical looks of surprise and disbelief.

"What's going on?" Indigo flicked up an eyebrow, crossed her arms over her chest, and settled most of her weight on one hip. If she wasn't one of my closest friends, I'd be sweating. "Why would kids leave a skull outside your apartment?"

"Why not? They think it's funny to scare people. We did worse when we were kids." I glanced into the apartment. I needed them gone, so I could deal with Lucian and the skull. Oh, and the death curse I'd been slapped in the face with.

Odessa scooped up Tuffin, who was nosing around the floor. "If it was kids, why knock me out of the way?"

"I panicked. Shall we box up the food? You can take the leftovers home."

"There's only one piece of brownie and the pizza crusts left." Luna's mouth was pursed, her gaze flickering around the corridor as if clue hunting.

"Take the brownie." I faked a yawn. "It's getting late."

"It's not even nine." Indigo hadn't moved from her suspicious witch pose.

"I've got an early start. Thanks for the food, though. We'll have to do this again." I headed past them into the apartment. Space. I needed space to work this out. No distractions, so I could form a plan.

Indigo, Luna, and Odessa followed me. They were all staring at me like I was a new exhibit at the modern art museum for magical mayhem.

I grabbed coats and bags and slung them at them. "This was fun."

"It was fun until a screaming skull showed up and that smooth-looking guy put in an appearance. What aren't you telling us?" Indigo slid her jacket on, but that was the only move she made to get out of my cursed hair.

"This is me being polite. I'm tired, and you need to leave." I pointed at the open door. "Or do you want Fire Fang to show you the way out?"

Fire Fang grunted in the back of his throat but wore a similarly curious expression on his furry face.

"We're going." Luna lifted a hand. "Come on, Earl. We know when we're not wanted."

Odessa hugged me. "You would say if anything was bothering you, right? If it's work, we can be discreet."

"It's not work. And I'm unbothered. Life is great. Almost as great as those brownies."

"You keep the last piece. I'll call you tomorrow." After another pumpkin scented hug, she walked out with Earl beside her.

Luna followed with Tuffin.

After giving me a hard look, Indigo shrugged. "See you later." She left with her three familiars.

I hurried to the door and eased it shut. I wasn't usually this curt with my friends, but I had to get them away from this situation.

Fire Fang stood in front of me, his eyes glowing. "So, shall we hunt Lucian? That jerk put the skull outside, right?"

"Right. To the death. That jerk just cursed me."

Chapter 5

I watched through the window until Indigo, Odessa, and Luna were out of sight before pounding down the stairs with Fire Fang beside me.

There was no need to hunt far for Lucian. His limo was parked along the road. I'd spotted it the second I'd looked outside.

I rapped a knuckle on the glass, and the back window slid down.

"Get in."

"You come up. I know where the weapons are in my apartment."

"There's no need for weapons. We both want the same thing."

"You dead?"

"The cursed skull destroyed and my friend's murder resolved."

"I don't give two moldy cheeseburgers about Delano Discord. And I hate to be tricked. If you want this to work, you come into the apartment, or the deal is off."

Lucian's gaze drifted to Fire Fang. "Your hellhound won't eat me?"

"I make no guarantees, but he has just had five slices of pizza."

"I could still make room for this goblin nobble," Fire Fang growled out.

"A goblin what?"

"Forget it. Let's move. You need to tell me everything you know about this screaming skull."

Lucian followed me back to the apartment, taking his time on the stairs. Once we were settled on the couch, I grabbed the last piece of brownie. And no, Lucian didn't get the offer of refreshments.

It was time to get to work.

"Who most wanted Delano dead?" I chewed on the brownie.

"He was a powerful man. That can make enemies. The Magic Council has been investigating those closest to him."

"Makes sense. Whoever did this had access to the house, so they could leave the skull there. Tell me about the locations where it was found."

"Sam discovered it when he opened the front door."

"And the skull just activated? It's not smart enough to know who it needs to curse?"

"I assume so. I did nothing to it when I left it outside your apartment."

"Which I'll deal with another time. Cursing someone to force them to work for you sucks." I glared at Lucian until he looked away. "So it was found outside the house on the first occasion. What about the second time?"

"Suzanne discovered it outside the kitchen door leading into the yard."

"And when Delano discovered it, it was outside his bedroom door, is that right?"

"Correct."

"So whoever did this couldn't get into the house the first two times, but must have found a way in. Or were they hoping Delano would leave through one of those doors? Or maybe the servants were test subjects. The killer needed to see if the skull worked."

"All of that is possible."

"You don't give much away."

"I focus on facts, rarely guesses."

"What was Delano's usual routine?"

"He was always up early. Business first and pleasure second. It was how he kept a grip on his fortune."

"What kind of magic user was he?"

"A jinn."

"Money and power hungry." Jinn could be benevolent wish givers, but they could twist into obsessive hoarders, hiding their wishes, money, and treasure.

"He was resourceful and smart. Delano rose by six, worked out, meditated, and then headed into work."

"From what I'm hearing about him, Delano doesn't strike me as all that Zen."

"More cudgel than Zen," Fire Fang said.

That earned him a smile from Lucian. "Delano could be a blunt instrument. It got the results he needed."

"Did you work with him every day?" I asked.

"Not face-to-face, but we spoke most days."

"And where did he work?"

"He had an office in the family's backyard."

"So it's possible he'd have used either of the doors where the skull was first seen to get to that office?"

"Very possible. Some mornings, he'd go into the kitchen, collect a cafetiere of coffee, and get to work. Sometimes, he'd work all night. I was often with him when that happened. We'd take some air and walk around the house and grounds."

"Which means the killer was targeting Delano from the beginning. The butler and serving girl got in the way." I finished the last bite of brownie. "Let's assume it was someone close to Delano. He was married?"

"He was. Delano had been married to the same woman for decades. Augusta was a loyal wife. They married when she was in her early twenties. She's the perfect accessory."

"A wife isn't an accessory."

"Forgive me. That was the wrong word. She was a compliment to Delano. She has breeding and influence and knows how to host an incredible party."

"What kind of thoroughbred breeding are we talking?"

"Augusta is a Crossfire witch."

"Crossfire? Those witches don't have power anymore. They lost it in the battle of Frost Wood."

"You know your history. After their defeat, alliances were forged. Delano saw an opportunity to assist the Crossfire witches and improve his social status."

"Their marriage was for convenience? Augusta needed protection, and Delano wanted to make a name for himself in certain magic social circles?"

"There was an element of convenience and opportunity to the marriage. But they were content. Augusta lives in luxury, had Delano's protection and access to his influence. Plus, the Crossfire witches' reputation was sustained. Other witches in that family did the same thing. They had no other option if they were to survive."

"Which must have been a dig in the gut for Augusta. She married a man she didn't love to protect her family."

"It was a small sacrifice. Delano was a decent husband. She had no complaints."

"You don't think Augusta planted the skull because she was unhappily married?"

"I'm aware she's a suspect with the Magic Council, but there's no evidence to suggest she did it or any reason for her to do such a thing. Their marriage was solid. It benefited both of them."

"Anyone else? What about children?"

"There's a son, Chilton."

"Tell me about him."

"He's a young man and single. He looks strikingly like Delano. They share the same distinct silver hair."

"Any problems between father and son?"

"Never. Chilton is a people pleaser. He charms and enchants. Delano had ambitions to train Chilton to take over when he was ready to retire. Although that was many years away. Of course, everything has changed now." Lucian pursed his lips. "Chilton isn't ready yet. But the business will need an anchor, now Delano has gone."

"Who else lived with him? Just the wife and son?"

"There's also Delano's brother. Erik. He's the younger brother. And I'll be honest with you, Erik resented Delano. He crossed the line several times, and Delano reprimanded him and reminded him of the family reputation. But it did no good."

"What did Erik do that crossed the line?"

"He dabbles with the darker side of magic. Usually gray spells. The ones that tread a thin line where the law is concerned. And he has an addiction to magic brothels. He wastes his time and spends too much money on darker spells and broken ladies." Lucian shook his head. "I wonder if it's because he realized he'd never inherit the family fortune. Delano had the reins and wasn't letting go. That left Erik with nothing to do. And he has no ambition to seek his own path."

"The baby brother squandered some of the family fortune and has been trying to ruin their name because he was jealous of Delano?"

"There was definitely jealousy stirring, but Erik's only interested in having a good time. And he has been distancing himself from the rest of the family. When he's home, you can usually find him drunk and sleeping it off. I doubt he has the mental capacity or magical stability to use a cursed skull. He likes dark magic, but he's not strong enough to contain it."

"You said he dabbles in gray magic. Gray to black is an easy transition. Perhaps he met someone at a magic brothel, and they offered him something he couldn't refuse. Use the skull to get his older brother out of the picture. Erik would then get access to the family fortune. He'd have everything he thought he'd never get his hands on. There's a motive."

"And I'd agree with you if I didn't know Erik as well as I do. He spends his life gazing into the bottom of a bottle. He thinks solutions will be given to him. Erik never works for anything."

"He had a change of heart. An opportunity arose, and he grabbed the screaming skull with both hands and used it on his brother."

"Reserve judgment until you've met him. Erik is too stupid and lazy to plan a murder. If he was ever going to kill, his method would be basic and crude."

"Such as?"

"Pushing Delano down the stairs or running him over. Something that requires little thought. Erik lives in the moment. He hasn't been thinking about how he can take over the Discord empire."

"He stays as a suspect. I don't like the sound of him." Dark magic twisted a person. It could have twisted Erik into a killer.

"Very well. I won't advise you how to conduct this investigation."

"Any other siblings?"

"There's Hattie. She lives at the house, too, along with Erik. They have their own wings. Hattie is... Well, she's a shadow. Almost silent, easy to overlook, forgettable. A nothing sort of woman."

"I hope you've complemented her using those terms. It'll do wonders for her self-esteem."

One side of Lucian's mouth lifted. "Delano once described Hattie as the disappointment in the family. She inherited nothing positive. It's as if the unwanted bits were squashed together to create Hattie. She's plump and plain and boring. No one remembers her."

"I'm sure some do. Just because she's not glamorous and doesn't fawn all over you doesn't mean she's not worth noticing."

He barked out a laugh. "She's never fawned over me or anyone. Hattie once said I had a smile and the moral compass of a shark. As you can see, she inherited no charm skills, either."

"That sounds like an accurate description to me." Fire Fang had settled himself across my feet, his attention on Lucian.

"You think Hattie wanted Delano dead?" I said.

"Sometimes, the way she speaks to people makes me think she wants them all dead. She's a difficult woman. Spiky."

"What would Hattie gain from Delano's death? What does she inherit?"

"Delano made provisions in a previous will for family members. Hattie would have gotten a small inheritance. Enough money to find a place to live and not worry about work. But she'd have needed to live carefully to ensure the money didn't run out. Her life would have been turned on its head. She may complain about the lifestyle she leads, but Hattie would be miserable if forced to leave the family home and no longer have the many cakes she devours from those fancy bone china plates."

"Was she aware of what her brother was leaving her?"

"Hattie snoops. And she always knows more than she lets on. If she'd found a way to learn what Delano had written in his will, she'd have done so."

"Which doesn't give her a great motive for wanting him dead."

"Perhaps not. But she needs to be investigated. There's something about that shrill little woman that sets my teeth on edge."

"You set my teeth on edge, you fluffy monkey," Fire Fang said. "Storm, can I eat him now?"

"Later. We still need to gather the evidence. Anyone else?"

Lucian steepled his fingers, and a smile crossed his face. "There's the lovely Rosina."

"And how is she related to the family?"

"No relation. She was Delano's girlfriend."

Fire Fang snorted a plume of smoke. "A wife and a girlfriend. What a chicken armpit."

"You said Delano had been married to the same woman for years. Where does the girlfriend fit?" I said.

"Rosina was the reason the marriage was so content. Delano had a voracious appetite for all things. He loved his wine, his food, and his women. Rosina was the latest in a long line of girlfriends who kept him entertained. As sweet as Augusta is, she could only do so much to please him."

I curled my top lip. "Delano openly cheated on Augusta?"

"He did. It was all aboveboard."

"I doubt it was aboveboard, according to their marriage vows. Augusta must have hated that."

"She was happy. Delano was a demanding man. I should know. We went to school together and have worked together ever since. He drove everyone to their limits. But that's what made him an incredible man. He showed you what you could achieve when you thought you had nothing left in the tank."

"It still doesn't let him off of cheating on his wife. Please don't tell me Rosina lives in the house, too."

"Of course she does. Delano needed the arrangement to be convenient. What's more convenient than having your girlfriend along the corridor, waiting to fulfil your latest fantasy?"

"This information puts Augusta at the top of the suspect list. She was forced into a marriage of convenience with a man who sounds like a nightmare and had her nose rubbed in it when he brought in his latest girlfriend. Not only brought her in, but moved her in. I'm surprised no one from the Magic Council has arrested Augusta and charged her with these murders."

"Don't get ahead of yourself. Augusta is a respectable woman, and she knew the arrangement she was going into. Although it was never openly discussed, Augusta and Delano had a passionless marriage. Augusta did what was required to ensure there was an heir, then Delano moved on."

"Once Augusta served her usefulness, you mean. It's no wonder Delano is dead."

"I don't expect you to like him, and I'm not looking for your acceptance regarding how he lived his life. I just need you to solve his murder."

"And I will, since you've given me no choice but to do that. Is that everyone?"

"That's it. All the people closest to Delano and everyone living in the house."

"We have left one person off the suspect list. You."

The merest flash of surprise emerged on Lucian's face. "I have nothing to gain from Delano's death. I've lost a friend."

"A friend who paid you a lot of money."

"Delano rewarded me for my loyalty."

"A friend you admitted pushed you to the edge. What if one of those pushes was too hard, and you snapped? You couldn't deal with his harsh rule, so you killed him."

"I tried to save him."

"But you weren't cursed. Is that because you knew not to look when the skull was screaming?"

"Miss Winter, I would have done anything to save Delano. It was only when I heard that bone shuddering scream that I knew what was happening. I bolted up the stairs and along the corridor, but I was too late. If I'd wanted Delano dead and to keep myself safe, I'd have stayed away."

"Or that was a clever attempt to hide your guilt."

"Losing Delano means I lose everything, too. I've only ever worked for him, and I'm known in the community as his right-hand man. That makes me unemployable. I'm not sure I could even work for anyone else."

"I'm sure you'd find a way around that if the offer was good enough. You're a calculating guy."

"What I've done to you may seem calculating, but I did it because I was desperate. The Magic Council has gotten nowhere in their investigation. Delano's murder must be avenged. That's why I came to you."

"And that's why you've cursed me. You're as bad as Delano."

"Delano wasn't a bad man. Perhaps he strayed from the right path now and again—"

"With one of his many girlfriends?" Fire Fang said.

Lucian didn't acknowledge that comment. "Delano did things for the right reasons. His alliance with the Crossfire witches saved an ancient magical family. His constant drive and pushing everyone he worked with brought out the best in them. I know it brought out the best in me. I owe Delano everything. Which is why I need you on this case. Whoever controls this skull is the killer. And they must still have control over it to make it vanish at will."

"The vanishing trick is strange," I said. Lucian had little to gain from murdering his employer, but I wasn't done grilling him. "Is that something you can do?"

"I have as much control over that thing as you do. It must be found and destroyed. Along with its creator."

I was still suspicious of Lucian, and he was staying on the suspect list, but there were others above him.

"How close were you to Delano's room when the skull screamed?"

"I was downstairs, refreshing my drink. I'd stopped by for dinner and was having a nightcap, then I planned to stay in a guest bedroom."

"You were alone?"

"I was. But before you jump to the assumption that makes me guilty, everyone else in the house was alone, too. Our word is our alibi."

"Which means you have no alibi, donkey helmet," Fire Fang said. He operated on the same logic path as me. Trust no one. Everyone hides things.

"I could still refuse to help you," I said. "I don't have time for this."

"You have seven days. And if you refuse to help, you'll lose all of this." Lucian splayed his hands and looked around, his gaze settling on the empty takeout cartons, the cardboard box that doubled as a side table, and my mismatching crockery.

"Fire Fang, you have permission to bite."

Lucian squeaked as Fire Fang jumped on him and latched his teeth around his throat. "Stop! Stop! I'm no good to you dead."

"I wouldn't say that. You'd make a great draft excluder until you rotted. And there's a stray cat outside that's always hungry." I left Fire Fang to chew on Lucian's throat and looked around the apartment, seeing it as he did. I had little in the way of material things, but why should that matter? My work and Eden were the only things I focused on.

Eden.

If I refused to take this case, that was it for her. I would never solve her mystery. I couldn't give up on my little sister.

"Get him off me," Lucian gasped from under Fire Fang's enormous bulk.

Every nerve told me not to take this case. I didn't want to help this smooth, devious warlock. But if

I didn't, any hope of finding Eden was gone once I was dead.

"Fire Fang, not today. I'll find you another snack," I said with obvious reluctance.

My sometimes obedient hellhound clambered off Lucian.

I grabbed Lucian's arm and hauled him to his feet. "Since the clock is ticking on my life, we'd better get started finding a triple murderer."

Chapter 6

"Everyone will be asleep." Lucian peered out the window of the limousine as it glided to a stop outside a mansion constructed of glass, steel, and concrete. Large floor-to-ceiling windows looked at me in unblinking blackness.

"They won't mind being woken. Since every second counts when it comes to keeping me alive, this investigation starts now. I need to speak to everyone in that house and find out what they know about Delano's murder," I said.

"You're sure this can't be done in the morning?" Lucian dabbed at the dull red marks on his neck, where Fire Fang had given him a little love bite.

"No." I climbed out of the limo, Fire Fang right behind me. The mansion was ridiculously large. Who needed this much space?

Lucian climbed out a few seconds later. He tapped on the front window, and it slid down. "Make sure the inside of the limo gets a full valet. That hound shed fur and drool everywhere."

"I wouldn't if you weren't such a monkey smell," Fire Fang said.

Lucian glared at him and shook his head. "I'll go inside and see who is awake."

"I want to start with Augusta," I said.

He sucked in a breath as if about to protest. "Very well. This way. Make sure you take your boots off. The carpets are white, and those things on your feet look like they've never seen boot polish."

My boots may be dirty, but these old faithfuls had carried me for miles.

Lucian cast an unlock spell by the front door to gain access.

"How many people know the spell to get inside?" I said.

"Only the family and key staff members. Although none of the staff is here at the moment. After the unfortunate deaths, it was decided we should send away everyone. It seemed the right thing to do while the skull was on the loose."

"It's a shame you didn't do that after Sam died. You would have saved Suzanne. Or wasn't she important enough to protect?"

"The connection between the curse, the screams, and the deaths wasn't made right away." Lucian turned to me before opening the door. "We're not coldhearted. If we could have stopped more deaths, we would have. Wait here. Boots off." Lucian stalked away, limping slightly. Fire Fang must have bruised him in their tussle on my couch.

I kept my boots on and walked into the nearest room. The walls were lined with what looked to my untrained eye like original artwork. The place was more like a museum gallery than a home. I had no appreciation for art, so I scooted around and went to the next room. This was an ostentatious dining room, with a table big enough to seat thirty and a faint smell of burned wood in the air.

I strode into a third room and stopped. A tall, slender woman with long dark hair down to her waist stood by a table. She had a proud tilt to her chin and a long straight nose.

"I didn't think anyone was still up," I said by way of an introduction.

She started and turned. "Who are you, and what are you doing in my home?"

"Augusta Discord?" I stayed by the door.

"That's me. How did you get in?"

"I came with Lucian. He twisted my arm to help figure out what happened to your husband. I'm Storm Winter. This is Fire Fang."

Recognition lit her pale green eyes. She was beautiful in an ice queen way. "Lucian has spoken of you. He said you were the best investigator out there." The haughty tilt of her chin was gone as she moved toward me, but there was a coolness in her eyes, almost a caution. It made me think she'd spent many years treading carefully around people. Perhaps one person in particular.

"I know how to do my job, if that's what you're interested in."

"Whatever you need to make this happen, just ask. Ever since the connection was made between the screaming skull and the three deaths, we've amassed as much information as we can. I am hopeful something useful will be discovered."

"I'd like to see that information."

"Right this way." She strode past me, ignoring Fire Fang even though she had to dodge around him, and led me into a dream room for any bibliophile nerd. There were books on shelves from floor to ceiling and several large tables scattered with open books, notepads, and maps.

I turned to inspect all the wood and paper. "This room must have a whole forest in it."

"Several. This is everything we've gathered on the skull." Augusta stopped by a cluttered table. "Lucian thought it would be helpful to discover the origin of the skull."

"Lucian has lots of thoughts. I'm yet to see many that are useful." I briefly looked over the papers.

"You don't think this is of value?"

"It could be, although this is all generic stuff. If we find out who created the skull, we can force its maker to reverse the curse. Then no one else needs to die."

"You don't think it'll come back, do you?" Augusta's long fingers wrapped around my forearm. "I didn't consider that. What if the skull is targeting everyone in this household? There have already been three deaths. Will there be more?"

"At the moment, only one more."

"Who?" Her hand tightened. "It's not Chilton, is it? Just the thought of losing him makes me feel like shrieking. Please, tell me my son isn't the next target."

"He's not. Probably. I'm the next target. That's how Lucian recruited me."

"Recruited you? I don't understand."

"Storm, there's no need to complicate the situation." Lucian strode in, not looking happy he'd found me spilling his dirty secrets. "Augusta, all you need to know is I have hired Storm to resolve this. I told you I'd get you the best."

I wasn't letting him off. "Lucian asked me to help, but I turned him down. So he placed the cursed skull outside my apartment door. It screamed at me, and now I'm cursed. If I don't solve the mystery of who murdered Delano, Sam, and Suzanne and figure out where the skull came from, I'll be the next victim."

A breathy gasp fluttered from Augusta's full lips. "Lucian, tell me you didn't do this. No one deserves to be cursed."

Lucian caught hold of Augusta's free hand. "It had to be done. The Magic Council has gotten nowhere."

"So you cursed an innocent witch?"

"For the family. For Delano. To make sure you get a resolution and move on. Chilton, too. He wants to know what happened to his father."

"Not by risking another's life. If I'd known you were planning this, I'd never have agreed to hire anyone." Augusta moved out of Lucian's reach, taking me with her, her grip tight on my arm, so I had no choice but to follow. "I'm so sorry. Lucian was wrong to do this. Of course, I want the murders solved. I'd pay a lot of money to know what happened to Delano and why someone targeted him. But I would never do this. This is wrong. Lucian, you should be ashamed."

"I'm ashamed of nothing. Delano deserves this. He always wanted the best. That's what I've given him."

"No, not this way. You must undo this."

"Even if he could, I doubt he would," I said, holding back a smile at the chastised expression on Lucian's face. "The only person who can undo the curse is the skull's creator. Have you found out who that is from your research?"

Augusta's eyelids fluttered. She squeezed my arm before letting go. "Not yet. But we will find a solution. And I'm not finished with you, Lucian. We need to discuss boundaries."

He simply nodded.

It was so satisfying to watch Augusta put him in his place.

"I'd like to speak to other members of the family," I said. "As soon as I get a full picture of who could be involved, I can make progress."

"Of course. Lucian, be useful. Round up everyone. Bring them here. The sooner, the better," Augusta said.

Looking like a scolded child who'd been told he wasn't getting pudding for the fifth night in a row, Lucian stomped out of the room.

Augusta's gaze was on the papers in front of her, her head shaking slightly. "I don't expect you to forgive Lucian for what he's done to you, but he was more like a brother to Delano than a friend. Delano took him under his wing from an early age. They boarded together, and Lucian was a scrawny child. I didn't know him back then, but I've seen pictures. He was picked on."

"Not really a surprise if he's always been that smug."

Fire Fang grunted a laugh as he wandered around the room.

"He can be... a know it all. And stubborn. One day, a bully made the mistake of saying a rude comment about Delano in front of Lucian. Lucian attacked him. Knocked him out. Delano learned about this and rewarded Lucian. The friendship blossomed, and they remained close. They've always looked out for each other. That doesn't mean I agree with Lucian's actions, but I understand them."

"I have friends. And I'd do a lot to protect them, too. But it sucks to be on the receiving end of that."

"I imagine it does. Well, there's only one thing for it. You have our assets and information at your disposal. Use them to find the answer. That way, the murders will be solved, and you can continue your life as you wish."

I flicked through a few of the pages. There were notes on sightings of where the skull had been seen and how many people had died. "How about you? Will you get the life you've always wanted now Delano is dead?"

Augusta sucked in a breath but kept her attention on the paperwork. "My life will be different now he's gone. It'll take some adjustment. We were married for a long time."

"Why stay with a man who repeatedly cheated on you?"

She flinched but remained statuesque as I examined her. "Lucian has been filling in the blanks about our situation?"

"He has. And the latest of those blanks is called Rosina. How many were there before her?"

"There's no need to be crude."

"Are we talking two or ten?"

Augusta slid her tongue across her teeth.

"More? Triple figures?"

"We all have situations in our lives that are less than perfect."

"A cheating husband is far from perfect. And a repeat cheater should have his important bits snipped off, so he's less eager to stray from home."

A smile traced across Augusta's lips. "I have had similar thoughts myself."

"You never acted on the snip-and-stay plan, though?"

"It was easier to deal with when Delano wasn't so obvious. Rosina was his most obvious acquisition."

People approaching the room put an end to our conversation, but I'd gotten enough out of Augusta to be certain the marriage was far from content, as Lucian had described.

Hurried footsteps approached the door and Lucian looked in. "Everyone is coming to join you. They'll just be a moment. Although I can't find Erik."

Augusta headed to the door. "If you'll excuse me, Storm, I'll dig out my brother-in-law." She walked away with Lucian, leaving me on my own with Fire Fang.

"What do you reckon about the wife?" I whispered to him, thumbing through the papers about the skull.

"She hated the dead guy. And why shouldn't she? Cheating on your wife should be a crime."

"You're always faithful to your ladies?"

"When I have one. Cheating is for losers."

"Augusta hated Delano less than she hated me."

I turned at the sound of a high female voice that had lifted at the end of the sentence.

Standing in the doorway was a woman in her mid-twenties, with shiny amber nineteen-sixties style bombshell hair. Her fitted red dress revealed cleavage and thigh, adding to the illusion she'd stepped off an old style movie set after filming her starring role.

"And you are?" I said.

She walked over, a hand stretched out, revealing polished red nails and sparkling jewels on her wrist. "Rosina Grail."

I shook her hand. "Storm Winter."

"You have stunning eyes, Storm. I sense fire in you."

I lifted a shoulder. "Better be careful not to get burned."

A light giggle drifted out. "I'm fireproof. And you're here because..." Her gaze went to the papers I'd been browsing.

"To figure out why a skull was used to kill three members of this household. You were Delano's girlfriend."

"Oh! Of course. And you've heard about me?" Her thick, dark lashes fluttered.

"Your name has come up in conversation. Especially since your living situation is far from normal."

"You mean the wife and the mistress sharing the same space? Aren't we terrible?" Rosina drifted to Fire Fang. Without seeking permission, she reached down and scratched his belly.

Fire Fang was a sucker for a belly rub. And although he was struggling to resist the delicious allure of long nails scratching through his fur, he didn't put up much of a fight and flopped on his side, exposing his undercarriage.

"You said Augusta hates you. Care to elaborate?" I said.

Rosina bent, revealing even more thigh as she continued petting Fire Fang. "She put on a brave face whenever Delano was around. He was quick to anger and hated when people objected to his plans. But when he was out of the way, her true face revealed itself. She's cold, cruel, and calculating. And she wants me gone."

"Is there any reason for you to stick around now Delano's dead?"

Rosina stood from petting Fire Fang. "This is my home. Although I am wondering if it's the right place for me. It's brimming with toxic betrayal and lies. It's hard to believe the people living here are related. When they're not smiling fake smiles at each other, they gossip behind backs and stick in the metaphorical knife."

"Rosina, you're still here?" Augusta stood in the doorway, drawn up to her full height, her hands on her slim hips. "It seems you find it impossible to take a hint. Is that because you're stubborn or stupid?"

Although the smile remained on Rosina's face, she looked more mannequin than human as she engaged in a stare off with Augusta. "A hint about what?"

Augusta glanced at me before striding into the room, her high heels cushioned by the thick white carpet underfoot. "I'll stop hinting and be plain with you. Delano has gone, which means your... services are no longer required. You won't get anything out of this family. No one wants you here. Leave."

"Other than you, everyone else likes me. They knew I made Delano happy. I deserve to be rewarded. Delano said he'd look after me."

"Delano told people whatever they needed to hear to make sure he got what he wanted out of them." Augusta's gaze flickered to me again. "We don't need to air your filthy laundry for anyone to find out about. You've caused enough scandal by being his mistress. It's time you found another target."

"Ladies, now's not the time to unpack your differences." Lucian dashed into the room and formed a physical barrier between Augusta and Rosina.

"She started it," Rosina said. "I've only ever been sweet to people who live here. I love to make other people happy. Creating happiness in others makes me happy."

"Then you're a deluded fool," Augusta said. "You have until the end of the week, and then you're out. If I have to throw you out myself, I'll do it. In fact, I'll take pleasure in removing you from this house."

"There's no need for harsh words." Lucian placed a placating hand on Augusta's shoulder. "We all want the same thing from this situation."

"Delano's mistress gone?" Augusta snapped out.

"Delano's murder solved. Everyone in this house, Rosina included, has valuable information about what happened that night. That's why Storm's here. She will discover the truth."

I was going to argue the point about why I was really there, but the room swiftly filled up with the rest of Delano's family. A guy in his early thirties appeared. The striking green eyes and flash of silver through his hair showed he must be the offspring of Augusta and Delano. Not far behind him was an older woman dressed in flat brown shoes, a calf-length plain brown dress, and her brunette hair was cut in a short pixie crop.

Whereas the guy was all smiles and greeting people, the older woman kept her eyes on the floor as if concerned she may trip over the ends of her pointed shoes.

"Is this everyone who was in the house the night Delano died?" I said to Augusta.

"Everyone other than my brother-in-law, Erik. I found him asleep. He's on his way and will join us shortly, when he's had a strong coffee."

"Allow me to make the introductions," Lucian said. "You've already met Rosina and Augusta. This handsome young devil is Chilton, Augusta and Delano's son." He pointed to the guy with the green eyes.

I nodded at Chilton, who greeted me with a sunny smile. "Lucian said you're going to solve my father's murder."

"That's the plan." My attention turned to the older woman, who still looked at the floor.

"This is Hattie," Lucian said. "Delano's younger sister."

Hattie didn't look at me, simply nodded, the white carpet capturing her attention as if it was the most fascinating floor covering she'd ever seen.

"Where do you want to start?" Lucian said. "I see Augusta has shown you the research materials. We hired a team to gather details about the skull."

"The history of the skull could be useful, but right now, I'm interested in present-day facts. I need your alibis. Where were you all when Delano was cursed?"

"That's simple. We all have the same alibi," Lucian said.

"You told me you were alone downstairs getting a drink," I said to him.

"Correct. I heard the scream and raced up the stairs."

"Everyone else was downstairs, too?"

"No, I was in the attached bathroom. It's next to the bedroom I share with Delano," Augusta said. "I'd just gotten out of the shower when I heard the scream."

I was surprised to hear Augusta shared a bedroom with Delano, given he had his mistress on hand. Maybe it was for appearance's sake, but from what Rosina said, everyone knew why she lived in the house.

"You were on your own in the bathroom?" I said.

"I was. I could hear Delano as he got ready for bed, but I had the door closed."

"Fortunately for you," Lucian said. "Otherwise, you could have been cursed too, if you'd looked out and seen the skull."

"Small mercies, I suppose," Augusta said.

I focused on Rosina. "How about you?"

"I was alone in my room when I heard that terrible scream. It sent a shiver down my spine. I didn't know what to do."

"Did you leave your room to see what the noise was?"

"I was too scared to do anything for a few moments. It was only when I heard Delano and Lucian talking in the corridor that I ventured out. Lucian had the skull hidden under his jacket. I couldn't believe it when I found out what was going on. My poor Delano, cursed."

"What about you, Chilton?" I said.

"The same as Rosina. I was in bed. It was late when it happened. Dad had gathered us for dinner to reveal his new plans. We spent a long time talking about what he would do with his money. After that, we went our separate ways."

I focused on Lucian. "You mentioned Delano's previous will looked after the family in the event of his death. That's changed? He wanted to do something different with his fortune?"

"It was to be flipped on its head and the assets used up," Lucian said.

"There was to be nothing left for anyone," Augusta said softly.

"It must have been a shock to discover Delano had this in mind. How did you take that news?" My attention was back on Chilton.

"Of course, it was a surprise," Augusta answered before Chilton could speak. "Delano was a traditionalist with his money. He always said he'd provide for those left behind."

Chilton nodded along. "Right. We were surprised. But the money was his. He could do what he liked with it."

"If Delano wasn't leaving the money to the family, what did he plan to do with it?" Some people gave their fortunes to charity. I had a feeling Delano wouldn't have done that.

"He intended to spend it. All of it," Augusta said.

"How much money would that be?" I said.

"Delano was a billionaire," Lucian said. "He invested wisely over the years and made a fortune buying struggling companies, pulling them apart, and selling the profitable bits."

"How could one man spend all that money?"

"He was talking about around the world trips, buying vacation houses, and going on a year-long gambling spree. The money wasn't coming to any of us if he'd changed his will," Augusta said.

"That's not true," Rosina said. "Delano planned to leave something to all of us."

"Is that what he told you to get you into bed?"

"Ladies, no cat talk," Lucian said. "And it doesn't matter now. Delano died before he changed his will and spent his fortune."

Ding, ding, ding! The motive was obvious. Someone in this room killed Delano to stop him from changing his will and squandering his fortune. Anyone here could have stepped up to the skull screaming plate for that motive. Especially with a billion at risk of being lost on vacations and gambling fun.

"Hattie, what were you doing that night?" I said.

She finally met my gaze. Her eyes matched the color of her dress, and frown lines framed a full, wonky mouth. "What's your authority here?"

"I hired her," Lucian said. "Storm is a private investigator."

"She isn't from the Magic Council?"

"They weren't delivering on the case. We need action to solve Delano's murder. Everyone I spoke to when seeking a skilled PI recommended Storm."

Hattie's nose crinkled. "I always go to bed early. The dinner was dragging on with everyone worrying about losing their fortune, so I made my excuses. I was asleep. The skull's scream woke me."

"Auntie Hattie gets up at five AM every morning," Chilton said. "I don't know how she does it. She's a superwoman."

"It's the quietest part of the day," Hattie said, sharing the briefest of smiles with her nephew. "There's no noise or distraction."

"So, all of you were on your own. No one can vouch for your whereabouts when Delano was cursed by the screaming skull," I said.

"I told you," Lucian said. "We all have the same alibi."

I looked around the group, hoping to see the weak link. Hattie was back to focusing on the carpet, Chilton was smiling broadly at me, Rosina was scratching Fire Fang's belly again, and Augusta and Lucian wore the same calm, composed expressions.

No one flinched. No one held up their hands and confessed guilt. No one looked guilty. Yet someone in this room was the killer.

"Any of you could have murdered Delano." There was no point offering any candy glaze to this situation. "If no one can vouch for where you were at the time the skull screamed, you all had an opportunity to place it outside Delano's bedroom. And you all have the same motive. You'd have lost out if Delano blew through the cash."

"Except me," Lucian said. "I'm not part of the family, so the fortune would never have come my way."

"Delano left you nothing in his will? When you spoke about him, you said how loyal you were to him and how close you were. Augusta even mentioned you were more like brothers."

"All of that is true, but I oversaw the drafting of Delano's last will. There was no mention of me in it, other than the gift of an antique pocket watch that belonged to his great grandfather."

"I had nothing to do with my brother's death," Hattie said. "Delano's excessive wealth was a terrible thing. He had so much, yet he kept looking for more. How much money does one man need?"

"You've never objected to living in his home, eating the food he paid for every night from his table, and accepting your monthly allowance," Augusta said coolly.

"I take what I need to survive," Hattie said. "I wouldn't hurt him to get my hands on the money he stashed away. I wouldn't know what to do with it."

"I keep suggesting a makeover and a closet of new clothes will turn you into a new woman," Rosina said. "We should go shopping together. You'd be pretty if you didn't wear so much brown."

"Auntie Hattie is perfect as she is." Chilton walked over and slung an arm around Hattie's shoulders. "And I love you in brown. It's your color."

Hattie's smile was small in response. "I have more important things to think about than the label on the back of my clothing. Brown is practical. You don't see the stains. I've had this dress for ten years."

"And it's a charming dress." Lucian's gaze was full of mirth as he looked my way. "Do you have more questions for us?"

"One person is missing," I said. "Where's Erik?"

"Oh, that useless man. He probably got lost on the way here," Augusta said. "He's as pointless as a soft spoon in a tub of hard ice cream."

"I know one way to get him here. Fire Fang, sniff out Erik. Follow the stench of alcohol," I said.

Fire Fang climbed to his paws, ending his prolonged belly rubbing session with Rosina, and loped out of the room.

"Your dog won't hurt him, will he?" Augusta said.

"Fire Fang only gives friendly nips. Although he has big teeth. So long as Erik keeps ahead of him while he's being herded here, he won't have any trouble."

"Erik can't be involved," Lucian said. "There's barely a day passes when the man can walk in a straight line. He's harmless because he's so drunk all the time."

"Uncle Erik's a good guy," Chilton said. "Sure, he likes a drink, but that's because he enjoys himself. He's a fun guy to spend time with. You'll like him, Storm."

"Erik is a disgusting lush," Hattie said. "And he's an embarrassment."

A yelp and something heavy hitting the floor had all our attention turning to the door. A few seconds later, a bedraggled guy with floppy silver-streaked hair and a crumpled suit staggered through the door. He collided with a side table, knocked it over, and crashed into another table, scattering papers everywhere.

Lucian shook his head. "Storm, allow me to introduce you to Delano's brother, Erik."

Erik looked over his shoulder. A squeak slid from his lips as he spotted Fire Fang in the doorway. "Is anyone else seeing that thing?"

"For the stars and moon's sake, pull yourself together, Erik." Augusta stalked over and attempted to brush wrinkles from his suit. She shouldn't have bothered. That suit had been slept in a dozen nights in a row, sat on by a hefty troll, and had stains on the lapels that would never come out.

Erik lifted a trembling hand and pointed at Fire Fang. "Tell me you see it, too."

"Of course. The dog is Storm's companion animal. You'd know that if you'd arrived on time. He was sent to bring you here, since you ignored my request. I suppose you fell asleep after I left?"

"I... I don't remember. You came and found me? Where was I?"

"Asleep on the pool table. You were using a ball as a pillow."

"Huh! I remember. I was in the middle of a game when I needed a five-minute nap." Erik massaged a round red mark on his cheek. "Pool balls aren't comfortable pillows."

Augusta snapped her fingers in his face. "Concentrate! We have an expert here helping us find out who cursed Delano. Don't you want to know what happened to your brother?"

"Delano? I couldn't care less about him."

She backed away. "Don't say that. You loved him."

"The guy was a huge jerk. He never said a decent word about me, so I know the feeling was mutual. He didn't like me because I wouldn't slither around him like all of you, your hands out for money." Erik hissed and waved his arms in the air, almost pitching over as he played snake. "This is a den of spine-backed, fang-toothed, devil adders."

"Be careful what you say," Lucian said. "Miss Winter is looking for Delano's killer. The way you're talking, it could put you on the top of her suspect list. From what I've learned of her investigative measures, she doesn't let go of her suspects easily."

I wasn't keen on agreeing with Lucian, but he had a point. "Erik, you thought little of your brother?"

His bleary, bloodshot eyes finally found me after his gaze wobbled around the room. "You're with the Magic Council?"

"I'm working freelance on this case. What did your brother do that made you hate him?"

Erik stood with his arms out as if he needed them to stay upright. "Bullied me, made fun of me in front of everyone, told me I'd amount to nothing. He didn't say that just to me. He was horrible to everyone who wouldn't toe his line. I'm not much of a line toer. I snap the line. Give it a yank and see what flips out on its rotten belly." He leaned forward, almost tumbling over. "There's lots of rot around here. It all needs cutting out."

"Erik! I give up on you." Augusta walked away, shaking her head.

"Can you remember where you were the night Delano was cursed?" I said.

"When did it happen again?"

"Five days ago," Lucian said. "And you most likely won't remember where you were. We discovered you passed out drunk in the kitchen. You got your hands on the chef's cooking sherry. You drank two bottles."

"Oh! That night! I remember. It was the night Chef served an enormous trifle covered in brandy cream. I got a taste for the stuff and went to congratulate her. She was kind enough to show me the bottles of sherry. Of course, I had to sample them. She had a small glass with me, too. Everything gets fuzzy after that."

"It would after downing two bottles of cooking sherry," Lucian said.

Fire Fang leaned against my hip. "Any of these sour slugs you want me to detain? You know, squash to the floor and bite a confession out of?"

"Not yet." Hearing another lousy alibi hadn't led me along a useful path. And although Erik wasn't hiding his hatred for Delano, would he have been in a fit enough state to sneak up the stairs and plant the skull without messing up?

"How long did the chef stay with you?" I said to him.

"A few minutes. She had a couple of sips and excused herself, saying it didn't seem right to drink with a member of the family."

"You were drinking alone?"

"I was. More for me."

"We keep out of Erik's way when he's on a bender," Lucian said. "He's a sloppy drunk and likes to fight when he's had too many."

"I never start the fights. I just finish them." Erik clapped his hands and rubbed them together briskly. "I need a pick me up. All this talk of murder is giving me a thirst."

Lucian shifted his attention from Erik, not bothering to hide his contempt. His cool gaze hit me. "Now you've heard everyone's alibis. Which one of us murdered Delano?"

Chapter 7

"Meow, meow, meeeeeooooow!"

I groaned and turned over, taking the pillow with me to use as a muffler against the persistent, grating noise outside.

"Meow, meooooooow, meow." The volume got turned up by several decibels. That cat knew I was trying to sleep in after a frustrating, progress-less night. She hated me.

"Why doesn't that cat pay attention to the hints? She's not moving in," I muttered into the pillow.

After visiting the Discord family yesterday and hearing the unhelpful alibis, I'd crashed out after midnight when I'd gotten back to my apartment. My dreams had been full of skulls, sweeping staircases, and secrets. That family was hiding a metric ton of secrets. And I needed to dig them out and get to the truth to find out who controlled that screaming skull.

The pained meowing continued, so I inched open an eye. Normally, Fire Fang was sprawled on the other side of the bed, his head on a pillow and his paws tucked over the top of the duvet. Not this morning. The space was empty.

I let go of the pillow and flopped onto my back. Fire Fang was levitating over the bed. "That's a new one. Did you get up there while you were sleeping?"

"Nope."

"How long have you been doing that?"

"About an hour."

"Why?"

"I felt the need to fly. I like feeling weightless. Besides, you were hogging the bed. And you kept muttering about skulls and idiots."

"That was my subconscious at work, figuring out what deception the Discord family is keeping from us." I reached up and scratched his belly. "You coming down?"

"In a minute."

I yawned until my jaw cracked and shuffled deeper under the duvet. Even though I had a clock counting down the time I had left to solve this case, I needed a few more minutes in bed. Unlike Hattie, I wasn't an early riser. My label read night owl.

"Meow, meow, meow."

"Urgh! Why does she have to start so early? She's not getting in."

"She must see something good in you," Fire Fang said. "Like I do. Even if you talk in your sleep."

"It's better than floating in my sleep." I pressed the button on the automatic coffee machine beside my bed, and while it brewed, I hit the bathroom, washed my face, and then jumped back on the bed, still in my faded T-shirt and shorts.

Fire Fang had made his way down and was in his usual position, flopped on the bed beside me.

Once the coffee was brewed, I grabbed a can of whipped cream from the drawer next to the bed. It wasn't kept there for kinky fun. Who'd waste good cream on that? It had a more important purpose. I squirted it over my coffee, then tilted the can, so I could shoot Fire Fang a huge globule of yummy goodness.

He gulped it down and swiped his tongue across his nose. "Delicious. It makes me want to levitate again."

"Go for it. Are you hiding any other powers? I'm used to you floating around, and you do that fun thing with flames sometimes, but is there anything else I need to look out for?"

"As far as I can tell, I'm an average hellhound. I've not met many others, though, so I've not got a frame of reference. I also have no memories of the time before I was a hell mutt."

Frame of reference? Fire Fang sometimes talked like a posh guy, not a cussing hellhound. "Before you were a mutt? You've been something before you were a hellhound?"

Fire Fang scratched behind one ear with a back paw. "I think so. I'm not sure what, though. I have my time as a hellhound, and then blank time. I know something was going on, and I'm sure I wasn't a hound. But I can't tell you what I was. A... something else."

"A shapeshifter? Although I've never heard of a shape shifting hellhound. But then some shapeshifters can be anything they want. You're not tricking me into giving you belly rubs and treats, are you?"

"You give those freely. I have no urge to change form. I like this one. Hellhound suits me."

I stroked a hand along his belly several times as I sipped my coffee and licked off my cream mustache. "So long as you're happy doing what you do now, I guess it doesn't matter what you were." Although I was intrigued. Was I sharing bed space with a magical creature that could change form but had lost its memories? When I had five minutes to call my own, I'd look into that.

"I like your thinking. Live in the moment. Be grateful for what you have. There's no use dwelling on my blank past."

"What if you were something incredible, like a phoenix or part dragon?"

"Being a phoenix must suck. Everything is going great, and then poof, you explode in a shower of flames, turn to ash, then hatch as a chick and have to do it all over again. No one needs to go back to their teenage years."

"You're right about that." I sipped more coffee.

"Did any of those weird dreams you were having help you with this case?"

"Nope. I have the same answer to give you as I did Lucian when he asked who killed Delano. I don't have enough information. No one has a decent alibi, they all have motives, and any of them could have done it."

"What do you think about Lucian claiming his innocence?"

"I'm not ruling him out, but I don't think it was him. The guy's smugger than a politician who's just won a major campaign even after his scandal with the intern was revealed, but he has the least to gain. Delano looked out for Lucian, set him up in business, and gave him a reputation most lawyers would die for. Now, all that is out on a limb. And the way Augusta spoke to him yesterday, she's unimpressed with his tactics."

"That leaves us with everyone else."

"Augusta looks good for it. In most of these investigations, the spouse is the first to be grilled. It must be tough living with the same person day after day, putting up with their disgusting habits—"

"You mean, the ones where they talk in their sleep, don't close the bathroom door, and leave takeout cartons in the lounge until a new form of fungus grows in them?"

"We're roommates. That's a different kind of relationship. We're allowed to be disgusting in front of each other. And don't forget, I get the joy of clearing up your mess, too."

"When do I ever leave any mess?"

"Have you forgotten the enormous, gross hairball you coughed up just before the speech spell took effect?"

Fire Fang lowered his muzzle, looking embarrassed. "It was a one-off. Hairballs are a rarity. But you're right. Augusta and Delano were married a long time. Love can turn dark. It can even turn to hate."

"And Augusta had a ton of reasons for wanting Delano dead and out of her hair for good."

"Meow, meow, meow."

"Hush up, cat!"

"She's hungry." Fire Fang nudged me with his muzzle. "So am I."

"If I feed her, it'll encourage her to keep yowling."

"Too late for that. You have kitty treats under the counter. You've been feeding her for months."

"She hasn't been around here for months."

"Yes, she has. Before we started hanging out, that cat was lurking around Witch Haven. I used to see her. She was always looking for something. Always hunting, hunting, hunting."

"You two were friends?"

"We're not enemies. She's never bothered me."

"Meow, meow, meow."

I clamped a hand over one ear. "That doesn't bother you?"

"Food. It comforts her. It also comforts me. Especially if there's lots of it."

I drew back my warm covers and slid out of bed. I peeked out the window, and the cat spotted me. She was a scrawny looking thing, with a raggedy tail and one eye that only half-opened. She needed not only a good meal but a groom. She didn't know how to take care of herself. Maybe someone kicked her out, so she wasn't great at fending for herself.

The meowing intensified the second she saw me, so I headed to the kitchen, opened the fridge, and pulled out some sliced meat. I opened the window and tossed out the meat, which she leaped upon and devoured within seconds.

"She'll take that as a sign of encouragement." Fire Fang grabbed the sliced ham I gave him.

"You told me to feed her."

"Correction. I told you what to do to keep her quiet. Got any more?"

"That cat can take my food offering however she likes, but she's not setting up home here." I kept watching the cat. I needed her gone. Life was complicated enough without a needy stray cat latching onto me. "Today's the day."

"For what?"

"To get that cat in a cage and to the shelter." I'd tried to catch her a dozen times, but she always got away.

Fire Fang grumbled a few times. "It'll be a no kill shelter, right?"

"Of course. I'm not a monster. Luna and Cole run a place. It'll be ideal for this kitty cat. But we won't find her a forever furry home while she's hanging about outside this apartment. She needs to go somewhere she can be properly cared for."

"Are you sure she can't move in? She's only small. I don't mind hanging out with cats. Although Nugget can be superior. And Tuffin is a food stealer."

"No more animals. I have enough problems with you levitating over my bed. What if you'd lost your mojo and landed on me?"

"I'd have had a comfy landing. Although you're bony. You don't eat enough."

"You make up for my lack of appetite. I should put you up for adoption, too. You know this is only a temporary thing."

"Yeah, if temporary means eternity. You're not getting rid of me." Fire Fang rolled onto his back and kicked his legs in the air. "Now, feed me more delicious deli meat and rub my belly."

I hid a grin behind my mug of coffee. I didn't want Fire Fang going anywhere soon. This wasn't the ideal place for him, and I needed to find some secure, outdoor space he could run around in without terrifying people, but this would do for now. For both of us.

I knelt and scratched his belly. "The screaming skull case will take some work to figure out, and it's not a problem I can solve in one day. But I can deal with that cat right now. It'll be good to have something positive ticked off the to-do list early on."

"How do you plan to capture her? She has that habit of vanishing without warning."

"Lots of treats. And you can help with herding her. I'll set the cage, cover it with something, put treats inside, and you send her in the right direction."

"There's some phrase about trying to herd cats. It never ends well."

"This will work. Give me ten minutes to get everything together, then we'll be ready to go stray cat catching."

After a quick shower, a change of clothes, and collecting a small animal cage from my office - I sometimes took on missing animal cases when the money was good - I headed down the stairs with Fire Fang and through my office. My pockets were full of treats, and my mind set to 'determined to achieve' mode. This cat was going in the cage and then to Luna's shelter. Luna could coo over her, spoil her, and find her a family to love her.

"Let's go around the back. That was the last place I saw her," I said.

I eased open the door, and we crept into the chilly morning air. The sun was rising, sending streaks of orange across a pale gray sky. There was a bite to the wind, and I tugged my sleeves down over my hands to keep out the worst of the cold.

As we rounded the building where the trash was stored, a small black shadow darted from behind a tree.

"That's her," I whispered. "You distract her while I set up the cage. I'll barricade it with trash bags, so she won't be able to dodge past easily."

Fire Fang loped away, heading in the direction the cat had gone.

I gently placed down the cage, opened the spring-loaded door, put a handful of treats inside, then set out a trail of treats leading to the cage to encourage her in. Hopefully, her hunger would override her suspicion, and she'd walk right in. Once she was inside, the door would automatically close. Job done.

After the treats were laid out, I bundled trash cans and bags around the cage. I'd forgotten to bring a cover for the cage, so I shrugged out of my jacket and laid it over the top. I didn't mind being cold if it meant I got rid of this cat.

I scanned the early morning gloom for any sign of the cat or Fire Fang, but it was silent out there. Only the breeze stirred the crispy leaves on the trees.

"Here, kitty. All the treats you need. Free bed and board for the rest of your life if you get in this comfortable, safe cage."

A bush close by me rustled, but nothing appeared out of it.

I headed farther from the cage, using the smallest light spell I could conjure so as not to startle the cat. I spotted the red glow of Fire Fang's eyes some distance away. Was the cat making a run for it?

The bush rustled again, and I jumped back. I ducked and looked under it. A large possum hissed at me and bared its teeth.

Holding up my hands, I backed away. "I'm not after you, buddy. You get back to whatever business you were doing."

It hissed again before shuffling off into the gloom.

I rubbed my arms to stay warm as I walked around, looking for the cat. She couldn't have gone far. She was always lurking about, making a racket and trying to guilt me into letting her in. It would never happen.

"Incoming! She's heading your way," Fire Fang yelled in the gloom.

I had barely a second to process what I saw. The cat sped out of the shadows and raced at the cage. She must have smelled the treats, or maybe Fire Fang had given her a nip of encouragement.

The cat wasn't slowing. If she kept going at that speed, she'd hit the wall. At the last second, she hoovered up the treats, then leaped, did a twist style parkour move, using the wall to bounce off, and landed on my head. Claws raked down one of my cheeks, and she kicked off, using my chest to propel herself away.

My arms pinwheeled. I lost my balance, and my knees hit a trash can as I went down. A bag of trash landed on my stomach as my head hit the cage.

I threw the bag of trash off me and clambered to my feet. One hand went to my cheek, and my fingers came away covered in blood. This little cat was mean. There was no need for such violence. Although I'd most likely put up a fight if someone tried to trick me into a cage.

Since the game was up, I cast a large light ball to see where the evil little scratcher had gone. She stood in front of Fire Fang, and he was giving her a thorough sniffing.

"Grab her!"

He kept sniffing. "It's weird, but she smells familiar."

"She could smell like tutti fruity ice cream, but don't let her go. Catch hold of her before she vanishes."

The cat glared at me and raced off, but Fire Fang was faster. He caught her tail under one paw and clamped his jaws around her back.

The cat may have been speedy, but she was also clever and knew not to fight when she was in the jaws of death. She went limp and howled.

I grabbed the cage and dashed over. "Put her in here. Quick, before she performs any more ninja tricks or casts a spell to vanish."

Fire Fang maneuvered his gigantic head into the cage, dropped the cat, and backed out.

I snapped the door shut and raised my hand for a high five.

Fire Fang slammed his enormous paw against my hand. "You're bleeding. It's dripping off your chin."

"I don't care about a little blood. This is a victory."

95

Chapter 8

The cage containing the unhappy cat was on the floor between my legs as we waited to be seen by the vet. I'd called Luna to make sure she had space for a cat at the animal sanctuary, and she was happy to take her in. But first, I had to get the angry fuzz ball checked over to make sure she was healthy.

Fire Fang was slumped next to the cage, not looking happy. "How much longer? This place gives me the chills."

"Relax. They won't do anything to you."

"You say that, but vets like to poke and prod where it's not appropriate. If they ask if I need any jabs, you say no. I'm a healthy hellhound. No medicine required. No needles, no potions, no nothing."

"It's not a bad idea to get you checked out while we're here. You have magic, but maybe the vet can figure out how powerful you are with a few spells."

"I'm all powerful. I don't need more power. My power is perfect."

I rested a hand on his head and scratched behind his ears to reassure him. It was no surprise any animal who came here, magical or otherwise, got twitchy. When they came to the vet, they knew it wouldn't be a fun experience.

While I waited to be called in, I pulled out my phone and called a research contact, John Smith. It wasn't his real name, but it was the name everyone knew him by. John kept a profile so low, he skimmed under all Magic Council radars. I could only imagine it was because of his shady past, which would mean instant arrest if his true identity was revealed.

"Hey, Storm. What do you need?"

That was one thing I liked about John. He got straight to the point. "I've got a job for you."

"Same as always. What's the deal?"

I looked around the waiting room, but other than an elderly lady sitting in the corner with a toy poodle on her lap, we were alone. "I'm dealing with an unusual case."

"Unusual dangerous or unusual weird?"

"Weird and personal. I need you to get me the inside scoop on cursed skulls that scream. I already have basic research, which I'll send you, but I need all the dirt."

"Interesting. Who's connected to this skull?"

"The Discord family. Have you heard of Delano Discord?"

"Sure. He's rich, arrogant, and makes his living out of other people's misery. He's one of those guys who buys failing companies and tears them apart."

"You got it. He's also a dead guy. Six days ago, someone left a cursed skull outside his bedroom door. He opened the door, it screamed, and a week later, he was dead. The family wants to know who did it."

"It's not something the Magic Council can deal with?"

"Not quickly. I also want any dirt on the family. They were all in the house when the curse triggered, so I figure one of them got that skull and set it up for Delano to find. They also murdered two servants before they got to Delano."

"Got it. Usual rates apply."

"Of course."

"You mentioned this was personal. You friends of this family?"

"Not friends. The guy who hired me to solve this case made sure I had no option but to get involved."

"Has he got dirt on you?" John chuckled.

"Something like that. And don't drag your heels with this investigation. The clock is ticking."

"I'm still intrigued by the dirt."

"It's none of your business. At least, not for now. You'll get ten percent on top of your usual fee if you get me the information in the next forty-eight hours."

"I'm already on it. How's that cute friend of yours, Odessa?"

"Still off-limits to slime bags. If you go near any of my friends and mess with them again, you'll know what it's like to be on my naughty list."

"Sounds like fun."

"It isn't. It involves Fire Fang and you in a room alone for half an hour."

John hissed out a breath. "I get it. I overstepped the mark with Odessa. It won't happen again."

"You bet it won't. Get back to me when you've got something useful." I ended the call and slid my phone into my pocket. John was a slimeball, but he knew all the other slime balls to talk to, and that made him useful. Not to be trusted, but useful.

"Excuse me, would you like a mint?" The old lady with the poodle held out half a packet of peppermints.

"I'm good, thanks."

"It's just there's a strange smell in here. It's unsettling my stomach. Can you smell it?" She tucked a peppermint into her mouth.

I discreetly sniffed my jacket and grimaced. "Nope. No idea where that's coming from. Maybe an animal had an upset stomach."

"It could be that. It smells like something is rotting, though. Like old trash."

I leaned away from her. Hopefully, a hot wash would get the smell from my clothing.

The cat howled out her misery and scratched the bars.

"Your little princess doesn't sound happy," the old lady said.

"She isn't. But she's not mine. She's a stray. I'm having her checked out to make sure she's healthy. She'll find a new home soon enough."

The door opened behind the reception area, and a woman wearing a white coat, her blonde hair pulled back from her face, looked out. "Storm Winter and stray, please."

I collected the cage, nodded at the old lady, and headed into the examination room. Fire Fang loped behind me, his head down and his tail between his legs.

"I'm Doctor Hooper. Set the cage on the table, please. Is she friendly?" The vet flicked through information on a screen in front of her. "I have little history here."

"Not so much." I pointed at my scratched cheek when she glanced at me.

"Did you clean the wound? Cat scratches often get infected. They have a lot of dirt trapped under their claws."

"I haven't had a chance. After I caught her, I came straight here."

Doctor Hooper passed me a packet of wipes. "These are for animals, but they contain antiseptic, so it's safe on your scratches. It should help." She bent and peered through the cage bars. "Hello, sad girl. There's no one looking after you?"

I dabbed a wipe on my cuts. "She's been hanging around my apartment for ages. I've been trying to catch her, but she keeps vanishing."

"Running off vanishing or literally vanishing?" Doctor Hooper still studied the cat.

"Both. She's got magic in her, but I know nothing about her other than that."

"Poor girl. Let's see if we can't get you happier. Then we'll have a think about your future." Doctor Hooper slid open the cage door.

The cat didn't move, just blinked large eyes at the vet and licked her nose.

"The cage becomes their best friend when they're here." Doctor Hooper eased the cat out.

She was limp, a boneless sack of fur, as the vet set her on the examination table.

"I feel her pain," Fire Fang muttered. He'd jammed himself into the corner of the room, trying to make himself as small as possible by sitting on his paws and curling his tail around his body.

"I don't have your hellhound booked for an exam, but I've got time if you want me to look him over, too," Doctor Hooper said.

"I'm good," Fire Fang said. "No health problems here."

Doctor Hooper examined the cat. "She's thin and needs feeding, but there are no external parasites causing problems. Let's see what's going on inside." She rubbed her hands together, and a pale purple glow drifted from her palms.

The cat relaxed, not seeming to mind magic being used on her.

Doctor Hooper ran her hands over the cat several times, from her nose to her tail. "That looks great. Other than being underweight and dehydrated, she's healthy. Not that old, either. In human years, maybe in her early twenties. She's got a couple of old injuries, but they must have happened a while ago, because they're healed. Just the scars left." She scratched under the cat's chin, and I was amazed when the cat gently purred.

"If there's nothing wrong with her, I've already found her a place in a nearby animal rescue. My friend runs it. She's great with animals."

"That's good news. Let me give her some boosters to be on the safe side, but then this little angel can go on her next adventure. We'll keep her overnight for observation, but then she's free."

The cat's eyes narrowed as Doctor Hooper pressed her fingers along her spine several times, but she didn't protest.

"All done." Doctor Hooper's gaze went to Fire Fang. "Are you planning on rehoming the hellhound, too? They can be difficult to find places for. It's the size, I think. It puts people off."

I bit the inside of my cheek. "I was thinking about that."

Fire Fang growled out his disapproval. "I'm going nowhere. I have a home with this ungrateful witch."

"He's your familiar?" Doctor Hooper stroked the cat.

"Not really. We're figuring things out." I leaned against the examination table. "Fire Fang has some unusual abilities. He breathes fire, which isn't odd for a hellhound, but he also levitates. And sometimes, he changes color."

"I've never heard of a hellhound doing that." Doctor Hooper's gaze moved to Fire Fang. "What are you mixed with?"

"Nothing." He turned his back on us.

"I've no idea. And he doesn't know either. He has some memory loss."

Doctor Hooper placed the cat in the cage before walking over to Fire Fang. "Have you been in any accidents or injured yourself? That can cause memory loss."

"No. And I don't need to be examined. There's nothing wrong with me."

"Relax, she's trying to help. You could get your memory back so you remember what you were before you were a hellhound."

"What's that?" Doctor Hooper hovered over Fire Fang, looking eager to examine him.

"Fire Fang said something odd to me. He thinks he was something else before he was a hellhound."

"Something else? How interesting. I love the complicated cases. Fire Fang, with your permission, I'd love to run tests on you."

"I told you this would happen." Fire Fang glared at me. "I don't need tests. I'm fine."

"You must want to know what you are, though. You could have a family somewhere or a home you've forgotten about," I said.

"I'm settled. I'm happy. I don't care about my past."

I kneeled beside him and rested my hand on his head. "But I do. I don't want you stuck with me when you could have an incredible life with someone else. You could belong to a powerful warlock."

"If you don't mind me saying, he looks like he's got a great life with you. Fire Fang is well-fed and healthy," Doctor Hooper said.

"I live in a one-bed apartment above my office. I have no outdoor space for him. And I work away a lot. I can't always take him with me. That's no life for such a huge animal."

"You ever heard me complain?" he muttered.

"Well, no. But we haven't been doing this long, and you've only just started to talk. It could get annoying in the long term."

"Fire Fang seems to be thriving." Doctor Hooper petted him.

She wasn't helping the situation. "Fire Fang, this is for your benefit. The tests will probably show nothing. But wouldn't it be great to know if you're a super hellhound?"

"I know I'm super enough without probing tests." His eyes glowed brilliant red as he glared at the vet.

"No probing," Doctor Hooper said. "Just magic. We can start with something simple."

"Absolutely no probing?"

"I'll begin with a health check. Then see how you feel."

He groaned. "You're going to probe. I know it. Run your tests, but they'd better not hurt."

The vet bit her lip, and her eyes flashed wide for a second. "One may hurt a tiny bit. To get a full profile of your ancestry, I'll need a blood sample. You'll get a big treat if you're a good boy and let me take some blood."

"This is so humiliating," he rumbled out.

"All I need to do is shave a tiny piece of fur from your paw and extract the blood. You'll barely feel it. I'll use the thinnest of needles." Doctor Hooper glanced at me and winked. "Storm, you may like to hold Fire Fang, just in case he finds it painful and needs comforting."

"He's being a wimp." I settled beside him on the floor and caught hold of his head, cradling it in my lap. I glanced at the cage and was surprised to see the cat paying attention. She seemed more relaxed and was probably grateful she had a warm place to stay. She'd be fine at the animal shelter. Someone would fall in love with her and take her home so she'd never have to howl outside my window again.

Doctor Hooper shaved off the fur and made swift work of drawing a vial of Fire Fang's blood.

My brave hellhound barely whimpered.

"All done, cutie pie. Now, for your treat." Doctor Hooper extracted a huge brown meaty smelling chew, almost the length of her arm, from a storage cupboard. She also brought out a smaller chew for the cat and fed it to her through the bars.

She handed the other to Fire Fang, and he pounced on it.

"Thanks for doing that," I said. "When will I get the results?"

"Should be within the next five or six days. Just make sure we have your contact details, and I'll phone them through when ready."

"That long?"

"They could come back earlier. It depends how busy the lab is."

"Great. I may not be dead by then."

Doctor Hooper's head jerked back. "You're sick?"

"No. Long story. Won't bore you with it. Just let me know when you get the results."

"Err... Of course. Take care of that cut on your cheek. No picking or it'll leave a scar."

A scar on my face was the least of my worries. After thanking the vet, I grabbed the cage and opened the door. Fire Fang bolted out, still chewing his treat. I paid the bill and headed outside.

A quick stop at Luna's animal shelter, and then it was back to the business of murder.

The cat was gone, Fire Fang was asleep in the corner of my office, and my cheek had stopped stinging.

I was deep in research mode, running a background check on Augusta Discord. And she had quite a background.

Fire Fang rolled over, yawned, climbed to his feet, and shook out his fur.

"Hey. No after-effects from your terrifying visit to the vet?" I said.

"I still smell strange, but I'll live. How's the research going?" He mooched over and rested his head on my lap so I could scratch behind his ears.

"Augusta is an aristocrat. She comes from old money and ancient power. At least she did. I knew she was a Crossfire witch, but my history on them is fuzzy. Do you know much about them?"

"They had their powers stolen."

"Taken in battle after they lost. Which is why Augusta forged an alliance with Delano. A witch with no power won't live long. There's always someone wanting to take her out."

"You're still thinking she's the most likely suspect for these murders?"

"She's got great motives for killing Delano, and Augusta was alone in the bathroom. She'd have needed to be sneaky to do it but must have crept out, left the skull by the door, and waited for the inevitable."

"If her power was taken, would she be strong enough to control such a weapon?"

"It's something to find out. It's time to talk to Augusta again and see how, and if, she got her hands on that cursed skull."

Chapter 9

I was back at the family home with Fire Fang by mid-afternoon. I'd called ahead to make sure Augusta would be in and we'd have time to talk about curses and skulls. We'd been interrupted the previous evening by the rest of the family showing up, but I already had a good idea there was no love lost between Augusta and Delano.

I was surprised when she opened the door, but remembered the servants had been sent home to avoid any more unfortunate deaths thanks to the skull popping up.

"How are you feeling?" she said in way of greeting.

"No complaints."

"I was wondering if the curse was making you feel strange. Before Delano died, he complained of headaches and said he felt tired. It could have been a side effect of being cursed."

"Nothing going on like that. But thanks for the warning. I'll look out for the symptoms."

"Come in. I had a full day today but cleared my afternoon when I heard you needed to speak to me." She caught hold of my arm as I stepped into the hallway. "Storm, I'm so sorry about Lucian. He shouldn't have done this to you. I'm not happy with him."

"Neither am I. And to be clear, I wouldn't have taken this case if I didn't have any other option."

Augusta's bottom teeth worried her lip. "Of course. I've been looking into your background. Well, I had someone do it for me. You have an incredible reputation for solving difficult cases. I understand why Lucian came to you."

"It won't be a great reputation for long if I don't figure out this case. This could be my last investigation."

"I hope you solve it for your own good. And of course, to find out what happened to Delano, Sam, and Suzanne."

"Me too. Shall we get going?"

"I've organized refreshments. I'm rather proud of myself. I did it on my own. It's been awhile since I've done any baking, so I can't vouch for how edible the cookies are, but with the servants gone... I wanted to make an effort." Augusta led me and Fire Fang into an elegant pink room, and I was happy to be greeted by a plate of delicious looking white iced cookies. There was also a large cafetiere of coffee.

We headed to some seats and settled in them. I took a cookie and offered it to Fire Fang. He bolted it down in two bites.

"I'm glad someone likes them," Augusta said, her tone a little sharp.

"He's my official taste tester." I took a cookie and had a bite. It was as tasty as it looked.

Augusta served the coffee and sat looking at me, an expectant expression on her face.

I finished the cookie. "Last time we spoke, you were open about the fact your marriage wasn't built on a romantic connection. That must have been tough to deal with."

A slow breath slid out of Augusta as she took her time to form her words. "Tough is an understatement. The marriage started fine. I was young, naïve, and desperate to please my family. And in the early days, Delano was charming. He was a handsome older man with money and power. He was exactly the person I needed to marry to ensure the Crossfire witches stayed relevant and, most importantly, alive. There had been several assassination attempts on the family after our power was taken."

"Were you in the battle of Frost Wood?"

"I was. Although not on the front lines. I hadn't long come into my power, and my defensive skills weren't as they should be. It was a brutal fight. The Valenti witches were relentless. The feud between the families had gone on for centuries, and that fight was the pinnacle. We only lost because they cheated and used illegal magic."

"And after the battle, you formed strategic alliances with other powerful families?"

"Those of us who could did. We'd have done anything to keep the coven safe. And as I said, to begin with, it wasn't a bad marriage. There was a time when I was fond of Delano. And I have my son, and I'm so grateful for that. I'm delighted he's taken after me, as opposed to his father. He's not power mad and obsessed with obtaining the latest thing. Chilton is a decent young man."

"How soon into the marriage did things change?"

"Within a few years, I regretted the marriage. No, that's the wrong word. The marriage helped save my family and gave me a son, but I was disappointed in how much Delano changed. He'd hidden his true self, or perhaps simply grown into a monster. I quickly learned not to ask too many questions. Delano loathed being questioned."

"You hated him?"

Another soft breath slid out. "Yes, I hated him. He was cold and cruel. And as he aged, all Delano wanted was more power. He became unkind, making it clear he only married me because of my family connection. When things were difficult between us, he even threatened to leave me and withdraw his protection from the Crossfire witches. Of course, I had to play nice and pretend there was nothing wrong or risk everything."

"You'd rather not have been married to him?"

"I am glad the marriage happened. Not for my sake, but to ensure the Crossfire witches weren't destroyed. But I wish he was a better man. He used to be. But he's so different from the man I agreed to a partnership with. I don't know, perhaps it was me. I annoyed him."

"Delano sounds like a guy who irritated easily. I doubt that was your fault."

She sipped her coffee. "Perhaps."

"Did you ever think about leaving?"

"Many times. Too many to remember. But it would have been risky, and I'd have dishonored my family. We all knew what we'd signed up for. If any of us break an alliance, we all become vulnerable. If

I left, it could reignite a war. And if that happened, the Crossfire witches would be destroyed. The Valenti witches are waiting for an opportunity to strike. Therefore, I needed Delano's name, fortune, and magic to protect myself and the coven."

"With him dead, does that make you vulnerable?"

Augusta hesitated for several seconds. "I have access to his resources. Delano has a magic vault in the cellar that I can use. And of course, I didn't just marry him. I married into the Discord family. They protect each other. Just because he's dead doesn't mean I'm alone."

"Do the Valenti witches know that? Or do they think, with Delano out of the way, you're a perfect target?"

Her hand slowed as she lifted the cup to her lips. "Our enemy operates on dumb luck and illegal moves, so anything is possible. Someone could have assumed, with Delano gone, I'm fair game. If they come for me, they'll regret it. Especially now I have my son to protect. I'll do whatever I have to, to keep him safe."

Augusta's desire to protect was clear. Had she killed Delano to protect her son from being negatively influenced by him? It was another motive worth considering.

"Talk me through your alibi again," I said. "I'm also interested in the other times the skull was used. You lost two servants, didn't you?"

"That's right. Samuel and Suzanne. They were valuable members of the household. Sam had been with us for over twenty years. He was a good man. Why kill our servants?"

"You tell me."

She lifted her hands. "I have no explanation."

"The killer could have been testing the effectiveness of the skull. Some people see servants as dispensable."

Her gaze grew glacial. "Not me. I always treat my staff fairly."

"Or the killer got the timing wrong. Their deaths were mistakes."

"Collateral damage," she murmured. "That happened a lot around Delano. People got hurt if they got in his way."

"Remind me where you were when Delano was cursed by the skull."

"In our private bathroom. It's next door to the bedroom, but you can access it from either the corridor or our room. Only the two of us use it. I heard the scream, but by the time I came out to see what was going on, Lucian had the skull and was with Delano. They both appeared shocked, as was I when I discovered what was going on."

"There's no way anyone can vouch for you being in the bathroom at that time?"

"I showered alone. There's no one who can verify that."

"Where were you when Sam and Suzanne were cursed?"

"You don't think... Well, of course, you must think the worst of all of us. And since the skull was the murder weapon in all three cases, it makes sense the same person killed them."

"My exact thoughts. So..."

"I was out of the house on both occasions." Augusta shook her head, sadness entering her eyes that hadn't been there when she'd spoken about Delano's death. "This place feels unstable. Everything is changing."

"Is it changing for the better?"

"It's impossible to tell." The sadness vanished, leaving a cold shrewdness behind. "I understand why you're focused on me. I have a good motive for wanting my husband dead. But I've been honest with you regarding my feelings for him. We tolerated each other because we had to. We'd found a way of working that functioned for both of us."

"Most of the time."

Her lips pursed. "Yes, most of the time."

"If you killed him, you took a risk. With Delano dead, your family could be vulnerable to a magic attack if a maverick Valenti witch wants to make a name for herself by taking you out."

"And you're asking yourself, how risk averse am I? Was my marriage to that odious man so dreadful, I'd rather go back into battle with the Valenti witches than spend another day with him?"

"It crossed my mind."

"Don't think I haven't been tempted to dispatch him myself and figure out how to fend off a new war. But I'm not just thinking about myself anymore. I'd never risk my coven or my son."

"Will your coven protect you if you leave this place?"

"They would do their best. And after Delano dropped his horrifying bombshell about wasting his wealth and power, the cogs started turning. I've thought up a dozen scenarios of where to go and who I should look to for protection."

"Again, it gives you an excellent motive for murder. Delano's plan left you exposed."

"I hold my hands up to having plenty of excellent motives. And I was alone when the skull screamed at Delano. But I was out of the house visiting family on both occasions when Samuel and Suzanne were cursed. I can give you the information so you can check."

"Do that." I sat back with another cookie in my hand. "But if you didn't kill Delano, who did?"

"That is for you to figure out. It's why Lucian found you."

"And cursed me."

Augusta paused as she wrote details of her alibis on a piece of paper. "Yes, true enough. And deeply regrettable."

I could see the pros and cons Augusta must have weighed up when considering killing Delano. She'd been living in a nightmare for a long time. A person can only take so much before something snaps, snaps hard, and never repairs. That could have been the case here. Augusta endured being married to Delano, but when he revealed he was taking away something she needed, she acted on feelings she'd had for most of her life.

For all that, I now doubted her guilt. Augusta was bonded to her coven and clearly loved her son. Killing Delano put many people at risk, and Augusta gave the impression of being calculating rather than a risk taker.

She gave me details of her alibis for the times Sam and Suzanne had been cursed, and I tucked the information in my pocket.

"Show me what magic you still have left," I said. "You'd need power to control a screaming skull."

"I'm embarrassed to say I have little. I could manage a light ball, but that's the extent of it. I can only cast a couple of spells a day before I'm drained." A haunted look drew her cheekbones up as Augusta inhaled. "I'm back at the level of beginner. Do you remember the spells they taught us in the first semester of witch school?"

I nodded. We'd all gone through it. "Show me what you've got."

Augusta held out her hands and closed her eyes. After a few seconds of concentration, lines firing across her forehead, a weak light ball hovered in the air before dissipating.

"That's it?"

"That is the full extent of my power. All the Crossfire witches were drained of magic on the battlefield. Adults and children alike. No one in my line was spared. We try to be grateful they didn't drain us completely and abandon us in the world of mortals."

"Why didn't they? It would have meant you were never a threat again."

"It's a question you'll have to ask the Valenti witches. But even an enemy respects tradition, power, and reputation. They wanted us fallen, but they didn't want to destroy us." Her expression hardened, and her fingers tightened around the cup she clasped. "Perhaps I'm being too benevolent, and they'd always planned to leave our broken shells behind so they could taunt us."

"Or as a reminder for other witches not to mess with them."

"That is also a possibility."

"You seem to have unfinished business with the Valenti witches."

"There will always be unfinished business between us." A haunting flash of malevolence marred her features before she was back to her composed self.

Although I was almost certain Augusta hadn't lied about her lack of magic, and she was as weak as she'd demonstrated, I needed to be doubly sure. Raising my hand, I slammed out a mid-level knockback spell. Not enough to kill, but enough to rattle bones.

Augusta threw out her hands as the spell approached, her eyes as wide as a hoot owl's who'd been caught with his beak in the mouse jar for the tenth time. The spell slammed into her, and she was shoved back against the couch. She lay there, her cup tipped over, the contents dripping onto the floor as she flailed her arms.

Fire Fang slurped up the spilled tea. "You could have been a little gentler."

I shrugged. "I had to be sure. If I'd used a mild spell, Augusta could have shaken it off. This way, we know she can't defend herself."

Augusta's breathing settled, and she pulled herself into a more refined seated position. "Are you convinced now of my lack of power?"

"I am. Thanks for your time and the information." I grabbed a final cookie. "I'd like to speak to Rosina if she's around."

Saying that name was like I'd yanked a piece of string attached to the top of Augusta's head. She sat ramrod straight, drew in a deep breath, and collected her cup off the floor.

"I shall ask her to meet you. If you'll excuse me." Augusta stood and strode from the room.

"What do you think of her?" I said to Fire Fang.

"Innocent. And she'll be feeling that knockback spell for a day or two."

"I had to know she wasn't an incredible liar. And I agree with you. Augusta's most likely innocent. It would have been so much easier if the wife had done it. Of course, we'll check her alibis to be sure, but I no longer consider her a suspect. Let's move on to the girlfriend and see what our bombshell mistress has to say for herself."

Chapter 10

Rather than Rosina coming to me, Augusta informed me she was exercising with a personal trainer, and I'd find them outside.

I was surprised they'd be in the backyard, or rather, the extensively manicured field, since there was a nip in the air, and a cool breeze fluffed Fire Fang's coarse fur as we left the house.

We headed around the side of the building, and I resisted the urge to roll my eyes. Of course, Rosina wasn't exercising outdoors. There was a huge, pale gray rough stone cut building with large glass windows in front of us. Inside the no doubt air conditioned room, Rosina was being worked out by a huge, muscular half-troll, wearing such tight exercise clothes that nothing was left to the imagination.

Fire Fang grumbled as he took in the scene. "Why can't people go for a run around a few acres of woodland if they want to get fit? All that tight clothing and walking mindlessly on a treadmill for hours. Where's the fun in that?"

"There's no fun. It's why people give up after a while and return to the couch and the cookies."

His muzzle turned my way. "You need to exercise more."

I snorted a laugh. "You want me to turn into a gym bunny?"

"No, but you should come running with me. It'll do you good. I keep encouraging you."

"Is your version of encouragement sticking your cold nose under the duvet when I'm sleeping?"

"It gets you moving."

"And yelling. At you."

"You spend too much time indoors. When you do that, you smell moth bally."

"I do not." I sniffed the sleeve of my jacket. Maybe I could get outdoors more often. But I already preferred to walk everywhere rather than drive, and I didn't own a car. I got my exercise walking around Witch Haven and taking Fire Fang out.

"Let's focus on the gym bunny in front of us, shall we, and not my workout routine?"

"What routine?"

We headed inside, and the personal trainer turned as the door closed behind us.

Rosina leaned to her left so she could look past him, while he held her knees as she did sit-ups. "Hey! You're welcome to join me. I've got more clothing in the changing room."

"We've already done our daily workout." I shot a warning look at Fire Fang. "I've got more questions about Delano."

"Of course you do. Give me ten minutes. I've got another hundred sit-ups to do and then my cool down."

"One hundred and fifty," the trainer said. "We're beating your personal best today."

"Berco, you're so strict with me." Rosina fluttered her long, overly made up lashes. Despite working out, she wore a full face of make-up.

"I'll ask the questions while you work out. It won't take long."

"Go ahead. All this exercise gets the blood pumping, so I can multitask. Just ask Berco. I'm amazing at compound moves."

Berco grunted out his agreement.

I stepped past the personal trainer, so I was standing by Rosina's head. "When we first met, you weren't sad Delano was dead. Was that because you killed him?"

Rosina jerked upright. "That'll be all, Berco."

He stood, and the look that hit me when he glanced my way was less than friendly. Maybe there was more to this relationship than client and trainer. "We'll work on your glutes next time."

"You flirt. You love working my glutes." She giggled and finger waved him away. Only when he'd gone did Rosina focus on me. "That wasn't a nice thing to say. People grieve in different ways. Just because I wasn't leaking tears when we met doesn't mean I don't care about Delano's murder."

"You don't seem to be grieving at all."

"I've shed tears, but I'm an ugly crier, so I never cry in public."

"Or you're not sad he's dead."

She sat in a cross-legged position and leaned forward to scratch Fire Fang. "Delano gave me everything I asked for. I'm sad things have changed.

And I am devastated I have to deal with the frosty Augusta and her demands I leave my home. And it is mine, no matter what she says. Delano promised he'd provide for me."

"That's quite a promise. How long had you been his girlfriend?"

"Six months."

"And Augusta and Delano were married for how long?"

"That's not the point. When you find the right one, you just know. And I knew with Delano. He was my forever." Rosina stood, collected a water bottle, and took a drink.

"How did you first meet?"

"He hired me as his personal assistant."

"To do the admin or meet his other needs?"

"Judge all you want, but I met his needs, professional and personal. And I enjoyed it. I like being around powerful, older men. They have an appeal. You must understand."

"I don't." I barely had time to eat, let alone date. "Where were you working before you joined this household?"

Rosina took another drink. "I worked for the Valenti witches."

"Valenti! The witches who destroyed the Crossfire coven? That's a coincidence."

"I'm not sure I understand."

"You do. You're smarter than your inflated lips give you credit for. Augusta is an enemy of the Valenti witches, and you sweep into this position, steal her husband, and get a foot in the door of a powerful family who've been protecting a Crossfire witch. Were you here for Delano, or so you could keep an eye on Augusta for your real employer?"

"I have no interest in spying on Augusta. I wanted Delano and everything he offered me. He gave me an incredible wage, high-class working conditions, and luxury accommodation. I grabbed it with both hands. Besides, he was charming. As soon as Delano saw me at a champagne business mixer, he said I had to work with him."

"What skills do you have to meet such a demanding role?"

A perfect eyebrow arched. "More than just my inflated lips. I went to business school."

"How hard did Delano have to work to convince you to leave the Valenti witches' employment?"

"He put in the effort. Men like it when you play a little hard to get. Not too much, because they get bored, but many find it stimulating to think they've won the challenge. So, I negotiated the terms and let Delano know my old employers wanted to keep me. Right away, he doubled the salary. He offered me something I could only have imagined in my wildest dreams. It was intoxicating. I couldn't refuse him. After a month of toying with his affections, I accepted. Our relationship has been idyllic."

"So the fact he was married to an enemy of the Valenti witches is simply one of those weird old coincidences."

"The Valenti witches had no problem with Delano. That's irrelevant. He was what I wanted, so I got him. I always get what I desire." Her fingers dug into Fire Fang's fur, making him grumble his appreciation. My hellhound companion was an embarrassment.

"When we met, you said this family is toxic, but I didn't get to find out why. Did you include Delano in that?"

Rosina adjusted the waistband of her fitted pants. "Forget I said that."

"I can't. It could be relevant to the murders. What's so toxic about the family?"

"You must already know. Everyone knows about the Discord family."

"Pretend I'm an idiot and don't listen to gossip."

Her appraising gaze ran over me. "Maybe you're dumber than you look. Always listen to gossip."

This time, I arched an eyebrow.

"Oh, fine. I have nothing to hide. Not anymore. Delano was all about amassing influence, wealth, and power. It was a game for him. He had so much, but wanted to add more bricks to his empire. I used to tease him one day he'd meet his match and those bricks would tumble down." Her bottom lip jutted out. "Perhaps he did, and this is the result. A result I didn't cause."

"Give me more details. How did Delano amass so much?"

"I will. But you should know, it wasn't just him I was talking about when I spoke of toxicity. All the family are involved. They enjoy stirring trouble. It must be in the genes."

"Who do they cause trouble for?"

"Anyone who gets in their way or has something they want. They also enjoy waving the occasional red flag at the Valenti witches."

"To protect Augusta? The rest of the family feels loyal to her and wants to ensure her old enemy is never settled?"

"I'm not a part of the family, so I don't get all the juicy scandal, but that could be a part of it."

"They're actively fighting with the Valenti witches?"

"Oh, no. The battlefield days are done. But they operate on stealth. In particular, they enjoy planting rumors to ruin other covens' reputations. I've seen it happen twice since I've been here."

"Gossiping about other witches is hardly a crime."

"It's not just that. They spread lies and plant evidence to show the rumors are true. It's their way of removing the competition without getting their hands dirty."

"And they're all involved in this?"

"Some more than others. Delano insisted they show their loyalty by providing a service to the family. If they refused, he'd cut them off."

"Did anyone refuse?"

Rosina shook out her hair. "Did you ever meet Delano when he was alive?"

"I didn't."

"He's not a man you say no to. And you never cross him. He demanded loyalty and respect from everyone. And if you didn't demonstrate that, then you were out."

"What did you do to demonstrate your loyalty?"

"I left the Valenti witches. He said, if I worked for him, I could never make contact with them again."

"You haven't spoken to a single Valenti witch since you left their employment?"

"I wouldn't risk what I have here. Or rather, what I had. Now everything will change." Rosina petted Fire Fang's side and looked around. "And I was just getting things how I liked them."

"What exactly do you have here? How were you able to handle being Delano's girlfriend but living in the same place as his wife?"

A smile flickered across Rosina's lips. "Our relationship wasn't as simple as that. I wasn't just a mistress."

"Then explain it to me. What were you?"

"Delano needed to be seen as a dominant alpha male. It wasn't enough for him to have a fabulous house, power, and influence. He needed to show dominance in all areas of his life. Being married to the same woman whose magic had been plundered meant he was lacking. I stepped in to fill the void."

"I get that bit. You're the mistress, doing all the fancy bedroom tricks to put a smile on his face."

"My looks deceive. It's what I excel in." Rosina flicked up her eyebrows. "Do you want to know a secret?"

"Only if it's relevant to this investigation."

She leaned forward. "I was his show mistress."

"Show mistress?"

"As far as the public was concerned, I made Delano happy in private."

"You lost me. Didn't you make him happy?"

"He wasn't unhappy. But none of it was real."

"You weren't in a physical relationship with him?"

"We had a kiss and a cuddle, but Delano's interests in the bedroom were too odd for my taste. He sated his urges in magic brothels. Of course, he didn't want rumors of his peculiar tastes getting out in public, but still needed to be seen as a virile man."

"You faked being his mistress?"

"Everyone sees me as a harmless floosy. Something pretty Delano put on his arm and paraded around. It worked for him. Not only did he have the wife with the incredible ancestral connections, but he also had a beautiful witch he could bend to his every whim. At least, she did when they were out together. That was what he really wanted from me. That was why he paid so well, so I would keep his secret."

My gaze flickered over Rosina. She was stunningly beautiful with her long amber curls and Bambi-like eyes, but behind those physical assets, there was a clever brain ticking.

"You can look. I know I'm beautiful. And that's what people pay attention to. The curves and the fluttering lashes and the sweet, obliging smile."

"It's all a distraction," I said.

"A distraction from what?" That girlish giggle slipped out, and I was on the receiving end of more eyelash fluttering.

"I'm uncertain. Why tell me this?"

The giggling faded. "To give you the full picture and make sure you know I didn't kill Delano or the servants. I had too much to lose."

"Is Augusta the reason you're here, not Delano? You've infiltrated your way into this house to get close to her to please the Valenti witches?"

"You think too much. I'm just a woman using her best assets for as long as possible. Looks fade, so

I need to gather my resources before I become irrelevant."

"What do you need the resources for? And that's not you denying you're involved with the Valenti witches. Are you?"

She winked at me, not once, but twice. "A lady needs to get her kicks somehow. And I don't do anything wrong."

"Other than betraying Augusta. Again. She thinks you were sleeping with her husband, but you're doing something worse. You're passing on information about her to a deadly enemy."

"Why would I do that? And deadly enemy is a stretch." She inspected her perfect fingernails. "It's better this way. So long as the Crossfire witches behave, there won't be another war. No one wants war."

"You're here to make sure Augusta remains weak. Or did your orders change? The Valenti witches insisted you get rid of Delano so they have easy access to Augusta."

"Storm, your overly active imagination is charming but wrong. Maybe, and I'm not saying I do, but maybe I have a foot in both camps. I check on Augusta now and again and make sure she's holding up her end of the treaty. At the same time, I get the luxury of living this lifestyle." She shook her head when I kept glaring at her. "If you don't believe me, arrange a coven meeting with the Valenti witches. You may survive it, if you're fast and lucky."

"We don't need luck. Storm will whip anyone." Fire Fang jumped up and stood loyally by my side.

I appreciated the support, but he'd never met a Valenti witch. They were as mean as a trodden on toadstool skunk with a hangover.

Rosina wriggled her fingers at him. "Would you like another belly rub, puppy?"

I pressed a hand on his head. "No, he doesn't."

He whined, but remained by my side.

She giggled. "I was tiring of this situation, anyway. Delano planned to get rid of his money and power, so there'd be nothing left when he died."

"That's something you actually seem sad about. You'd have lost out too if he'd frittered everything away."

"I'm sure some of that frittering would have come to me in the way of vacations and jewels. But I would have lost a lot."

"Which gives you two excellent motives. The Valenti witches ordered you to get rid of Delano or simply the fact you didn't want to lose out on the luxurious lifestyle you'd gotten used to."

Rosina pulled up one leg and stretched it out. "You're a smart witch, but that line of investigation will take you in the wrong direction. Delano thought it was amusing to dispose of his wealth. For him, it was another challenge. That was how he operated, seeing life as an experiment to see what boundaries he could push."

"And he pushed things so far that someone killed him."

A shimmer appeared in Rosina's eyes. "He did. And for that, I am genuinely sad. But I had no reason to kill Delano."

"I just gave you the reasons."

"They're the wrong ones. It was a family member. They all had more to lose than me. Augusta, in particular."

"You think she did it?"

"I try not to think. It gives me wrinkles."

"Have a go. You might surprise yourself."

Rosina's eyes widened before that innocent smile reappeared. "You're the expert. If you believe Augusta is innocent, and I see by the look on your face you do, that's the decision you must make."

"Remind me of your alibi, again."

"It's simple. I was in my bedroom alone. No one saw me go in, and no one came in while I was in there." She giggled again. "It's a terrible alibi. If I was going to make one up, I'd have come up with a much better option. But that's the barefaced truth. I was on my own. Someone so lovely should never be left alone for long, or she'll get swooped up."

"Not if she talks about herself in the third person, she won't. With your motives, lack of alibi, and your opportunity, you could have done it."

"I see why you think that." Rosina lowered the leg she was stretching. "Speak to Erik before you put me in shackles."

"Why him?"

"He's dangerous. He used to put Delano in risky situations and not by accident. I warned Delano about Erik and told him not to go anywhere with him on his own, but Delano laughed it off. He considered himself invulnerable. And, of course, Erik is usually drunk on alcohol or magic, so he is never seen as a threat."

"You think he is?"

"Erik has a dark side. He dabbles in spells he can barely control and often uses illegal magic."

"So he's shady. Why would Erik want Delano dead?"

"You'll have to ask him. But I've got a feeling about him. I get these feelings, and they're always right. And I can recognize a person's integrity as soon as we meet. With you, I see goodness but also sense turmoil buried beneath the surface."

"There's no turmoil. My life is one big dream of unicorns who poop rainbow stars."

Fire Fang snorted out his disbelief, which I chose to ignore.

"I'm never wrong. It's an ability I'm blessed with. I also know you won't rest until you find out the truth about what happened to Delano and the servants."

"Which means, if you're guilty, you're in trouble."

"I'm not, so I have nothing to worry about."

Her confidence rankled me. "You're wrong about me. I'm solving this case to save myself, nothing more."

"If you say so." Rosina's mischievous smile faded. "I heard what Lucian did to you. I will have words with him. Not that they'll do any good. But Lucian had a fierce loyalty toward Delano. He'd die for him."

"So I've heard."

She gathered a towel and her water bottle. "Keep me on your suspect list if you must, but I suggest you look at Erik. Now, if there's nothing else, I'm overdue a delicious massage from my personal trainer. The things he can do with his hands..."

"Don't go anywhere before this investigation is over. I may have more questions for you."

"Don't worry about me leaving just yet. I plan to dig in my heels and stay for a bit more fun."

"Because your real bosses, the Valenti witches, insist upon it?"

"No, sweetie. Because I'm not giving up this luxury without a fight." Rosina sashayed away.

I nudged Fire Fang when I noticed his attention was on the sway of her hips. "Less drooling, more interviewing suspects."

"I wasn't drooling. I was studying a potential killer."

"You think Rosina was involved?"

"I think she's not as dumb as she makes out."

"I got that, too. Come on. Let's see what the drunken brother knows about cursed skulls and dark magic."

Chapter 11

"This place looks fun." I stood outside a building with a sagging, moss covered roof. There was a blinking sign outside with half the letters refusing to light up. I could figure out what it said, though. *Girls, booze, gambling.*

And this was where Erik Discord supposedly spent most of his time.

"The place stinks like crusty feet," Fire Fang muttered. "Sometimes, I wish I didn't have such a sensitive nose."

"I share your pain. Even I can smell that." The air drifting out of the partially open door at the front of the club contained second-hand smoke, cheap booze, and sweat. But I needed to speak to Erik, so that's where we were going.

I pulled open the door, took a few steps inside, and was blocked by a large, muscular male chest. My gaze travelled up a foot before I met the head attached to that body. It was an ogre, and from the scowl on his face and the old scars on his cheeks, a mean one who enjoyed a brawl.

"What do you want?" he grumbled, stepping into my personal space.

I shuffled my toes closer until they touched his and grinned up at him. "We heard this is the best place in town. We've come to have fun."

"You're not a member. I don't know you. You're not welcome." He leaned down and growled in my face, his onion breath wafting over me.

His growl was drowned out by Fire Fang's rumbling roar as he stepped up beside me, his teeth bared and drool sliding from his exposed fangs and dropping onto the ogre's black boots.

The ogre flinched but didn't back down. "Those are the rules. If you're not a member, you don't get in."

"And how do you become a member of this amazing establishment?" I said.

"You don't. No witches allowed. No stinking mutts, either."

That comment earned him another vicious growl from Fire Fang. It was accompanied by a small jet of flames that shot over the ogre's head.

I settled a hand on Fire Fang. "Easy now, both of you. No one wants trouble."

"I'm always happy for a little trouble," Fire Fang said.

"We just need a quick look inside to see if a friend is here," I said. "We'll be in and out in ten minutes."

"You'll be thrown out in ten seconds. Leave." The ogre scrubbed the toe of his drool covered boot on the stained carpet.

The external door behind me opened, and I turned to see two shady-looking warlocks with their collars pulled up approaching.

The ogre stepped back, opened the door leading into the club, and nodded at them as they flashed cards at him. "Have a fun evening, gentlemen."

I dodged past the ogre to get through the door, but his large, calloused hand wrapped around the back of my neck and yanked me off my feet so my legs dangled in the air.

I pressed my hands together, splayed my fingers, and unleashed a lightning bolt. It slammed through the roof of the club and onto the floor beside the ogre.

He staggered out of the way, dazzled by the brilliant light. His grip on me vanished, and I landed in a crouch. I spun toward him, ready to unleash a more accurate lightning bolt if he wanted to play rough.

In the second it took me to turn, Fire Fang had pounced. He was on top of the ogre, who was sprawled on his back. Fire Fang's teeth were clamped around the ogre's throat.

I took a few seconds to get comfortable, resting a hip against the wall and crossing one foot over the other. "None of this would have happened if you'd let us through that door. We'd have gone in, checked things out, had a friendly chat with our buddy, and been on our way. Now there's a hole in your roof, a hellhound about to take a chunk out of you, and my fingers are itching to unleash magic all over this place. How would your customers feel about a permanent torrential rain cloud over this wonderful venue?"

The ogre gurgled out several unintelligible words, which were almost drowned out by Fire Fang's continuous growling. We hadn't known each other long, but this bitter, grumpy hound fit perfectly into my life.

More gurgling and grunts came out of the ogre.

"I think I've deciphered that noise. You made a mistake. We're welcome inside the club, and you'll even pay for our first round of drinks. How generous. Fire Fang, let the nice ogre go."

Fire Fang made a show of huffing acrid smoke into the ogre's face. He dropped his hold on him, jumped up and down on his chest a couple of times, and slid to my side. "You should have let me eat this goblin nobble."

"He'd be chewy. Look at all that muscle. And he's most likely the reason this place smells of crusty feet. You sure you want to take that risk?"

The ogre scuttled back on his hands and knees, his glare pinned on Fire Fang. "I'm calling the boss about you. The club rules are on the wall. Obey them." He pointed at a wonky sign with a red stain smeared down the middle of it. The rules were: no unpaid debt, no photography, no unnecessary violence.

"I've broken no rule. The violence was necessary to get you to see sense. I'm heading in now. And call your boss. I'll be happy to blast him off his feet, too." I dashed through the door while the ogre was still grumbling to himself, Fire Fang by my side.

I quickly learned it was important to breathe shallowly in a dive like this so as not to inhale anything toxic or too pungent. The lights were low, the floor sticky underfoot, and the cologne in the air was cheap and overpowering. Mingled with that stink was the tang of dangerous magic. And it was on the loose.

"Let's make this fast. If that ogre calls for backup, we'll have a real fight on our hands."

"I'm always up for a fight," Fire Fang said. "Although I need a bowl of something strong to take the taste of rancid ogre out of my mouth."

"Let's find Erik, pull apart his alibi, and see what he can tell us about putting his brother's life at risk. If he brought him here, he wasn't looking out for Delano's wellbeing."

My attention was drawn to a table buzzing with energy. There were six scantily dressed women watching a card game in progress.

I approached the table with Fire Fang, nudged one woman aside with a less than friendly shove from my hip, and discovered Erik. He was swaying in his seat, his eyes bloodshot and a wonky smile on his face as he tossed a heap of gold coins into the center of the table.

"Beat that. I met your offer and I raise you," he slurred.

Two card players folded, but one sharp-eyed guy with a pointed chin and a goatee beard remained in the game. "I'll see you. Show me your cards." He pushed a pile of gold coins into the center of the table.

Erik's wonky smile faded. "You can't beat this hand."

"Stop talking. Let's see what you've got."

Erik's bleary gaze wavered around the table. It passed over me, but he didn't seem to recognize me through the haze of alcohol and, most likely, illegal magic he was high on. He flipped his cards and pushed them away.

The guy with the goatee beard smiled, revealing pointed teeth. He turned over his own cards. He had three aces.

"How?" Erik leaped to his feet. "You cheated."

"I play fairly." The guy shoved back his seat. "But if you keep accusing me of being a cheater, you'll discover I fight dirty."

No one spoke for several seconds, and the only sounds around the table were Erik's deep breathing and the slap of his damp palms as he clenched and unclenched his fingers.

"I hated this game, anyway." Erik shoved past his seat, sending it sprawling to the floor. He staggered away to the bar.

I brushed aside two women who tried to assist him. "He's mine. You can have him after I'm done."

Neither of them looked impressed, but when Fire Fang blocked their path, they backed away.

I caught hold of Erik's arm. "Hey. Remember me?"

He glanced at me and shook his head. "Why are you wearing so many clothes? And most of the girls here are tanned. You're pale. Are you sick? I'm not into Goth."

I wasn't offended he didn't find me memorable. More like relieved. "I'm not working here. I met you at your home. I'm Storm Winter. I'm investigating what happened to Delano."

Erik leaned against the bar and shuffled around. His gaze slid up and down me several times, making me feel like a slimy tongue was sliding over me. "Oh.

Sure. But why are you here?" He raised a hand at the bartender, who nodded and pulled down a glass.

He was being blunt with me, so it was time to return the favor. "Because I want to find out if you murdered your brother."

Erik's eyes widened and his head lurched back. He waved his hands up and down. "Keep quiet. I have a reputation to maintain."

"You don't want your wonderful friends, who are cheating you out of a fortune, to know you could be a killer? It could add sparkle to your reputation."

"I... Well, Huh! I guess it would make some hesitate before cheating me at the card table. Did you see what Gideon did? He must have had an extra ace up his sleeve. No one draws three aces. He'd only been playing for ten minutes." Erik scrubbed his hands through his silver streaked hair.

"I'm glad that's your focus and not that you're a suspect in a triple murder investigation."

"Stop flapping your lips about murder. I don't need some nosy witch messing things up for me here."

"Because this is the nicest place you've been able to find in this neighborhood?"

"It's not so bad. It suits me. That's all you need to know." He grabbed the shot glass off the bar and downed it in one, before gesturing for a top up. "Hit me again, Rene."

The bartender obliged and glanced at me. "What will it be?"

"I'm good, thanks."

"If you want to stay and talk, you'll drink with me," Erik said. "Give her a shot."

"No shot." My gaze slid over the row of drink options behind the bar. I wasn't a drinker. It always gave me a headache and made me sleep badly. "A clean glass and something cold and non-alcoholic over ice."

"Coming right up," Rene said.

"I need to get back to the game," Erik said. "I don't want to lose my spot. There's a big buy-in at that table."

"You should lose your spot. You're a terrible player."

"It's a bluff. I lull the others into a false sense of security. They think I'm a loser, and then I turn things around. Well, most of the time."

"Sure you do. So I'll make this easy on you. You answer my questions, and I'll leave you to lose all your money. How does that sound?"

"I'm walking out of this place a winner." Erik chortled to himself. "I'm one of life's winners. Go on then, what do you need to know?"

"When I spoke to the family, you made it clear you thought little of Delano. Why would that be?"

"It's no secret the guy was a massive jerk."

"What made you think he was such a jerk?"

"He was a gold obsessed jinn, who hoarded anything pretty, including women." Erik snorted out a laugh. "He was getting desperate to prove he was the top dog as he got older. He thought he had to have someone young and pretty on his arm to show he was still a man. It was pathetic."

"You're talking about Rosina?"

"Her and the others. She's not the first girlfriend he brought home. He had two on the go at once, and they lived in the house for a few weeks before he got bored and kicked them out."

"You didn't approve of him cheating on Augusta?"

"What's to approve of? It was gross. And disrespectful to Augusta. She has heritage. She's classy."

"What did Augusta think about the situation? Did you talk to her about it?"

Erik gestured the bartender over as he emptied his glass again. "She hated it but had no choice but to accept it. I suppose you've talked to her about their marriage of convenience?" He framed the last three words in air quotes.

"Augusta's been honest with me about her situation. I don't think you're being honest, though."

"What am I lying about?"

"How jealous you were about Delano. As the elder brother, he had the family money, the power, and the women. Where did that leave you?" I deliberately took a long, slow look around the dingy club.

"I wanted none of that." Erik spilled his shot over his hand, cursing as he flicked off the drink.

Rene cleaned up the spill and re-filled the glass. "Take it easy, Sharky. That's the expensive stuff you're cleaning my bar with."

"It's all good, Rene. Put it on my tab. And add one for yourself."

I accepted my drink with a nod of thanks to the bartender. "What's with the nickname? Does Sharky mean something?"

"It's nothing," Erik said.

Rene raised his eyebrows at me but said nothing before walking away. There was a story there, which I intended to find out.

"Returning to Augusta for a moment, you must have seen the marriage go through difficult times over the years," I said.

"That's an understatement. Delano wasn't always such a jerk, but he never made life easy for Augusta. The opposite."

"Do you think she could have snapped? She killed him?"

Erik didn't speak for a long time. "You'll have to ask her about that."

"I'm asking you. Have you always lived in the house with them?"

"There's no reason for me to live anywhere else."

"So you have an opinion about Augusta and her relationship with Delano."

"Yeah, and it's my opinion."

"Which I need to hear, since I'm looking for your brother's killer. And if I'm not looking at Augusta, I'm staring hard at you."

Erik glared into his shot glass. "Augusta used to be sweet, but Delano broke her. It was little things to begin with. He used to criticize what she wore or how she styled her hair, but as she got older, he told her she was past her prime. I never thought that. She's a good-looking lady. Always has been."

"You're fond of her?"

"Sure. She didn't want into this mess, but her hand was forced. She dealt with it the best way she could. Augusta has remained dignified for most of it, but I could tell it hurt her. That's not the worst bit." Now

Erik was slurring out his words, he didn't seem to want to stop, and I was happy to listen.

"What else did Delano do to Augusta?"

"It started about a year ago. When we were all together, he'd get this evil look in his eyes and talk about how he was considering breaking the alliance with the Crossfire witches. He wanted rid of Augusta. He said their reputation was no longer important to him, and he had everything he needed."

"Did he ever do anything about that, or was it another way to grind down Augusta?"

Erik clamped a hand over his mouth before lowering it. "How should I know? He never consulted me about anything. I've told you too much. You should go."

"You've not told me enough. Did your brother find a way to break the alliance with Augusta?"

"They were still married when he died, weren't they?"

I sipped from the cold glass of sparkling water as I considered what Erik had told me. Although I'd placed Augusta at the bottom of the suspect list, this information meant she had an amazing motive for wanting Delano dead. If he'd been working on breaking the alliance through a divorce, she'd have been left penniless and vulnerable. If Augusta found out what Delano was planning, she'd have acted to keep herself safe. And she'd already told me she'd do anything to protect her coven and her son.

"I have to get back to the table." Erik staggered away, but I yanked him back and slammed him against the bar. "Let's talk for a minute more.

Delano had everything you desired. Did you hate that?"

"No! And he didn't have everything."

"He had a fortune. His business was raking in money, and he had an impressive reputation. And with him dead, most of that must pass to you. You weren't tempted to remove him from the family so you could claim what was yours?"

Erik rolled the empty shot glass along the bar. "It would have been good to get the wealth. You know what jinns are like. We're stingy with the handouts. Did you know he destroyed his wishing lamp so he couldn't grant any wishes? What sort of jinn does that make him?"

"We both know the answer to that question."

He scratched his fingers through his hair again. "Yeah, Delano only ever thought about himself. Whenever he went into a situation, he was looking for the angle that favored him."

"You could have done with Delano sharing his hoard with you. If you come here all the time, you must burn through your assets."

"Maybe. I'm having a bad run at the moment, that's all." Erik's gaze shifted to the table, and a desirous look entered his eyes. "I'll turn things around. Although right now, I don't seem any good at keeping assets for long. Everything slips through my fingers."

My grip tightened on his arm. "That gives you a motive for killing Delano."

"It does. But I was passed out in the kitchen the night he was cursed. Whenever I've had too much to drink, I never make it upstairs and crash on a couch. It's my routine. Ask anyone. There's no way I'd have made it up those stairs with a screeching skull without being noticed. Or with my current luck, I'd have dropped the thing and watched it bounce down the steps and shatter."

"I'm assuming you were alone that night?"

"I was." Erik kept his gaze on the card game. "I didn't kill Delano. I've thought about it, so I'm happy the universe nudged things into happening, but it wasn't me. Although I'd like to shake the hand of the guy who did it. It's gotten rid of a huge problem. And as you said, I'm the next in line to inherit. And I have plans for the fortune that's coming my way."

Again, that was a tick in the 'Erik killed Delano' box.

"Did you bring Delano here?" I said.

"Sure. All the time."

"Did you ever get into trouble when you were here?"

"Nothing we couldn't handle. Delano had a big mouth. That riled people up."

"Are you sure it was him with the big mouth?"

His gaze flicked my way then back to the card game. "What do you mean?"

"You brought Delano here to get him in trouble. Then you'd look the other way, hoping something fatal would happen to him."

Erik's back straightened. "Who have you been talking to?"

"Plenty of people. Other suspects."

"Those other suspects don't know what they're talking about. Sure, you come to a place like this and expect things to get rough. And if you were a smug, entitled jerk like my brother, you guarantee trouble finds you. But he handled himself. He'd shove his hand into his pocket and throw money at the problem until it went away. Or brag about the family name. That sent most people scuttling."

"Sharky, get your butt over here if you want to keep in this game," a guy at the table yelled.

"Are we done?" Erik was already staggering away.

"Sure. I'll catch up with you back at the house if I decide you're guilty."

"Of being a drunken idiot," Fire Fang grumbled.

Erik raised a hand in acknowledgement, not bothering to look back at me.

I turned to face the bar, pulled out some money, and gestured Rene over. I slid him a pile of notes. "Tell me everything you know about Delano and Erik Discord."

Chapter 12

Rene slid the notes into his back pocket and topped up my glass. "You don't work for the Magic Council."

"Maybe I do."

"They never tip as well as you just did. What's with the questions?" He filled a bowl with water and set it on the floor for Fire Fang.

"I'm a private investigator. Are you able to give me information about Delano and Erik, or should I ask for that tip back?"

"You found the way to my heart." Rene patted his back pocket. "What do you need to know?"

"Why the Sharky nickname?"

He smirked. "Sharky is short for card shark. Erik also thinks he's a ladies' man. He calls it sharking when he goes on the hunt."

"Is he good at either of those things?"

"It's an ironic nickname. Not that Erik gets that."

I took another sip of my drink. "What was Delano and Erik's relationship like?"

"Bad. They argued all the time. Some siblings do that. It's a weird love/hate relationship. You know what I mean?"

I nodded as a flash of memory of bickering with Eden hit, making my heart lurch and a flicker of pain dig into my guts. My little sister had bugged the patience right out of me, and I'd end up yelling at her. But we always made up.

"How bad did things get between them?" I downed more drink until my throat relaxed.

"I was listening to your conversation." Rene lifted one shoulder. "It's a bartender's hazard. You stay in the background and keep your ears open. And when my ears were open around those two, I knew things were bad between them. Erik was always jabbing Delano, trying to get a reaction."

"How did Delano respond?"

"Usually with sarcasm. Although he sometimes jabbed back. He even used magic on his brother. But he needed to be careful, because Erik dabbles in shady spells. And those spells have been getting darker. It gets you that way, the dark magic. You have a play and think it's fine, then before you know it, it's got you around the throat and is choking the life out of you."

"Erik is that bad?"

"He's not that good. He's in trouble. Although when he came in a week ago, he said he was celebrating."

"Did he tell you what he was celebrating?"

"He wouldn't give details, but he's been like that the past few days. He staggers in, all smiles and clapping people on the back, and saying fortune is coming his way. He even said he planned on dusting off his jinn lamp and offering a few wishes since he was in such a good mood."

"Erik is a reluctant jinn, like his brother was?"

"He must be. I've never seen him grant a wish. And I don't know what he's got to be happy about. The guy is sinking in debt. He owes money to everyone around that table, and he has a tab at this bar he's yet to clear. He gets around to it, eventually, but only when things get sticky for him."

"Sticky as in he gets roughed up or threatened?"

"You got it. Guys like that have to be in a certain amount of pain before they react."

"Erik mentioned nothing about Delano being the source of his good fortune, did he?"

"No, but I keep my ear to the ground. I heard Delano was dead. Something about a cursed skull, wasn't it?"

I nodded, but didn't furnish him with more detail. "What else has Erik said about Delano?"

"Ooooh! Is this how you operate? I don't get answers to my questions?"

"Did I see you slip a pile of cash my way?"

Rene laughed. "True fact. I know enough about their relationship to be confident Erik hated Delano. He talked about getting even with him, but it was only ever drunk talk."

"You're sure? Since Delano is dead and Erik's walking around telling everyone what good luck he's about to come into, maybe he created his own luck."

"Not Erik. He's dumb and selfish, but over the years, I've gotten to know the type. There are guys who come in here and want to be the big man, like Erik. They brag about being the best, but when the chips are down, they run with their tails between their legs. That's Erik. He's all talk and no action. I know when I come face-to-face with someone who acts on their threats. You strike me as that kind of someone."

"I take that as a compliment."

"You should. You must get the job done, whatever it is."

"I need to with this case. Anything else you can tell me about Erik?"

"Plenty. How about another drink?"

It looked like my money had run out. While Rene filled a bowl with peanuts and placed them in front of me, I slid him more money.

He flipped through it and nodded before sliding it into his pocket. "Erik uses his family name to get what he wants. And if that doesn't work, he mentions Delano. Well, he used to. He's on his own now."

"How's that going for him?"

"He's surviving. Everyone knows that family. And everyone knew Delano took no prisoners. He was the same here. What he wanted, he got, and he didn't care what means were used to secure something. A game, a girl, a new spell. That was how he rolled. Erik tries to be the same, but it's not always a success. He's a more timid version of his older brother. It's sad to watch. Delano got everything Erik wanted. Including the hot wife."

"You've met Augusta?"

"Only once, but I've seen pictures of her. She came here one evening after Delano and Erik had been gambling for three days straight. We have rooms upstairs, so the high-paying customers can crash if they need a break from the tables. She came in, looking for Delano."

"How did Augusta seem?"

"Angry, but she kept it civil. She's one dignified lady. I liked her." Rene leaned closer. "And did you know she was supposed to marry Erik, not Delano?"

"No kidding. What went wrong?"

"From what I've heard, a formal introduction was set up between the families. Erik, being the loser he is, showed up drunk and late to the dinner the Crossfire witches had arranged. He staggered in, slurring his speech and almost unable to stand. The family was appalled. They declined the match."

"Which was a risky move, considering their situation. Erik must have been a real mess."

"I guess he must have been. We all know how desperate the Crossfire witches were to secure powerful alliances before they were crushed."

"Why would he do that, though? An alliance with a Crossfire witch would have given him status. It could have gotten him out of Delano's shadow."

"Yeah, and here's the interesting bit. Erik claims he was drugged, or someone used a spell on him, so he showed up in that condition. But look at the guy." Rene jerked his chin in the direction of the card game, where Erik was slumped in a chair. "He's a disaster. He probably got nervous, had a few drinks, and took things too far. So Augusta went with Delano. There were some quick renegotiations of the alliance, and the formal match was made."

I turned my head so I could study Erik as he fumbled with what was left of his gold coins and drank more booze. He had every reason to hate

Delano. Delano had the lifestyle he'd dreamed of, and he'd taken Augusta.

"Are you looking at Erik as Delano's killer?" Rene's question pulled me from my pondering.

"Among others." I finished my drink. "I appreciate the information."

He patted his pocket once more. "Always a pleasure. I'd say drop by again, but I have a feeling this isn't your kind of place."

"I'll be back the next time I have a criminal to drag out of here."

Rene's chuckle followed me out of the club as I left with Fire Fang.

"I feel like a hot bath after being in there," Fire Fang said. "I stink of despair and poor decision making."

"You and me both."

We walked along in silence for a moment.

Fire Fang nudged my leg with his head. "We could share."

"Share what?"

"A bath."

"And have your dog fur clogging the plug hole. I'll pass. You get the hose out the back once we're home."

He growled and shook his head. "You go in the bath first so you get the clean water. I don't mind tepid seconds."

My nose wrinkled. "Still a pass." I headed back to my rented car and sat in the driver's seat for a minute.

"What do you reckon?" Fire Fang was in the back seat, taking up the entire length as he sprawled across it.

"I think Erik hated Delano. And with Delano dead, Erik will get a huge part of his fortune."

"Don't forget the wife he lost. Maybe Erik can take Augusta on as well now Delano's gone."

"He could. And when Erik spoke about Augusta, there was affection there. He could still want her. And he must be thinking, with Delano gone and Augusta still needing protection, she'll look his way. Erik may be working up to a proposal."

"That poor woman. To be saddled with two donkey helmets from the same family."

"We need to keep a watch on Erik's movements. If he makes a play for Augusta, he's most likely the killer. Although how someone that messed up worked out how to get and control a cursed skull may have to remain a mystery."

"He's our new prime suspect?"

I started the car. "Yep. Along with everyone else."

My footsteps were heavy as I shuffled around the kitchen, drinking strong coffee. I forced myself to accept another day had slid open, and I was no closer to figuring out who killed Delano, Samuel, and Suzanne, and where that cursed skull had come from.

Although my suspicions about Augusta had been reignited after speaking to Erik, her alibis checked out. She wasn't at the house when Samuel and Suzanne were cursed.

I was another day closer to my death, and that put no one in a positive mood. Although I shouldn't complain. Wasn't everyone else in the same position?

Fire Fang rolled off the couch, where he'd been dozing since I'd dragged us out of bed. "Are you sure sleeping in is a bad idea? If you don't get enough rest, the curse could catch up to you sooner."

"Nice try, but neither of us is getting a lie-in until this is solved. One way or the other." I slid a finger slowly across my throat.

Fire Fang bared his teeth. "You're not dying on my watch."

I tossed him a handful of dog biscuits. "You say the sweetest things. I'm amazed you don't have a string of fluffy girlfriends hankering to spend time with you with all the smooth chat and silky lines."

"Maybe I do, and you just don't get to see them." He scarfed down the food and walked to the front door. "What are you waiting for?"

I glanced at the crumpled, oversized T-shirt I'd slept in. "Clothing when leaving the apartment isn't optional."

"You're dressed. That'll do. You can't die because you stopped to change your shirt."

"I won't. At least, I'll do my best not to die within the next week." I dumped my coffee mug in the sink, got dressed, and headed to the door. I pulled it open and almost stepped on a small black cat sleeping on the mat.

It wasn't just any small black cat. It was the one I'd rounded up and taken to the shelter.

I groaned. "What are you doing here?"

The cat turned her head, narrowed her eyes, and hissed at me.

"You were supposed to be starting a new life and waiting to be adopted by your forever family. How did you get out? And why come back here?"

The cat simply hissed again.

"Fire Fang, grab her."

The cat leaped up, hackles raised, and raced away.

I pointed along the corridor. "Why aren't you chasing her? She'll only start howling if we don't get her back to the shelter."

Fire Fang sniffed the air and then the mat the cat had been on. "She's not your average cat."

"We know that. We've been on the receiving end of her strange magic. But we don't need her in our lives. We've got enough going on without a sassy cat to complicate the situation."

"There must be a reason she keeps coming back." His red-rimmed eyes skimmed over me. "It can't be for your warm and friendly company or the leftover food you toss out for her."

"I should stop doing that. It's making things worse." I stepped out and locked the door behind me. "I haven't got time to deal with her today, even though she needs to leave. I'll call the vets and tell them they have a runaway to collect."

We headed outside. I'd only gone a few steps when I heard my name called. I turned and spotted Indigo striding toward me.

"Where have you been hiding?" she said in way of a greeting.

"Nowhere. Just working a case."

"Anything good?"

"Nope."

"I'm at a loose end if you need a hand." She passed me a takeout cup of coffee. "This was meant for Olympus, but you look like you need it more. Have you been burning the midnight witch oil again?"

"Something like that. I thought you were busy with the house renovation."

Indigo fell into step with me as I strode along. "It's almost done. I'm just waiting for some finishing touches. Of course, the house isn't cooperating. But the builder can't get back till the afternoon, so if you need a hand..."

"It's all good."

She nudged me with her hip. "I have solved a mystery or two in my time. I could be useful."

"This case is unique. You wouldn't be any help."

Indigo blew on her coffee. "Has it got anything to do with that weird screaming skull that showed up at your apartment door?"

"I'd forgotten about that."

Indigo's shrewd expression told me exactly what she thought of that lie. "Those kids haven't been back, have they?"

"Kids?"

"The ones that left the skull."

"Oh, no. I must have scared them off for good this time. I need to get going. Busy day." I tried to outwalk her, but she kept up.

There was no way I was getting my friends involved with this cursed skull mystery. If whoever had the skull learned other people were involved in figuring out the murders, they could sneak into Witch Haven and curse them, too.

Indigo was almost jogging to keep up with me. "You know where I am if you need any help."

I kept power walking. "Sure. Thanks for the coffee."

"And don't forget, it's girls' night tomorrow. You'll be there? Odessa is hosting."

"So it'll be pumpkin pie for dessert?" I glanced over my shoulder, relieved to see Indigo had gotten the hint and slowed down.

"You love pumpkin pie."

"Everything she gives us always tastes like pumpkin."

"Not this time. She's promised homemade apple pie. It's your favorite."

It was. But dessert couldn't distract me. "I won't be able to make it."

"Yes, you will," Indigo yelled. "You need time out the same as the rest of us. Be there at seven. No excuses."

"Catch you later." I dashed off before Indigo could keep twisting my arm. The less time I spent around my friends, the better. Whoever had control of that cursed skull was sneaky. I wouldn't put it past them to eliminate any threat they discovered.

And Indigo was smart, just like Odessa and Luna. If they got involved and found out I'd been cursed, it would put them in a vulnerable position. They'd meddle, thinking they were saving me, and that wasn't something I needed. I could save myself. And if I didn't... well, no one else would get hurt.

Fire Fang was grumbling and puffing smoke out of his nostrils.

"What's wrong with you?"

"You're not going to girls' night, are you? Or accepting any help."

"No. Is that a problem?"

"I want the apple pie. I'd even take the pumpkin pie. Odessa makes amazing pies. And I don't want you dead."

"I'll get you a pie from the bakery. You won't miss out. Luna's uncle makes great pies, too. And he has all different flavors."

"You say that, but you'll forget. And you need help with the not being dead part. Ignoring it doesn't make it go away."

"I'm not ignoring it. By solving these murders, I'm thinking about not dying. Come on, less obsessing over desserts and my demise. We need to question Augusta again. Even though those alibis checked out, there's a lot she didn't tell us."

Chapter 13

"Augusta's not here." Lucian stood in the doorway of the Discord house, his tie loose around his neck. "She left early today."

"When will she be back? I have more questions about the skull."

He gestured me inside, then closed the door. "I'm not sure. How's the investigation going? I intended to call you today and see what progress you'd made."

"Sure you did. Or is that a guilty conscience forcing you to stay in touch because your skull signed my death warrant?" I followed him into a tidy study with an antique desk at one end of the room.

"I feel no guilt for doing anything I can to ensure my best friend's killer is discovered."

"Even if that means you kill me?"

His level gaze met mine. "Your reputation revealed you can solve any mystery."

I kept my gaze down as I settled in a seat. I could solve almost any mystery a client came to me with, but there was one mystery that had always eluded me.

"Would you like refreshments?" Lucian asked.

"This isn't a social call."

"That's a relief. With the servants gone, we're fending for ourselves. The novelty has swiftly worn off."

"It must be a struggle to make your own meals and brew the coffee."

"Sarcasm is beneath you, Miss Winter."

"I enjoy it. And as for solving the mystery of the skull, I'm still interviewing suspects. One name in particular keeps rising to the top."

Lucian wore the same impassive, hard-to-read expression he always did as he gestured for me to continue.

"Augusta. The motives for her wanting Delano dead keep piling up."

His expression didn't alter. "That is unfortunate. But I understand why you consider her the prime suspect."

"I didn't say I did. Do you think she's guilty?"

"That's not for me to judge."

"You've seen how toxic their relationship was, despite telling me they were content. You also told me you've been friends with Delano for a long time. You must have known Augusta for almost that long, too."

"Almost. And perhaps I have seen Delano do a few things in his relationship I hope he wasn't proud of."

"Cheating?"

"Maybe."

"Stealing other people's wives?"

"It's possible."

"Anything worse?"

"I couldn't possibly comment."

"A perfect lawyer response. The picture I'm developing of Delano is of a man with no conscience. If he wanted something, he took it and didn't care if it badly affected others."

Lucian ruminated on his words before speaking. "Delano had his moments, but he was decent to me. An excellent friend."

"You're the only one saying he was decent and excellent. Perhaps your loyalty was misplaced."

"Or perhaps I'm the only one who knew the real Delano. He had a public persona he maintained."

"Being a greedy, selfish narcissist?"

"It's one way to look at his actions. But his focus was on ensuring he remained at the top of a fierce market. Someone was always looking to take him down."

"And to stay on top, he felt he had to tread on people?"

"Maybe one or two got squashed along the way."

"And the cheating? How do you feel about that?"

"Powerful men attract attention. And Delano enjoyed the ladies."

"That was a non-answer. You saw no harm in that?"

"It wasn't ideal for everyone, but the situation was outlined when Delano and Augusta formed their alliance. Augusta was free to have other men, providing she was discreet."

"Were you involved with creating their alliance?"

"I was. I sat in on the negotiations with the Crossfire witches."

"So you'll know Erik was the original choice to marry Augusta."

A flicker of emotion crossed Lucian's face, but it was so fast I couldn't grab its meaning. "You have been thorough."

"I'm the best. It's the reason you cursed me."

He pursed his lips a fraction. "Yes, I was aware of the original arrangement. But as I'm sure you've discovered, Erik wasn't an ideal candidate."

"Why was he chosen to marry Augusta if that was the case?"

"They're closer in age. And the Crossfire witches had lost many in the war. They hoped for several children to expand their ranks. Delano was focused on building his career and making a name for himself, so it was decided Erik would be the better choice. He'd be more focused on family. There were fewer expectations set against him. Unlike Delano."

"Erik believed something was done to him, so when he showed up at the meeting to complete the alliance, he looked incompetent."

"He would say that. After all, he lost everything. But Erik was dabbling with the wrong kind of magic and drinking too much, even back then. He must have overestimated what he could handle. He only has himself to blame."

"Perhaps Delano was to blame. Delano decided he wanted Augusta, so he took matters into his own hands. Maybe Erik never forgave him, so he dealt the killer blow with this skull."

"So you're not only focused on Augusta. You also consider Erik a suspect?"

"With your dubious alibis, you're all suspects."

"Even me?"

"Any man who curses another person to death because he wants them to do something for him can't be considered a sound character."

There was that flicker of emotion again. "My methods were unscrupulous, but my reason is pure. Delano's murder must be resolved."

As much as I hated a death curse ticking away in the background, I saw the logic to Lucian's cold actions against me. But it was no comfort, given I was on the receiving end of his determination to get justice for his friend.

"Returning to Augusta, does she consult you when she has legal matters to resolve?" I said.

"Always. I deal with the entire family's affairs. It's what they pay me for."

"What can you tell me about the planned divorce?"

"Divorce? You're mistaken. There was no divorce."

"Are you sure? Delano had been talking about getting rid of Augusta before he died. I assumed he would use your services to find a way out of the marriage. Or perhaps you were helping Augusta. That must have been a conflict of interest if you were involved with both parties."

Lucian dismissed my comment with a sharp gesture. "You're getting ahead of yourself. Delano talked about a lot of things. He could be impetuous, but he understood the alliance. He'd never have broken it."

"Perhaps he would if he was having his arm twisted by a special girlfriend. Rosina seems persuasive. And smart. Probably even smarter than you."

"Highly unlikely. Rosina is irrelevant. She'll soon be out of this house and become an unpleasant memory. She had no sway over Delano and would never have convinced him to divorce Augusta. He wouldn't want a woman of low morals becoming his wife."

"What about Augusta? Did she confide in you about leaving Delano or finding a way out of the alliance that would ensure her family remained protected?"

"Conversations I have with my clients are confidential."

"Which suggests you two did talk about her leaving Delano. How far did that go?"

Lucian didn't respond.

"What you tell me could solve your best friend's murder. That must be your top priority if you were a true friend."

"I was a true friend. And I remain loyal." Lucian leaned forward in his seat and rested his elbows on his knees.

"To Delano? Or to everyone?"

"I'm the family lawyer."

"That doesn't answer the question."

"Augusta knows I'm discreet. And I never discuss another family member's legal matters with anyone else."

"Not even with Delano?"

"Not even him. He valued loyalty but understood people have matters in their life that require the utmost discretion. It's why he kept me around. He could trust me with his darkest secrets. And the secrets of others."

"Did Augusta come to you and ask about how she could get out of her hideous marriage?"

Lucian paused again, looking like he was moving words around in his head to reveal a truth without betraying his best friend. "Not so much. But she asked where to hide money. And she showed me the lease on an apartment. She wanted to make sure there was nothing in it to trap her into a long-term commitment. Augusta wasn't leaving, though. She described it as a backup plan in case things got too difficult and she needed a short respite."

"Having a secret stash of money and a bolt hole no one knows about sounds a lot like she was planning to leave."

"Augusta was unhappy, but she'll admit that to you. I saw it more as her looking for an alternative, so she didn't feel trapped. She didn't want to leave, but needed to know she could if she decided to. Even having that would have been a comfort. Augusta would have been able to stay with Delano, knowing there was another option."

"How much money has she squirrelled away in her not-going-to-escape-fund?"

"Not a huge amount. Delano was vigilant with his income and treasure. If she'd been careful, she'd have been able to live on what she had for two or three years."

"And did Augusta sign the lease on that apartment?"

"Not that I'm aware of. She simply asked me to look through it. I did, and I saw no problems. But I advised her against proceeding. If Delano had found out, he'd have considered it a betrayal."

I sat back in my seat. This information suggested it was even more likely Augusta killed Delano. Maybe he had discovered she'd been hiding money and viewing apartments, so she had a safe place to go. A secret place, so Delano couldn't drag her back into a loveless situation. He tried to take that away from her, so she killed him. But the servants' deaths and her lack of power were a problem. And Augusta had alibis for Sam and Suzanne's murders. Could she have faked those alibis?

"I see the cogs turning, Storm. You think Augusta killed him. But that's not possible. When I was running toward that skull, there was no sign of Augusta. She came out of the bathroom. She was behind Delano."

"That doesn't mean she didn't sneak out and plant the skull. There's a separate door in the hallway leading out of that bathroom. She could have done it."

"Where did she get the skull from? And how can Augusta control such a powerful object? She mentioned you tested her magic, so you know she has barely any power. She's been that way since the Crossfire witches were defeated. If she'd tried to control the skull, it would have turned on her. She'd have been cursed."

That was another problem I hadn't figured out. Augusta had so little magic.

"I do need to speak to her," I said.

Lucian stifled a sigh. "Then I suggest you come back later. She should be here late afternoon."

The door leading into the study opened, and Hattie appeared. She took a step back and began to close the door behind her. "Sorry. I didn't know anyone was in here."

"If you've got a few minutes, I'd like to talk to you," I said.

Hattie stopped like she was a unicorn caught in a hunter's light ball. Her pale brown eyes drifted over me. "Why?"

"To go over the night of Delano's murder. You could have useful information to help me find his killer." Or she could be the killer.

"I'm busy. You'll have to arrange an appointment for another time."

"It won't take long."

"I was about to take a walk. And—"

"Great. I have legs. I can walk with you. And Fire Fang needs to burn off some energy." I nodded at Lucian, then stood and strode over to Hattie. "Lead the way."

"I... This can't take long. I really am busy." Hattie turned on her sensible low-heeled brown shoes and walked to the front door.

"This should be fun," Fire Fang muttered. "Is it me, or is Hattie giving out an unfriendly vibe?"

"It's not you."

"You already know my alibi," Hattie said, not looking at me as she strode out the door. "I was in bed alone. Everyone knows what time I go to bed every night. I never deviate from that. It's important to keep to a routine."

"Even when your brother has just revealed he's giving away his fortune and you'll get nothing when he dies? Surely, a routine deviation would be acceptable, then."

She gripped her hands tight in front of her and then let go, wriggling out her fingers. "It didn't matter to me."

"It should. You'd have been left with nothing."

"I have everything I need."

"What would you have done once Delano spent everything? I'm assuming he was planning to sell this place, too."

"That was for him to decide. It was his fortune and his house." Gravel crunched under Hattie's feet as she marched along the driveway. She headed around the side of the house and took a path toward some trees.

Fire Fang loped off a few steps, enjoying sniffing around in the grass.

I kept up with Hattie, despite the brisk pace. "Were you close to Delano?"

"No."

"Did you have any problem with him?"

"No."

"Did you like him?"

"Let me guess, she's going to say no," Fire Fang said.

Hattie sucked in a breath and glared at him. "We had nothing in common. I didn't dislike him. I just didn't know him."

"But you lived together. You must have known him. Didn't you grow up together, too?"

We reached the tree line, and she plunged in, not minding the brambles snagging her woolen stockings. "I went to boarding school. I was sent away when I was six. I only saw Delano on family vacations and when I came home for Christmas. He was older than me and wanted nothing to do with his younger sister. I felt the same about him. We had nothing in common."

"What made you so different?"

"He was brash and greedy. All he cared about was material things. You only have to look around that enormous house to see how much he cared about impressing other people. It was all show, show, show. It repulses me."

"You don't like the finer things in life?" I hopped over a fallen log as we continued deeper into the trees.

"Do you see me wearing designer clothes or carrying an expensive purse?"

"You said you liked practical clothes because they don't show the stains."

"Exactly. There's nothing practical about owning such a big house or buying expensive gadgets or wasting money on art. You should give back. Delano had too much, but it was never enough."

"If you disliked the situation so much, why stay in the house?"

"It's not as if I had a choice."

"Delano forced you to stay?"

Her gaze cut my way. Her cheeks were flushed, and she was wheezing. "You must have heard about me. Everyone makes fun of me."

"No one's made fun of you when I've been around. Why would they do that?"

She finally looked me full in the face, and there was surprise in her eyes. "Really?"

"I know little about you. Why do you have to stay here? Does Delano have something on you?"

"This way. I'll show you why I'm stuck here."

We walked for a few more minutes until we came to a small, secure, brick built building. Hattie took a key from her pocket and unlocked the padlock on the door. She opened it and flicked on a light. Inside was a bare concrete floor, and shelves lined the walls. On those shelves were jinn lamps. Probably a hundred if I had to guess.

"Family heirlooms?" I said.

"That's mine. Top shelf, far right corner."

"Your family keeps their wishing lamps here?" I stepped inside and looked around.

"All our lamps are here, along with the decoys. It makes it hard for people to control us if they don't know which lamp belongs to us."

"Why are you showing me your lamp? Aren't you worried I'll grab it and make outlandish wishes?" I wouldn't. You had to be careful with jinn magic. Get the wish wrong or fudge the request, and you'd pay. It was much like all magic. If you got sloppy, you got stung.

A smirk slid across Hattie's thin lips. "You can try. Take it down and make a wish. I permit you to access my jinn magic."

I glanced at Fire Fang, who hovered outside, before lifting down the lamp. It was plain, with no decoration. Jinn lamps were often elaborate, highly polished, and engraved with artwork. This one had a dent in the side and a film of dust covering it.

"What are you waiting for? Most people get excited when gifted wishes from a jinn. I won't cheat you. You have three wishes, Storm Winter. Use them wisely."

"What size of wish should I ask for?"

"Start with something small."

"Ask for cake," Fire Fang said. "I'm hungry. I'm still thinking about that apple pie we're going to miss out on."

I rubbed the lamp. "Jinn, my wish is for a salted caramel cupcake with white icing."

"Your wish is granted." Hattie lifted her arms, her hands palms out, and rotated them in a circle in front of her. She completed the circle. There was a puff of smoke, and she grabbed a cupcake as it materialized. She handed it to me.

"It looks like what I asked for." My stomach growled almost as loudly as Fire Fang when I disturbed him from his sleep.

"Have a taste," Hattie said.

I pulled down the paper wrapper on the cupcake and took a bite. It took a few seconds before a sour, gritty taste kicked in. It also had fishy undertones. I grabbed a tissue from my pocket and spat out the cupcake.

"Let me try." Fire Fang grabbed a big bite before I could stop him. He also spat it out. "What in the flaming goblin nobble is in this?"

"That's my problem," Hattie said. "I don't work. Every time someone asks me for a wish, it backfires. On the surface, everything seems fine, but then the problems start."

"Have you always been like this?"

"All my life. I once overheard my parents call me the runt of the litter. And I know I'm nothing much to look at. I didn't inherit any of the family traits like the silver hair, charm, or good looks. I arrived dowdy and plain and with my magic misfiring. I hate it. I have to rely on other people's charity to survive. That's why I'm stuck here. I can't amass a jinn hoard, because every time I try, it goes wrong. The last time I found some money, it turned out it had been stolen and had to be turned in to the Magic Council."

"Maybe you need to practice your magic more. Sometimes it takes me a few tries before I get a spell right."

"Believe me, I've practiced and practiced and practiced. I'm just the same. Even the wish lamp I was given when I turned eighteen was damaged. It was dropped before it was given to me. The dent in the side has been there ever since. No amount of magic or hammering gets rid of it. It's lumpy and misshapen, just like me."

"Because your lamp is damaged, you are, too?"

"They're probably connected. But it has more to do with the fact my magic never worked. It was why my parents sent me to boarding school. I'm the family embarrassment. I'm useless to them. Delano teased me about it. I wanted to leave him and all this behind, but where would I go? How would I live? My bad luck follows me."

"You don't use any magic?"

"Not unless I have to. All I want, and what I would wish for if I was ever given a wish, is to be mortal."

Fire Fang growled, and I couldn't suppress my grimace. Being mortal sounded difficult, dangerous, and miserable.

"I've seen that expression on so many faces when I reveal my desire to leave the world of magic, but I'd be on a level playing field with everyone else. If no one around me had magic, we'd be the same. I'd leave behind my jinn lamp and broken spells and be ordinary. I would blend in and never have to worry about putting a foot wrong and casting a misfiring wish."

I handed her the lamp. "I'm sorry about your messed up magic. But there must be another way than wanting to be mortal."

"Not as far as I can see." She looked at the lamp. "You're not going to ask for your other wishes? You're entitled to them."

"I could wish to—"

"Careful! You finish that sentence, and I must grant the wish."

"I was going to ask for information on who killed your brother."

"Oh! Well, you could try, but that wish would lead you to an innocent person who's been framed for these murders. Not particularly helpful. Perhaps another cake? I'm obligated to give you the wishes."

"Then, Hattie Discord, I wish I didn't have my last two wishes."

"Nicely done. That is a wish I can grant." Hattie circled her arms again, and there was another puff of smoke.

I tensed, waiting to see if a dragon would appear and devour me or a horde of imps would race out of the trees and attack, but nothing happened.

"Is that it?" I said. "I thought your wishes went wrong."

"You were fortunate in that you asked for nothing. Nothing creates nothing. No wrong can come from nothing. Although watch your step for the next hour or two, just in case." She replaced the lamp on the shelf. "I respect magic in this family, but we simply have different values. I'm not magical. I'm mundane."

Fire Fang whined softly, and even I felt a little sorry for this washed up jinn everyone overlooked.

The softness on her face vanished. "There's no use feeling pity for me. I've always felt differently about magic." Hattie locked the door, and we walked back through the trees.

"Did Delano point out those differences to you?"

"All the time. But usually when he was bored and looking for amusement. I learned to ignore him or avoid him. But sometimes, he'd seek me out and torment me."

"You could have left. Found a job or even settled with the mortals and tried it out."

"I did once, but Delano refused to set me free. He had so much wealth, but wouldn't let any of it go. I would have been happy living on a pittance, but he refused me even that. I was trapped. Forced to endure a cruel brother who thought I was a misfit."

There was a motive. Delano had misused his sister, and the quiet mouse had snapped and roared like a thorn-stabbed lion.

"Weren't you ever tempted to get revenge on Delano? After years of being bullied, you must have thought about it."

"How would I have done that? Delano was all powerful. He had everything, and I had nothing."

"You had something. You still do."

"What's that?"

"Your ability to be invisible. I barely noticed you when we were with the other family members. It takes skill to fly under the radar in a room full of people. Perhaps you used that to get the cursed skull and sneak it outside your brother's room."

"You make me sound like a super spy. I almost wish I was. But my ability to be invisible has less to do with my behavior and more to do with other people's opinion of me. Every time I enter a room, they don't notice me."

"Because you choose to blend in. It must mean you've overheard a lot you shouldn't."

"Nothing of interest. At least not to me. And I don't snoop on my family. Like I said, I respect them. But it's as if I was born into the wrong family. We have nothing in common. I long to be free."

"You are. Delano's hold over you is gone. You can leave. You're finally free."

"I am." Hattie was quiet as we approached the house. "And because of that, you think I used that skull on him?"

"It's as good a motive as any I've discovered."

"I disagree. There are other people who'd gain so much more from Delano's murder. And if you're talking about freedom as a motive, focus on Augusta. He pinned her down like she was an exotic butterfly on a specimen board. He humiliated her again and again. And he took it to the next level when he moved Rosina in and flaunted her."

"I'm talking to Augusta, too, but I'm not ruling anyone out. And so far, everyone's alibi is flimsy. Yours included."

"With my misfiring magic, do you think I'd be able to control a screaming skull? If I tried, it would turn around and bite me, then scream and explode in my face. Trust me, I know not to meddle with powerful magic. I had to learn that the hard way." She pushed up the sleeve of her brown sweater to reveal an old white scar running across her forearm.

"What happened?"

"A misfiring spell. Delano had been goading me for days about getting better at my jinn magic. So I tried a new spell. I activated my lamp, cast out the magic, and it hit me. My arm was badly burned. And although healing spells were used, it never fully healed. I'll always have this."

We reached the house, and I turned to Hattie. "You must hate magic. It's done nothing but mess with you."

"I have no love for it, just like I had no love for my brother. I wanted them both out of my life, and I finally got something I truly desired."

"Maybe someone granted you a wish that worked," I said.

"I doubt that. Now, I really do need to go." She nodded at me and hurried inside.

I remained outside. This spiky little mouse could have more bite to her than she was letting on. Hattie was still a suspect.

My phone buzzed in my back pocket, and I pulled it out to see a message from John Smith.

I got your screaming skull information. Meet you in the usual place in two hours.

Chapter 14

The usual meeting place was a gloomy, low-ceilinged bar a few miles outside of Witch Haven. John was a man of routine. He always wore the same clothes, drank the same ale, and sat in the same seat when he visited this bar.

John kept his life simple and his fees high, but I paid them. He got me what I needed without causing me too much hassle, which meant I didn't have to grub around in the gutter too often for results.

"What have you got for me?" I sat in the seat opposite him, not surprised to find a tall glass of sparkling water waiting for me.

"Everything you need about the screaming skull. It's a nasty piece of kit. You shouldn't be messing with it."

"It messed with me, so I have no other option." My gaze settled on the file in front of him on the table. "That looks like it'll take a while to get through."

"The skull has got a long history. And a dark one."

"Of course it has. When it screams, it's not singing an off-key version of the Monster Mash. Give me the highlights. I'll read the rest in bed."

John chuckled. "You live an exciting life. Is that the most fun you have in the bedroom?"

"It's all I need."

He pulled a bone-shaped dog treat from his pocket and held it out for Fire Fang, who loomed close beside me. Fire Fang thought little of John, and, as usual, he rejected the treat.

"One day, I'll get that hound to like me." John pocketed the treat.

"He's choosy about his friends. And he has good instincts for people."

"Yeah, and those instincts tell me you're not to be trusted, goblin nobble," Fire Fang said.

It was rare to see John startled, but he lurched in his seat, his gaze intent on Fire Fang. "When did he start talking?"

"A few days ago. We finally figured out a spell to unlock his voice."

"And I've got things to say to you, turkey goblet," Fire Fang said.

John's brow wrinkled. "Are you sure that speech spell worked?"

"It worked perfectly, thanks to Odessa and her hatred of cussing. Fire Fang likes to cuss, so Odessa added a tweak to the spell to make sure he keeps everything PG. He's not happy about that."

John roared out a laugh. He tipped back in his seat and continued to study Fire Fang like he was an exciting new toy he'd love to get his hands on. "Odessa is something else."

"Don't even think about her. She's not for you."

"I know. Stay away from your friends. I heard you loud and clear after you slammed me into a wall and told me I'd be wearing my colon as a scarf if I made a move on any of them."

"And the same goes for Fire Fang. I've seen that lecherous look in your eyes before."

"I draw the line at dating furries."

"Don't be cute."

"You can't blame me for having interesting thoughts about him. A talking hellhound with extra abilities is a prize."

"He's no one's prize. Back off."

"How much do you want for him?" John wasn't getting the hint.

"I'm not for sale." Fire Fang stomped into John's personal space and growled in his face.

"He's his own hellhound. Fire Fang goes where he likes, with whoever he likes. And from the way he's growling at you, you're bottom of the list of people he wants to spend time with."

"He's not even on the list." Fire Fang planted a large paw in the center of John's chest, claws out.

John raised his hands, although there was a sharp glint in his eyes. "You can name your price. I'll be able to double it with the right gullible customer."

"You're speaking like you want to be roasted on an open flame and tossed out the door of this place still smoking." I sipped my drink, waiting to see if Fire Fang would make a move. I wouldn't stop him if he did.

"I collect interesting facts and things. And Fire Fang has gotten a lot more interesting now the conversation is two-way."

Fire Fang shoved John in the chest with his paw, making him yelp, then grabbed the front of John's shirt in his teeth and growled, deep and low, so the floor shook.

"You keep talking, and Fire Fang keeps getting madder."

"If I die, you get no more information." There was a wobble in John's voice, but he held my stare. "You need me."

It was a punch in the gut to acknowledge that. "You're only getting away with this because you're useful. Fire Fang, let him go."

With obvious reluctance, Fire Fang dumped John back in his chair. "We need to find a new turkey giblet to give us information."

I told myself the same thing every time I dealt with John, but there was no sleazebag smarter or swifter. "So, this skull? The short version."

John straightened his shirt and downed half his pint of ale. "Potted history. It's been around about eight hundred years. It's been called many things. The Death Skull, the Bone Destroyer, the Shrieking Scare. The name changes, but it's the same skull."

"We're talking ancient magic," I said. "Who's the creator?"

"Unknown. Although it's got to be someone powerful. A long line of ancient magic users who dabble in the seriously dark stuff. They're most likely dangerous and unstable if any are still alive. That kind of magic user dies young in a blaze of destructive spells."

"Keep digging. I need the name of who created it and their descendants. They'll be able to get rid of the skull. They should have the power to recall it and cancel the curse."

"I'll keep looking, but the further I go back in the records, the less reliable the sources become. Even though most magic users live hundreds of years, the original witch who created this will be long gone."

"We can only hope. If she's still around, no one will want to go up against her."

John drank more ale. "I get the sense you're prepared to, in order to solve this case."

"I have no choice. Hand over the file, and I'll leave you to it."

John picked up the file and held it against his chest. "Not yet. I want to know why you're putting your life on the line for the Discord family. I've been looking into them, and there are various lines of scum and scandal tracing through their history. The dead guy's business in particular."

"He was a piece of work, that's for sure. But the rest of the family doesn't seem so bad. One suspect said they're all toxic, though, and not to be trusted."

"That'll be no problem for you. You trust no one."

"It's the motto I should have tattooed on my behind. Now, the file."

"You're not telling me everything."

"You've heard everything you need to know."

"I haven't. You're not attached to this family, and you have no friends connected to them, yet you want to find the dark witch who created this screaming skull and start a fight. Is the pay that good?"

"It's worth dying for."

"Now I'm intrigued. Tell me everything, or I walk away with this file."

Fire Fang lurched at John, and only my hand on his back leg stopped him from biting down on the arm he'd grabbed.

"So you do have control over this hellhound." John remained still, knowing it would be a dumb move to fight. "I thought you said he was a free mutt."

"We have a working relationship. Give me the file. I've already deposited half the money in your account. You won't get any more until it's in my hands."

"I'm prepared to take the hit. Just tell me why you're involved."

John always loved to get the full facts, and I knew he'd dig his heels in and walk away from the rest of the money if I didn't give him what he wanted.

"This is between us," I said.

"Always. I don't gossip about my clients to anyone."

After a quick assessment of the risk, I figured John knowing I was cursed wouldn't harm me. "I refused this job, so the victim's best friend, Lucian Barkridge, got hold of the screaming skull and left it outside my apartment. I saw it, it screamed, and now I'm cursed. I have seven days to solve the mystery. Or rather, I had seven days. I've got a clock ticking down against my life. If I don't find out everything I can about the curse and destroy the skull, I'll be dead."

John didn't even blink at the news. "I hope you don't die. You're a great customer."

"Of course, you'll only miss my money."

"And your charming conversation."

I gestured to him to hand over the file, and he gave it willingly enough.

"Since it's you, and I don't dislike you, I'll keep looking for the originator of the curse. No extra charge. You can call it a parting gift, in case you don't make it," John said.

I nodded my appreciation, already flicking through the file. There were copies of old documents written in ancient magic that would take a while to decipher.

"To save your brain, I've had everything translated. It's on the flip side of the copy." John tapped the table to get my attention. "And I got you a freebie. This one's on me." He pulled a sheet of paper out of his pocket and passed it to me.

The world froze. A grainy picture of what looked like my sister stared at me.

I slapped my hand on the wooden table. "Why didn't you reveal this sooner? You had a lead on Eden and didn't tell me?"

He shrugged. "Maybe it's her. Maybe it's not. How do you know what she looks like after all these years?"

I grabbed the picture and held it close. It wasn't a clear image, but the shape of her face and those eyes. It was an older version of the sister I'd lost. I kept staring at it. There were differences, too, though. And she was frowning. Eden was the smiley one. She loved to laugh. This young woman looked bitter and had lines etched on either side of her mouth. She was hunched up, her arms wrapped around herself as if trying to make herself small.

I rubbed at the indigestion-like pain in my chest. "What else have you got, other than this picture?"

"Nothing to make you happy. That was taken in a non-magical village. Eden was caught on camera using magic on mortals."

"She'd never do that. Eden was young when she vanished, but we all know the basic rules of magic."

"Are you sure? After all, you've been out of touch a long time. And if Eden didn't have a mentor when learning her craft, she could be up to anything. There are magic users who care nothing about exploiting mortals."

I gritted my teeth, holding back a sharp retort. I hated John could be right about my sister going rogue.

"The details of where she was last seen are on the back of the photo." John stood, downed the rest of his drink, and pushed back his chair. "Try not to die. Good luck." He walked away and out of the bar.

I stayed where I was, studying the grainy image and rubbing my chest as the indigestion pain grew worse. She must be so scared and desperate if she was using magic on mortals. Perhaps the person who took her had trained her to do that. They'd created a magic wielding weapon.

If Eden was captured by law enforcers who dealt with mortals, she'd go into one of their jails. It would be chaos. Magic users and mortals weren't meant to mix. We were too dangerous to be around them, and they were too weak to be near us.

Fire Fang rested his chin on my lap, his gaze on the photo. "I've seen all the pictures of Eden you have. That doesn't look much like her to me."

"But you've never met her. This picture isn't good quality. It could be her. She looks around the right age." I sat back in my seat and let out a long sigh, trying to ease the tension in my chest. I wanted to go after Eden, track this sighting, and bring her back. But if I did, the screaming skull case would get away from me. If I failed to solve this, I was dead and wouldn't be around to help Eden get out of whatever mess she was in.

"Storm, I know you never listen to advice—"

"Not true. I listen to good advice. I get little of that anymore."

"I'm going to give you some. Put yourself first, for once. Save yourself before you look for Eden. You're no good to her as a ghost. When you get her back, she'll need support. Especially if she's been hanging out with mortals. You need to be here to look out for her. Which means you have to focus on this case."

"What if it's her in this picture? What if Eden is out there, and I don't follow this lead, and she slips away again?"

"Then you'll get a new lead. Someone else will see her and report it. Anyone using magic around mortals is picked out as an oddity. There are cameras everywhere in the mortal world. Although they won't see the magic, they'll know there's something odd about Eden. That information will get back to you. Then you can find her. But not until you're free from this curse. A dead Storm would be even less fun than a living one."

I absently patted Fire Fang's head. I didn't want to make this decision. "I'm no fun?"

"You can be when you let your guard down. You've got contacts all over the place. Use them. Pick your best and send them to this location. If Eden is there, they'll find her. And even if they can't bring her back, they'll keep tabs on her until you're ready to collect your sister."

I scratched behind his ears. "You make a lot of sense. I'm glad you're talking now."

"Even when I cuss like a sailor?"

"Especially that. I wish I knew what a goblin nobble was, though."

"It's exactly that. A goblin nobble."

I mustered a smile, then pulled out my phone and sent a message to a private investigator I didn't distrust.

Tulip, got an urgent job for you. You available?

I tapped my fingers on top of the table and played with my glass as I waited for a response.

Just finishing up a job. What's the deal?

I've got a sighting of Eden I need checking out. No contact. Just watch.

When and where?

Immediately. I'll send you the details.

It'll cost you. I've got three more jobs lined up after this one.

Double your rate?

Triple and you got a deal.

Done. I fired off the information about where Eden was and took a picture of the image John had given me and sent it, too.

Perfect. I'll let you know what I find. You know how to pay me. xx

I wired half the fee, as per our usual agreement.

"Good choice. Right choice," Fire Fang said.

"If it's the right choice, why do I feel so bad? I need to look for Eden, not deal with rich people and their issues."

"Right now, you need to focus on saving your life. And maybe mine, too. My stomach feels like my throat's been cut. When was the last time we ate?"

"I don't know. A while ago." I stared at my phone. "If anything comes of this sighting of Eden, I'll make the journey there straightaway."

"After you've solved the cursed skull case?"

I checked the time. It should be late enough for Augusta to be back at the house. "Let's hope so. Let's head to the Discord house. We'll pay an unannounced visit to Augusta. And I want to speak to her son. We need to get through all the suspects fast, make an arrest, and get on with what's important."

"Saving your life."

"Saving my sister."

Chapter 15

Erik stood in front of me, swaying from side to side, an almost empty bottle of whiskey in one hand. "You again. You're bad luck. I lost everything at that game you interfered with."

"I'm not bad luck. You're a lousy player, and you play with cheats. No one ever wins at gambling," I said.

"I have won! In the past. I had a great winning streak to begin with."

I had no time for Erik's drunken gambling ramblings. "You had a winning streak at the beginning because your con artist buddies lulled you into a false sense of security. You've been played. That place is bad for you. Stop gambling and ease off the booze, and your life will be a lot brighter."

"What are you, my therapist?"

"Thankfully, not. I'm here to see Augusta and Chilton."

"Ha! Bad luck does follow you. They're out."

"Are you sure? Lucian said Augusta would be back by now."

"She was, but didn't hang around for long. She came home, changed into some fancy dress, picked up Chilton, and they left."

I pressed my hand against the door as he tried to close it in my face. "Where did they go?"

"It's nothing to do with you. It's a private matter. Get your foot out of this door." Erik stumbled back when Fire Fang growled at him.

"Nothing is private in this investigation if it'll solve your brother's murder. Tell me where they are."

"If you don't, I'll shake it out of you," Fire Fang said. "Since Storm's forgotten to feed me, again, I might take a few chunks out of your podgy belly, too. I imagine you're well marinated."

Erik dropped the bottle he held. "There's no need for that. I'll tell you. They've gone to a posh dinner to commemorate Delano."

"And where is this posh dinner being held?" I said.

"There's an invitation on the table." He staggered away and returned a moment later, a fresh bottle of booze in one hand. He thrust a thick piece of cream card at me.

I took it and scanned the details, Fire Fang nudging my elbow so he could look.

The Zanti Foundation kindly requests the company of the esteemed Augusta Discord and family at a commemorative dinner for Delano Discord. The evening will be a celebration of his life's work and an opportunity for friends and family to gather to remember a great man lost too soon.

I skimmed through the time and address information, storing it to memory. "Why aren't you there, if this event is for family members?"

Erik shrugged. "Augusta said it was a bad idea. Something about me being an embarrassment. I wasn't paying attention. Besides, who wants to go to a stuffy dinner when I've got everything I need here?" He raised the bottle and took a drink.

I pocketed the invitation and walked away.

"You know where that place is, right?" Fire Fang hopped into the back seat of the rented car as I climbed in the front.

I pulled out the card again. "Sure. I've never been to the Magic Embassy."

"There'll be high security, lots of magic wards, and strict rules."

"How would you know that?"

Fire Fang scratched behind his ear with a back paw. "I must have been there."

"They let fire breathing hellhounds in?"

"Doubtful. But I know the place. I remember the layout. There are marble steps up to the front door. Loads of expensive antiques. Huge open rooms. There's even some ancient bit of wood the founders use as a dining table. It has magical symbols carved into it. Weird. Where's that memory coming from?"

"Maybe you've been reincarnated. You could have been a lapdog to a powerful warlock in a former life, and he dined at the Embassy."

He growled. "I'm no one's lapdog. You're sure you want to do this? We could grab Augusta tomorrow."

"Time isn't on my side. I'll find a way into this dinner so we can talk to Augusta and Chilton." I started the car, keyed in the directions on the GPS, and we headed off.

The Embassy was an hour's drive away, and Fire Fang snoozed on the back seat while I focused on the driving.

We passed through magical and mortal towns. Whenever I was waiting at traffic lights, I peered around, focusing on anyone who looked like Eden. I never stopped looking, and I never would. My sister was out there, I knew it. Even though she used to wind me up, banging on my bedroom door and demanding we play together, I'd do anything to get her back. Although playtime was over for us. We were grown witches with power.

I struggled to reconcile that with the image of my sweet, annoying baby sister in my head. When I got her home, we'd have to make some serious adjustments.

I pulled into a parking spot reserved for dignitaries outside the Embassy and climbed out with Fire Fang.

We made it up the marble steps and to the front door. It was locked, although the lights blazing inside suggested lots of people were home.

"Are you going to ring that bell, or shall we go in the stealthy way?" Fire Fang said.

"Let's try stealthy first and see how far we get." Although weather magic was my specialty, I had other tricks up my sleeve, and an unlock spell got us through the main door.

I made it a few steps before a heavy wave of hot energy hit me. I backed up and glowered at the magic barrier preventing me from getting any farther.

Fire Fang paced along the length of the barrier. "I don't feel any weak spots. This won't be easy to smash through."

"And hitting that barrier probably triggered a security alert, so we don't have long. Let's see if there's a back way in."

We headed out the door, around the side of the building, and discovered another entrance. There was a sign beside it saying staff only.

"We can be staff," Fire Fang said.

"I don't think you'll pass as a cater waiter but nice idea." I used an unlock spell again, and we snuck through the door.

The bustle of noise and smells drifting along the corridor told me we were close to the kitchen.

I glanced at Fire Fang. "We'll march through and act like we're supposed to be here. No one will stop us."

"Have you seen us? We stick out."

"We can blend."

"I could scare everyone out of the kitchen. Give you an easy passage."

"Scaring is our Plan B." I dashed along the corridor with Fire Fang, trying a few doors we passed, but they were storage or cleaning closets and didn't lead into the dinner.

We reached the double doors to the kitchen, and I peered through a round window. There were twenty people dashing around, busily plating tiny portions of food on huge plates and splattering sauce over steaming morsels. I wasn't a fan of posh dinners. I liked my food simple and uncomplicated, but my stomach growled, reminding me I'd neglected several meal times.

"You ready?" I whispered.

"Let's do this."

I shoved open the door and marched in. I kept my eyes on the doors the wait staff were dashing in and out of. That was the target. Through there, and all we needed to do was find Augusta and Chilton.

A large guy in chef whites holding a meat cleaver stepped into my path. "What are you doing in my kitchen?"

"Hey! Great food. Loved the entrees. I got lost on my way back from the bathroom. If you'll excuse me."

He moved to block my path again. "You're not telling me you're a dinner guest." His gaze slid over my black boots, jeans, and sweater.

"Of course. Don't you know who I am?"

"No clue. Someone call security. We have an intruder."

"I'll deal with him. You go." Fire Fang grabbed the hand holding the meat cleaver and dropped the guy to the floor. He blasted flames whenever anyone got close, leaving the path free for me to race through the doors.

I grabbed a chair and wedged it under the handles so no one could get through and cause me trouble.

Taking in a deep breath, I turned. Elegance hit me like a sparkled fairy kiss. The lighting was subdued, soft music played in the background, and the scent of expensive perfume filled the air.

I remained by the doors as I looked for my targets. It could take a while. There were over two hundred and fifty people in this room.

There was a shriek and something crashed to the floor in the kitchen, causing a few diners to look my way. I hurried away, remaining by the wall as I scanned the tables.

Augusta and Chilton were at a table on the opposite side of the room, along with a dozen other people, all dressed expensively and reeking of entitled power.

I jogged past startled looking diners and straight over to them.

Augusta was about to take a sip of wine when her gaze locked onto me. Surprise flickered across her face, and she lowered her glass. "Storm. What are you doing here?"

"I've been trying to speak to you all day. Are you avoiding me for a reason? Guilty conscience, perhaps?"

"What's this?" Chilton's cheerful smile faded as he glanced at his mother.

"Now's not a good time," Augusta said. "As you can see, we're in the middle of something."

"You need to get out of this something. Although I'm happy to ask my questions right here, but I don't think you want everyone overhearing."

Two burly women in black suits appeared by the table on either side of me. The weight of their intimidation pressed in on me, as did a warning sting of magic.

"Is there a problem, Mrs. Discord?" one of them inquired. "Chef reported an intruder."

Augusta's gaze met mine. "No problem. Thank you."

The women gave me a thorough visual onceover before backing off.

"I can only spare a few minutes. And not here. Let's go into the corridor." Augusta set aside her napkin and stood.

"I'll come with you." Chilton pushed back his chair and held his arm out for Augusta to take.

I followed them out of the dining room, aware all eyes were on us but not caring.

"This had better be important," Augusta said. "The people in there are influential. They could make life difficult for me."

"They're meaningless to me. And this is important, given I've been death cursed, so I have to solve your husband's murder."

A pained look crossed Augusta's face. "Of course. Forgive me. I've been so caught up with everything going on, I sometimes forget what Lucian did to you. What do you need from me?"

"I need to know if you faked your alibis and killed your husband."

Augusta gasped and grabbed Chilton's arm.

"My mother didn't kill anyone," Chilton said. "None of us had anything to do with it. Why would you say that?"

"Because everything I'm uncovering keeps leading me back to your mother."

Augusta squeezed Chilton's arm, her knuckles white. "What have you found out? Why do you think I'm the killer?"

"Because you're leasing a secret apartment and hiding money from your husband. Why would you do that?"

Chilton shook his head. "You're making a mistake."

Augusta patted him on the arm, her expression tight and her cheeks ghostly white. "Go get us drinks from the bar. It was so hot in that room, and I need something to help me cool down."

"I don't want to leave you alone with her." Chilton scowled at me. "Sorry to be rude, but you're not being nice. My mother would never kill my father."

"I'll be fine, Chilton. We just have a few things to discuss. Five minutes. That's all I need to sort this out."

"And I'll need five minutes with you, too, Chilton, when I'm done here," I said.

"That won't be necessary. My son's not involved in this." Augusta's tone was icy, her maternal protective instinct firing up.

"Is that a confession?" I said.

"No, it's not. Chilton, if you'll excuse us." Augusta grasped my arm and turned me away from Chilton.

He didn't look happy but finally left us alone.

"How did you find out about the money and the apartment?" she said, her tone low and clogged with urgency.

"I know how to do my job. And some people like slipping out secrets."

Augusta closed her eyes for a second before opening them. "I've already admitted to you the horror of my marriage. Delano enjoyed humiliating me with his parade of mistresses. He was a revolting man, and I was a desperate woman. I knew it was dangerous, but I had to have a way out."

"And when that failed, you cursed him?"

"I didn't kill him. Why would I create a haven for myself and a stash of assets, then ruin it all and murder my husband?"

"Because he found out."

"Delano knew nothing of my plans. I made sure of it."

"That you know of. Even if he didn't find out, he could have done something truly abhorrent to you, and that pushed you over the edge."

"Pushed an almost powerless witch over the edge, you mean? I couldn't control that skull even if I wanted to. It wasn't me." She pushed her hair off her face, her eyes shimmering.

She had me there. I still hadn't figured out how Augusta would have been able to control the skull.

"I just want to forget about Delano," she whispered.

"Which is why you're at this elaborate dinner?"

"Some of his business partners arranged it. They were toadies to Delano when he was alive, and him dying hasn't altered their behavior. Only now, they're sliming around me, hoping to get a cut of his assets. I've had to fend off six conversations about buying his businesses. I even had one odious individual suggest I should look for a new husband. I sent him away with his tail between his legs. After my experience with marriage, I have little interest in a relationship."

"I can't say I blame you. Maybe try a different kind of guy if you go there again."

"Any suggestions?"

"One who's less interested in power and more interested in making you happy."

The ghost of a smile flickered to life. "Good advice. Are you married?"

"You won't catch me doing anything so dumb." Every time I got a new piece of information in this investigation, it led me to Augusta, but when I spoke to her, the doubts crept back in.

Augusta arched one eyebrow. "If you're not going to arrest me, I have several overly ambitious individuals to disappoint tonight."

"Not tonight, I won't. You don't have plans to sell Delano's assets to any of them, do you?"

Augusta paused by the door. "I'm considering the options, but none of the men or women here tonight will get their hands on what Delano had. Even though Erik will inherit the assets, I plan to make the decisions about the future of this family and its wealth." She swept away in a cloud of expensive perfume and silk, leaving the door open.

A blast of flame shot into the dining hall, and Fire Fang swiftly followed. He skidded across the wooden floor, his gaze shifting until he saw me.

He bounded over. "The food is great, although the portions are too small. Did you get what you needed?"

"I mainly got confused." I hurried away as chaos engulfed the room. People tried to put out the flames, although a few were looking in our direction. And those looks weren't friendly. We were almost out of time.

"We should leave. That chef wants me sliced and marinated, and I'm not ready to go out in a blaze of pickled ginger and fondue just yet."

I slowed as I passed the members' bar. "Before we go, I need a drink."

"Shouldn't we get out of here, you know, before I'm diced and you're arrested?"

"Most likely. But there's another suspect in my sights, and I'm not letting him go."

Chapter 16

The private members' bar was separate to the dining area, and the chaos Fire Fang had caused had yet to reach the ears of the drinkers in here. The atmosphere was calm, and the air smelled of whiskey and wine.

I spotted Chilton at the bar, talking to a server. I stood beside him and waited until he turned to look at me.

His cheeks flushed, and he stepped back. He surprised me by catching hold of my hand. "I owe you another apology. I never speak to people like that, but you surprised me when you threw around accusations of murder. I hope I didn't offend you."

I was equally surprised he was apologizing to me. I eased away my hand. "You were standing up for a member of your family. Anyone would have done the same."

"Of course. I'm sure you always defend your parents."

"I would, but they're dead."

"Ah. Again, I've made an error. Let me make it up to you. May I get you a drink?"

"There's no need. And there's no making up to do. Murder suspects get tetchy when they're questioned. It happens. And I've been treated much worse."

"Even so, it couldn't have been pleasant for you." Chilton brought over a stool, along with a plump cushion, which he set in front of me. "Make yourself comfortable."

"I don't need a drink, a cushion, or a seat. I just need you to answer a few questions."

"Are you certain? There's nothing I can do to make you more comfortable?"

"I'm already more comfortable than a kitten in a perfectly sized shoebox."

"A... shoebox?"

"Yep."

"And no drink?"

"Not while I'm working."

Chilton glanced at the door as footsteps hurried past. It wouldn't be long before word reached him about what we'd done in the kitchen.

"How did you feel about your dad's plans for the family fortune?" I said.

He seemed to have an internal battle as he considered the question, his forehead wrinkling and straightening several times. "Initially shocked. I worked with him, you see. We'd had discussions about me taking over."

"And you were looking forward to that?"

Chilton took another few seconds to ponder. "I was. But I had my own plans for his fortune. I wanted to use the money for good."

"That's unusual for a jinn. You're hoarders."

"True. And I have my own hoard, which I'm proud of. But it's different when you inherit a fortune. You're less attached. At least, I'm not as attached to my father's fortune as I am to my own assets. It comes from the fact you generate the wealth rather than are given it. I made my first purchase of gold coins when I was a teenager."

"So what are your plans for your dad's fortune?"

"I want to invest it ethically. And I've set up a charity to help the less fortunate. Magic users who fall on hard times. There are more out there than many realize."

"Again, a bit weird, being you're a jinn."

He looked offended. "We're not all heartless money grubbers."

I tilted my head from side to side. "From the outside, it often looks like you are. You came up with these plans on your own? No one told you to do that with your dad's money?"

"It was a mix of my mother's input and my own ideas. I talked to a few friends, too. I admired Dad and part of me wanted to be like him, but my mother thought we had enough. In truth, we have too much. If you could see inside the vault... Well, you can't, but it's impressive. We could make a big difference to the community with the assets left behind."

"Which wouldn't have been the case if your dad had frittered everything away before he died."

"That's true. But there was nothing I could do. My father was a stubborn man. When he got an idea, he dug in his heels, even if people suggested there was another way."

"You really think he could have blown through all that money?"

"If that was the plan, he'd have done it. Father failed at nothing. I had concerns about what he wanted to do, but he had more knowledge than me. He was a clever man. I took after him looks-wise but not with intellect. Are you sure I can't get you a drink?"

"Absolutely sure."

The server behind the bar came up to us. "Excuse the interruption, but guests are being asked to gather outside. There's been a fire in the dining room."

Chilton jumped to his feet. "Has anyone been hurt? Can I help in any way?"

"Everything is under control, and they're hoping to continue the dinner. They're asking people to leave the building to be on the safe side. If I could get you to..." He gestured at the door.

"We'd better go," Chilton said. "Is there anything else you need to know from me? Have I been helpful? It's such a sad business. But please, don't accuse my mother. She wasn't always happy with my father, but she'd never hurt him."

It was unlikely Chilton knew just how bad things had been between his parents. "Remind me of your alibi for the night your father was cursed."

"I was in bed alone. It's a rather sad alibi, isn't it?"

"No one was with you or came to speak to you at any point?"

"No, I was all alone. I really think we should go. And I must check on my mother and the other guests." Chilton went to guide me out of the room by putting his hand on the small of my back.

I stepped away. "I know the way out."

"Of course. If you'll excuse me." Chilton hurried away.

I slowed when I reached the dining room and looked in at the chaos, flames, and smoke. There was a movie playing, showing pictures of Delano. While I watched the over the top compliments and praise flashed over the images from people who knew him, I considered what Chilton had told me. He didn't have much of a motive and seemed too affable to be a danger to anyone. Although maybe he had more desire for his father's assets than he let on.

"Chilton seemed like a friendly guy," Fire Fang said. "No murder creep vibe."

"That's what I was thinking. Chilton admired his dad and didn't seem bothered about getting the money. Although he has a lousy alibi."

"Just like everyone else in this investigation."

"The nice guy thing could also be an act. Chilton was coveting his dad's fortune, and when he learned he wasn't getting his hands on it, he killed him."

After a minute of watching the movie showing Delano's amazing achievements and what a great man he was, I'd had enough. "Let's get out of here. After seeing that propaganda, I need a drink and a huge pie."

"Pie. Now you're talking. Will it be apple?"

I'd found a quiet café that didn't mind hellhounds being inside and was sipping my second strong coffee while polishing off a delicious slab of warm apple pie with custard.

Fire Fang had gone for a foot-long meat feast baguette and a side order of apple pie. I didn't mind overindulging him. I'd been neglectful about regular feeding over the last couple of days. For both of us. I must get better at remembering meal times.

"Is this seat taken?" A tall guy with brilliant blue eyes looked at the empty seat next to me hopefully and smiled.

"It is."

"Oh. It's just that I saw you dining alone. You've been on your own since you got here."

"I'm not alone." I gestured at Fire Fang.

"Would you like company? I never enjoy eating on my own."

"I do."

Confusion marred his not unattractive face. "You do want company?"

"No, I like eating on my own. There's no one to object when I drop stuff down me." The guy was good-looking enough, but I wasn't in the mood for company. And I had too much stuffed in my head to even consider flirting.

He opened his mouth, but then closed it and looked over his shoulder.

I glanced up at him when he remained by the table. "Is there anything you need? Ketchup? Mustard?"

"She's being polite. Get lost, donkey helmet," Fire Fang said. "She's with me."

The guy's eyes widened, and he backed away. "Sorry. My mistake." He dashed to a table on the other side of the café and sat with his back to us.

I smirked as Fire Fang growled a warning at the other diners, just in case they were dumb enough to attempt a conversation. "I'm with you, am I? When did that happen?"

"He was being a creep."

I glanced at the guy and shrugged. My friends told me my love life was as dire as my decorative skills, but I liked simple and unfussy. Relationships were anything but that.

Fire Fang rested his chin on my lap, and I scratched his head.

"You may not like it, but I look out for you," he grumbled.

"I didn't say I didn't like it. But this... relationship is only temporary—"

"It's not. I'm staying."

"Do I get a say in that?"

He growled. "No."

"If a guy said that to me, he'd feel my boot on his behind, and he'd be blocked everywhere. When you talk to your fluffy girlfriends, don't say that kind of thing. It makes you sound like an alpha pig."

"An alpha pig?"

"You know, trying to be the dominant force, while sticking your snout where it doesn't belong. No one needs that in their life."

Fire Fang growled again. "What are we going to do next?"

"I'm working on a plan." I pulled out my phone to see if there were any messages and discovered a missed call from the vet. I was about to hit redial, but my attention was caught by Rosina striding past the café. "Hey. Heads up. I'd recognize that auburn hair anywhere."

Fire Fang's eyes narrowed. "What's she doing here? You don't think she was invited to the dinner, do you?"

I shoved back my seat and hurried to the window, watching her strut along the sidewalk in a pair of dangerous-looking red high heels. At least, they'd be dangerous if I walked in them. I'd break both ankles within thirty seconds.

"If Augusta had anything to do with that dinner, Rosina definitely wouldn't have been invited," I said.

Fire Fang joined me at the window. "She looks like she's on a mission."

"Let's go see what she's up to. You watch. I'll pay the bill."

Within a minute, we were out of the café and tracking Rosina. She was holding a large purse over one arm. She occasionally checked her phone, but otherwise seemed to know where she was going.

"She could be shopping," Fire Fang said. "She's always wearing new clothes whenever we see her."

"We've only seen her a couple of times."

"Yeah, but I'm not used to it. You wear the same thing for weeks on end before changing."

"Not true. And I always have clean underwear on." Most days.

"Rosina teases herself up to look like a peacock."

"And you like that?"

"It's what's inside that counts." He glanced at me. "Although a T-shirt with less food stains wouldn't do you any harm."

"You know the fancy peacocks are male, don't you? Pea hens are the dowdy ones. It's the guys that get gussied up to impress the ladies. I like the pea hen's style. I wish it was how things worked around here."

"Why does that bother you? You're not into flashy guys."

"How do you know what kind of guy I like?"

He growled, low and deep. "I see you with a guy who's rough around the edges but has a brain. And you need someone to keep you on your toes and to remind you to change your sweater more than once a month."

I looked down and grimaced. Maybe there were a couple of stains on my sweater that shouldn't be there. But when life got busy, my priorities changed. Making sure I looked like some cute daisy waiting to be plucked by a guy was never one of them.

"Rosina is slowing down. What's that place she's looking at?" Fire Fang said.

We hung back until she went inside the store and then moved closer.

I read the sign outside. *The Magic Emporium. Find a treasure, sell a treasure.* "It's a pawnshop."

"Why does Rosina need to pawn her things?"

"Since her rich honey is dead, she won't have an income. She could be getting desperate and selling off things Delano gave her, getting money together for when Augusta kicks her out."

We peered through the glass front window of the store, ignoring the curious looks of passersby.

Rosina spent twenty minutes pulling things out of her large purse and handing them to a tall, plump guy behind the counter.

The glass was smoked, so it was hard to see what Rosina was handing over, but she seemed happy when she pocketed what the guy gave her and even kissed his cheek before heading to the door.

We shuffled into the alleyway by the side of the store and waited until she'd left.

"Fire Fang, you tail Rosina. I'll see what the guy inside has to reveal."

He nodded and loped away.

I pushed open the door and walked inside.

"Greetings. Welcome to the Magic Emporium. You'll find all the treats you desire in here. What do you wish to do today? A trade or a sale?" The plump man smiled at me and spread his hands out. "Take a look around if you need a minute."

"I'm not here to trade. But I am looking for information."

He indulged me with a wide smile, but his eyes were sharp. "Sadly, that's not free these days. Only browsing is free."

I pulled out my wallet and passed him some money. "I want to know about the woman you just did business with."

The money disappeared behind the counter.

"A charming lady. And a regular customer. She often teases me she's fleecing her boyfriend of his fortune piece by piece." He chuckled. "That was a joke. At least, I'm almost certain she doesn't mean it. But it pays not to quiz too much when undertaking a business transaction."

"When did she start coming here?"

"Her visits started a few months ago. Maybe longer. She's friendly and always happy to chat. She shows up with a bag full of goodies and hands them over."

"What kind of goodies?"

"Mainly magic trinkets. A few enchanted gems. I've even had some gold coins. That's not the most exciting thing she's given me, though."

"What's that?"

"Look to your right." His eyes sparkled.

There was a tall glass cabinet full of vials of magic. They shimmered in different shades of red, green, and gold.

I took a step closer. "She's been selling you her magic?"

"Not her magic. But she's been acquiring others."

"With the consent of the magic user, naturally." It was illegal to drain another magic user without their permission, although it went on from time to time.

"I assume so. I test the legitimacy of the magic, and if it's something I need, I hand over payment."

"Does she tell you where the magic comes from?"

"Most likely from the same individual she's borrowing her magic trinkets from."

"Borrowing. Right. You have no problem dealing with stolen goods?"

"If questions were ever raised as to the legitimacy of the goods or the magic, I'm able to plead ignorance. I ask everyone who trades with me to sign a form showing they have full responsibility if ever there are any problems with the transaction."

"So you avoid blame if the Magic Council comes snooping?"

"It works better that way." His sharp gaze flickered over me. "May I ask you a question?"

"You can try. If I don't like it, I won't answer."

"Why the interest? Has my beautiful patron acquired something of yours and you want it back? If so, my rates are fair."

In my eyes, sleazy charm was as popular as a rare steak at a vegan barbecue. Maybe a shock to this guy's system would shake the truth out of him. "Your client, Rosina, is a suspect in a triple murder investigation."

The effect was exactly what I'd hoped for. He backed away, lifting his hands and shaking his head. "No, no, no! I want no part of that. Tell her she's no longer welcome. I won't trade with anyone dangerous."

"I can understand why. How about you let me see what she sold you? The items could be connected to her victims. If word gets out you deal with dangerous criminals, it won't do your reputation any good."

"Of course. It's under the counter. I haven't sorted it." He grabbed a tray and slammed it down in front of me. "Is this what you're looking for?"

There were three gold coins engraved with four-leaf clovers, two necklaces, and six jewel encrusted bracelets, along with two rings. Other than the coins, these could have been gifts Delano gave Rosina.

"This is everything? Rosina didn't give you any magic this time?"

"No. She said she wouldn't be bringing in more magic. Is that how she killed people? She drained them until they died?"

"That wasn't the method used. And Rosina is just a person of interest in these murders." I took a picture of the items, then pocketed my phone. "What about the other things she traded with you? Anything unusual?"

"More of the same. Mainly jewelry. A couple of coins, but that's it. It was standard stuff. Pretty, but nothing to alarm me."

"Other than the magic?"

His cheeks flushed. "Yes, other than that. I... Perhaps I should have asked a few more questions."

The door behind me banged open, and Fire Fang stood there. "You need to see this. It's weird."

I nodded at the store owner, who was staring in startled alarm at Fire Fang. "Thanks for the information." I turned and hurried out. "What's Rosina up to?"

"This way. I figured she'd deposit the money in a bank or spend it on clothes or purses."

"But she's not doing that?"

"She's gone into a discount warehouse and is loading a cart with food, clothing, and blankets."

"For herself?"

"It's not the kind of thing she wears. It's practical stuff like T-shirts and fleece jackets." Fire Fang led me to a huge set of automatic doors, and we headed inside the discount warehouse.

The overhead lighting was unflattering, the shelves metal and packed with cheap goods you could buy in bulk.

"The last place I saw her was in the food aisle. She was loading up sacks of rice."

I followed Fire Fang, and we discovered Rosina heading toward the checkouts.

"Rosina! I didn't expect to see you here." I stood in front of her piled shopping cart.

She glanced at me, and her eyes widened. She dropped her hold on the cart and raced away.

"Fire Fang, will you do the honors? Bring her down," I said.

He bounded after Rosina, who made it twenty steps before Fire Fang jumped on her back and shoved her to the floor. She squeaked and stumbled, landing on her hands and knees.

Several people had stopped to watch the hellhound take down the auburn-haired bombshell. A few even had their phones out.

I shooed them away. "This is official business. This woman is wanted by the Magic Council for murder."

Most of them drifted off, but a couple of guys stayed. Most likely, they wanted to step in and help the damsel in distress. I glared at them until they moved away.

"Get off me," Rosina said. "Storm, call off your dog."

"Only if you promise not to run. I hate cardio." I walked over and petted Fire Fang on the head. "Good boy."

"I won't. I know I won't be able to get away. Not in these heels."

I gestured at Fire Fang, and he moved off her but remained close, growling softly.

Rosina clambered to her feet and smoothed down her rumpled skirt. She turned and ran, knocking over a shopping cart and scattering the contents all over the floor.

I groaned. "Really?"

Her speed was impressive, as were her vaulting skills. She leaped a cashier and was out the door before Fire Fang had even moved.

"Let's get her. Again." I jogged past startled shoppers and out the door. Fire Fang was way ahead of me.

Rosina turned and looked at us. She squeaked and sped up, flipping off her heels and running barefoot. But it was no good. Four paws were faster than two feet. Within a minute, she was face down on the concrete.

"Are you following me?" Rosina looked up from underneath Fire Fang.

I jogged up beside her. "No. But it was our lucky day. You walked past us, and we decided to see what you were doing. Why are you pawning your jewels?"

"Does it matter? They belong to me. I can do what I like with them."

"I doubt the gold coins belonged to you. Did you steal them from Delano, just like you stole his magic?"

Her plump lips pressed together. "Maybe I did. This isn't what it looks like, though."

"It looks a lot like you were stealing from Delano. Fill me in on the truth."

Rosina squirmed under Fire Fang, but he wasn't letting her go. "Okay! You know our relationship wasn't everything it seemed. Delano needed a pretty accessory on his arm."

"I get that. You were faking being his mistress. Where does the stealing come in? Did something go wrong, and he wanted more than you were willing to give, so you needed an escape fund?"

"No. It's just as I told you. We put on a show, and he left me alone. That was it."

"You were using Delano."

"We used each other. He just didn't realize how much he was being played." She risked nudging Fire Fang with her elbow. "Can I get up?"

"Not yet. Did Delano know you were taking his magic?" I said.

She let out a small sigh. "No. I admit I went a little too far. But Delano had so much, and magic is worth a fortune. Almost as much as his gold. And I only got those coins because he let slip he kept some in his sock drawer."

"Did Delano find out what you were doing? Is that why you killed him?"

"He had no idea what I was up to. He thought I was an airhead piece of fluff. That was exactly what I wanted him to think."

"I don't believe you. Delano's dead, and you're amassing as much money as possible before Augusta kicks you out of the house."

"No. The money isn't for me. You've got it all wrong."

"Did you have a debt to pay off? Getting your hands on a screaming skull wouldn't have been cheap. You must owe someone for that magic. Are they pressing for a repayment, so you're scrambling to get your hands on the money fast?"

"I... No. The skull had nothing to do with me. I had an arrangement with Delano that suited us both. Why would I ruin that?"

"Because the arrangement became more trouble than it was worth. You claimed to be alone in your room the night Delano was cursed."

"That's true. I was."

"Where exactly is your bedroom?"

"Delano set me up in the room opposite his. He used to torment Augusta by saying it gave him easy access to me." Rosina winced. "That wasn't something I enjoyed taking part in, but I had to make it look good."

"What's going on?"

I turned at the sound of Chilton's voice.

He got out of a black limousine and hurried over. "Rosina, why is that dog sitting on you?"

Her cheeks flushed. "It's a misunderstanding. Storm saw something and jumped to conclusions. Wrong conclusions."

"The conclusion is clear. Ever since you got involved with Delano, you've been stealing from him. But you took it to another level when you stole his magic. He found out, threatened you, so you needed him dead. And you have no alibi for the night he was cursed. And let's not forget your connection to the Valenti witches. You picked up bad habits from them. Habits that led to triple murder."

Chilton shook his head. "Rosina wouldn't do that. She's a good person."

"You're sticking up for your dad's mistress?" I said.

His face turned several shades of pink as his mouth opened and closed. "Of course not. But she's sweet to everyone. She can't be a killer."

"You can be sweet and a killer. You're coming with me, Rosina. You have questions to answer." I grabbed her arm before she could protest, placed a hand on Fire Fang's head, and translocated us to Olympus Duke's office in Witch Haven.

The Magic Council could take it from here, but the evidence was clear. This case was solved.

Chapter 17

I rolled over in bed and smiled. Even though I could hear the high-pitched howls of the stray cat outside the apartment, it wasn't messing with my good mood. Delano's killer had been found. I just needed to deal with the skull problem, and I could get on with my life.

Fire Fang took up the other side of my double bed. He opened one eye. "What's wrong?"

"Why do you think anything is wrong?"

"You're smiling. I always get worried when you smile."

"We figured out what happened to Delano."

He wriggled around on the bed. "You're sure about Rosina?"

"We found out she was conning Delano. Her life is one big lie. For all we know, she could have been having a proper relationship with him and things went sour. Then he discovered she was cheating him out of his jinn fortune and threatened to expose her. She panicked, called in a favor from her former employer, and took it way too far."

"What about the other suspects' motives? You were sure it was Augusta to begin with."

"Augusta has no power." I rolled onto my back and stared at the ceiling. "And every time I've spoken to her, I got the impression she wanted this horrible part of her life forgotten. She married Delano because she needed to save her family, but it brought her misery. I'm sure she imagined killing Delano multiple times, but didn't have the power to do it. Rosina did. Even if she had to make a bargain with some powerful witches to get it."

"What about Erik and his hatred for Delano? No longer an issue?"

"He's a drunk loser with no prospects. He's too mixed up in his own messy world to think through a plan to use a screaming skull to curse his brother."

"Or Hattie, the bitter sister who wants to be... mortal."

"Again, her magic is faulty. And she wants rid of the family. I imagine she'll be moving on soon. Maybe even to the world of mortals. What a horrible thought."

"And you're dismissing the sleazy best friend as a suspect?"

"I don't like Lucian, and he's too smooth, but what would he gain from murdering his best friend? Not any of Delano's fortune. And perhaps Augusta will decide to use a different legal adviser. Lucian could be out of a job before long." I rolled over, so I faced Fire Fang, snug in my bed and happy to be lounging with my furry friend. "Rosina was manipulating the situation and got caught out. She had to act fast, or everything would have gone wrong."

"By just happening to find a cursed skull in her purse?"

"You're only defending her because she gives amazing belly rubs."

"The best. It's the fake nails. They dig in. But you haven't explained why she was bulk buying that stuff in the discount store. Why would she use the money to buy that?"

I huffed out a breath. Fire Fang wouldn't spoil my rare cheerful mood. "Some mysteries have to remain just that."

"If Rosina needed the money to pay a debt to whoever gave her the screaming skull, she'd use it on that."

"She could be economizing. I don't know. And I don't care. Let the Magic Council tidy up the loose ends. Rosina is the killer. And now that's off our hands, we can focus on the important things."

"Like finding the skull and getting you uncursed?"

"That's one item on my list of things to do I must not fail to achieve."

He shuffled closer and stuck his damp nose on my arm. "We only have a few days left."

"That's all we need. Get up. We have work to do."

After a quick shower and a change of clothes, making sure I picked a sweater without stains, I settled on the couch with a huge mug of coffee and a plate of waffles and sifted through the information John had given me about the cursed skull.

It took several hours to look through it all, and by the time I'd finished, I'd placed the information into three neat piles. Ancient history, recent history, and present-day sightings and use of the skull. I'd been making notes as I read through the information and had discovered several references to bone witches.

Fire Fang was also on the couch, his head in my lap as he looked at the notes I'd made. "You've underlined that. You think a bone witch is important?"

"I've not had much to do with bone witches. There aren't many left. But they get mentioned. It could be important."

"I'm glad there aren't many left. Bone witches are creepy. Any witch who has the power to manipulate bone isn't one you mess with. And there's not much that stops them. They know that, too, so most of them do what they like."

"They are creepy, but I wouldn't mind an introduction to see if there have been rumors circulating about the skull. Without finding the source, the cursed skull will kill me."

Fire Fang rolled off the couch. "Then let's go. What are we doing lounging about here?"

"Putting a plan into place. There's no point rushing around like a headless goblin trying to figure things out. The solution is in these papers. We just need to find it." I stood and refreshed my coffee.

As I headed back to the couch, the stray cat howled again. I set down my mug and pulled out my phone, calling the vet I'd delivered her to.

"Harvest Hill veterinary clinic."

"I'm calling about a stray cat I brought in the other day. She's black, kind of skinny, and loud. She's found her way back to my apartment."

"Oh! That cat. I know who you're talking about. She belongs to you?"

"No, she's a stray. But she's back. I need her gone."

"It was so strange. She poofed out of her cage when our backs were turned. We'd just finished giving her some shots and multivitamins, and she vanished. She's come back to you?"

"Unfortunately, she has."

"She must like you. Do you have a connection with her? Maybe a partial familiar bond gone wrong?"

"Nothing like that. The cat just won't take a hint. You need to come get her. She's causing a nuisance. Someone will report her to animal control."

"There's no one available to pick up a stray cat. And I know the shelters are busy today. They always are. Can you bring her back? Or take her in for a few days? Maybe foster her?"

The last time I'd captured that cat, I'd ended up on the ground with bags of trash covering me. "I'll see what I can do. I'm also waiting for the bloodwork results on my hellhound. I missed a call from the vet, so I figured they were ready."

"Let me check. What's the name?"

"Storm Winter."

"Of the animal being tested."

"Sure. Fire Fang."

The sound of fingers hitting the keyboard came down the line. "They're back. But there's a note to say the vet wants to speak to you about the results."

My gaze flicked to Fire Fang, who was pacing by the front door. "Is it something bad?" He wasn't mine, but I didn't like to think of him suffering.

"Most likely not. Doctor Hooper is thorough, though. I expect she wants to talk through all the results and answer questions you have. She does that with all patients. It's nothing to worry about."

"I'll speak to her now."

"She's in an emergency surgery. We had an injured griffin brought in less than an hour ago that got into a fight with a helicopter. I'll let her know you called. She'll be in touch as soon as she can. And don't worry about Fire Fang. Give him a kiss and a treat. He'll be fine."

I ended the call and immediately contacted John Smith.

"Hey, Winter. Not dead yet?"

"Getting there. Have you got more information for me?"

"Patience. These things take time."

"That's the one thing I don't have. I need you to look into the bone witches for me, too."

There was silence for several heartbeats. "Why do you want to mess around with those crazy old crones?"

"The information you gave me mentioned bone witches several times. And it makes sense they're connected to a cursed skull."

"Stay away from them. Nothing good will come of you poking a bone witch. I tangled with one once, and I've got the scars on my back to prove it."

"I don't want the details of how you got those."

"Sadly, it's not what you think. She had information I needed, but we couldn't come to a compromise. She didn't like it when I wouldn't take no for an answer. Those scars still sting."

"I still need the information. I need a contact. A bone witch who likes to chat."

"No such thing. And you don't know for definite it was a bone witch who created that skull. Someone with enough magic and money may have made it."

"Temporarily. But the records on this thing show it has been around for almost a thousand years. This is bone witch magic. Nothing else would hold that much power for such a long time. I need a contact in that community. Who do you know?"

He didn't speak again for several seconds. "Do you have a specific coven in mind?"

"Not yet. But I'll speak to any bone witch about the skull. She'll point me in the right direction."

"Or suck the bones from your body and use them for a spell. You tangle with the wrong bone witch and you won't get out the other side in one piece. She'll want something from you."

"I have resources."

"You know what I'm talking about. Bone witches take their payment in one currency. Are you willing to offer that in exchange for the information you need?"

I wriggled my fingers and toes. These witches traded in bones. It was what made their magic so strong. And they took those bones from the dead and the living.

"I hear from the silence you understand me. Stay away from the bone witches."

"No. I need answers."

"Or an early funeral."

"I have to. I'm dead anyway if I don't break this curse."

He hissed down the phone. "I can't lose my best paying client. I'll put out feelers, see if anyone bites. But I'm promising nothing. Most of the bone witches are experts at remaining hidden."

"Do what you can. I like being alive."

"Yeah, I don't hate you being alive either." The line went dead.

I had one more call to make. I dialed Tulip, the private investigator I'd sent Eden's lead to. It went to voicemail, which I wasn't surprised about. When she worked on a case, she usually kept her phone on silent.

I sent her a message instead. *Any news on Eden?*

The reply came back a moment later.

No joy so far. I'm still asking around. Be in touch if I have news.

I sat back on the couch and sipped my coffee.

"We're not leaving?" Fire Fang returned to the couch but, after turning several times and pawing the cushion, couldn't seem to get comfortable.

"Soon. I need to think." Every lead I'd gotten on Eden over the years had gone cold quickly. It was as if she didn't want to be found. Or maybe whoever took her was making sure she could never be found.

I jumped up and dumped my empty mug on the table with a thud. "Let's take a walk. I need fresh air."

Fire Fang hopped off the couch, followed me down the stairs and out the back door. He was used to my mood swings and barely complained about them anymore.

He looked over his shoulder a couple of times as we headed along the quiet streets of Witch Haven.

"Something bothering you?" I said.

"We're being followed."

I shot a look over my shoulder and discovered the stray black cat following at a distance. "I have to hand it to her, she's one stubborn cat."

"It's not such a terrible idea to consider keeping her. She wouldn't take up much space."

"And who would feed her when I'm away on a case? And what's to say you wouldn't get hungry one night and eat her?"

"I'd never eat her. I like her."

"You don't even know her."

"I sort of do. I can't explain it, but I like her scent. It's homey. It smells safe."

I regarded Fire Fang with interest. His background was a mystery to him and me both. "Maybe you knew her in a former life. If you think you were another creature before you were a hellhound, you could have known that cat, too. Maybe you used to be a cat."

He didn't rise to my jab. "Where magic is concerned, anything is possible. You should think about it. We can figure out a feeding schedule. Luna loves animals. She can drop by and feed her when we go on a mission."

"Just because you've been hanging out with me for a while doesn't mean we're working every case together. It's not convenient to have a hulking hellhound treading on your toes and tagging along like a needy ghost in a haunted house."

"Tagging along! I'm an essential part of your business. The sidekick you never knew you needed. If nothing else, I can be the growling muscle you depend upon when we get attacked by a group of angry demons. Or did you forget about that?"

"That doesn't happen often."

"It happens enough for me to know you need me, even if you don't like to admit it."

"You're not staying. Not for good. Your position in my life is as temporary as that cat's."

"It's not quite that bad. I get to sleep in your bed, after all."

"Because you sneak on when I've gone to sleep. I should shut you in the living room."

"I'd only burn down the door to get in. That would get expensive for you, having to replace the door every week. Besides, you sleep better when I'm with you."

"I've noticed no difference in the quality of my sleep since you entered my life." That was a small lie. And I did like waking and seeing Fire Fang every morning, even when he hogged the duvet.

We walked along in silence for a few minutes.

I slowed as I reached the cemetery and pulled open the heavy metal gate.

"Is there someone you want to pay your respects to?" Fire Fang asked.

"Silvaria Digby knows about the dead. She could also know something about bone witches. I expect she's chased a few out of this graveyard when they've skulked around looking for bones for their spells."

"Do we have to? I don't like Silvaria. That walking cane she uses is made of human bone."

"It just looks like that. It's a part of her act to scare people out of the cemetery and make sure they don't bother her or her dead companions." At least,

I was fairly certain she didn't walk around with a hulking great bit of fused bone in her hand.

A quick circuit around the cemetery revealed an absence of anyone living.

"She's not here. Let's go." Fire Fang nudged me to the gate.

I brushed him away and headed to the back of the cemetery. Silvaria had a small place around here she lived in, but it was well-concealed and hard to find.

Something snapped under my foot. I hoped it was a twig and not a small piece of bone I'd accidentally shattered. That wouldn't put Silvaria in a good mood. Not that I'd ever seen her cheerful. Unless she was dancing. This bitter old witch loved to boogie.

A moment later, there was a scuffle, and a flash of magic skimmed my head and hit a rock close by.

"Who goes there? This is private property."

I recognized the familiar rasp of Silvaria's voice. "It's Storm Winter. I have a question about a cursed skull and the bone witches."

There was silence. Even the air seemed still, as if waiting to see whether Silvaria would welcome us in. She shuffled into view, leaning heavily on the long stick Fire Fang was convinced was a human bone. She was a small witch, withered before her years for some unknown reason. She disliked everyone and everything and was quick to take offence, so I had to tread carefully. And since that wasn't my forte, this could get interesting.

"Bone witch, you say? I know nothing about them." She turned away. "Don't tread on any graves as you leave."

"You must have met a few bone witches in your time. You have a resource they covet."

"Maybe I have. That doesn't make them my friends." She kept shuffling away.

"I need to speak to one."

"Then you're an idiot. Go home. Find something less dangerous to do."

"Silvaria, wait. I've been cursed by a skull. It's a death curse, and I only have a few days to live. I think a bone witch created the skull that cursed me. I need to find her so she can tell me how to undo the curse or how to destroy the skull."

She turned back slowly. There'd been a flicker of alarm in her shrewd gaze when her eyes met mine, but it vanished in an instant. "It's a sad thing to happen to someone so young, but a bone witch won't help you."

"Because she can't, or she won't?" I strode toward Silvaria and caught hold of her arm. "Tell me what you know about the bone witches."

She yanked her arm away and hissed at me. "Do you have a death wish?"

"I may as well. If I don't destroy this curse, I'm dead, anyway."

Silvaria was silent. She flexed her fingers around her walking stick. "How can you be certain a bone witch made this skull?"

"I can't. But I've done my research, and this is an ancient skull with significant power. It's already killed three times, and I'm next. I have to stop it."

She sucked air in-between her teeth, whistling it out slowly. "If a bone witch made such a weapon, she wouldn't have handed it over easily. Such an object would be precious to her."

"It's precious to me, too. I have to reverse the curse."

"You missed my point. Such an object would not be given out lightly. There'd have been a cost."

"I understand that."

"Then you'll also understand the bone witches demand a high payment when gifting cursed skulls to another magic user."

"And they only take payment in bone," I said. "Whoever acquired this skull would have needed a collection of bones for the witch? Have you heard of any bones going missing from local graveyards?"

"No, and none have been taken from here. But they don't want just any bones. The witch would have demanded a personal payment." Silvaria ran a hand across my rib cage. "A bone from the receiver of the skull. If this connection is true, then your killer will be missing something significant."

I considered Rosina. She had all her limbs intact as well as her fingers. If she'd lost a bone, she wouldn't have been able to grow it back with magic that quickly. There'd be a sign she was injured. Had I got the wrong person for the murders?

"Silvaria, I know you don't want to help, but if you have any contacts in a bone witch coven, I need to speak to them. I have to narrow down who gifted this cursed skull."

"It won't do you any good. You'll have to accept your fate. We all die sometime. You're just going sooner than expected. Get your affairs in order and make your peace. Or don't. I don't care."

A gasp behind me had me turning. Odessa, Luna, and Indigo stood in front of me.

Chapter 18

"You're going to die?" Odessa rushed over and engulfed me in a pumpkin scented hug.

I struggled out of her grip and backed away, shooting a warning look at Silvaria to be quiet. "No, you misunderstood. We were just... talking."

Indigo and Luna marched over.

"We heard you. We may not have heard all the conversation, but we know enough. The skull that showed up at your apartment and screamed cursed you?" Luna said. "You blasted Odessa out of the way, so she wouldn't be cursed, didn't you?"

"And it's a death curse?" Indigo said.

I looked at the ground and rocked back on my heels. "It's nothing. I'm sorting it."

Silvaria snorted her disbelief.

"Why didn't you tell us when it happened?" Indigo said. "We could have helped."

"How? Do you know how to destroy a cursed skull? Or maybe you're best buddies with a bone witch?"

My friends glanced at each other. They all wore matching shocked expressions.

"Thought not. Stay out of my business. You can't help, so you'll only get in my way if you get involved. What are you all doing here, anyway?"

Indigo caught hold of my arm, keeping it in her grasp even though I tried to turn away. "We know you prefer to work alone. Sometimes, you can't do everything alone. You need people to help you. That's what we're here for."

I shook my head. I'd kept them out of the loop for a reason. If they got involved, they'd get hurt. I'd already lost my sister. I wasn't losing anyone else. "Since you know me so well, you'll know to turn around and walk away from this. I've got it figured out. If anyone else gets involved, it'll complicate things. Simple works best."

"You've still got a lot to figure out by the sounds of it," Silvaria said. "And you're not doing it in my cemetery. All of you leave. You're disturbing the dead."

"That would be impossible," Fire Fang muttered.

"Out!" Silvaria pointed along the path. "Deal with your mess on your own time and out of my earshot."

Indigo marched over to Silvaria. "Enough of that rudeness, or there'll be no dance classes for you. I came by to give you the schedule for next month. And I know you don't want to miss out on the Sparkles and Sequins show coming up. We've been practicing for weeks."

Silvaria's lips vanished as she pressed them together. She thumped her stick on the ground. "You can't threaten to take away my dancing. I've already got my new dress."

"I can. I'm your partner. I won't dance with you if you don't help Storm. All she needs are names. We'll do the rest."

"We won't do anything," I snapped. "You're not getting tangled up in my mess."

"Too late. We already are," Odessa said. "You could have solved this by now if you'd kept us involved. We would have researched the skull together."

"That's exactly why I don't want you involved. You get messed up in this, and whoever controls that skull will come for you. We'll all be cursed. Then we'll die. At least, this way, it's only me."

My friends gathered around me until they'd trapped me in a circle. The warmth of their friendship and love was like a cheap perfume I refused to inhale. They didn't need my problems. Why couldn't they understand that?

"You're too hard on yourself," Luna said. "You're our friend, so of course, we'll look out for you. We've beaten worse things than this."

"Not without my help," Silvaria said.

I looked over at her with narrowed eyes. "Will you help?"

"No dancing if you don't," Indigo said.

"Oh, very well. But Indigo, I insist on doing the solo performance. I know you've mastered the steps better than me, but—"

"It's all yours," Indigo said. "You'll be magnificent. Just give Storm what she needs to solve this mystery."

Silvaria limped away, grumbling to herself.

"You didn't have to do that," I said. "Even though I can't figure out why you enjoy them, you love those dance lessons with Silvaria. And you haven't stopped going on about the event you're dragging us to."

"The dance gala will come around again. And it's nothing compared to this. Your life is at stake. I can afford to miss out on a few shimmies and slides to keep you safe. Now, stop being stubborn and let us help," Indigo said.

Silvaria returned and thrust a piece of paper at me. "You didn't get this from me. Start at the top and work down. If you're still alive by the time you get to the bottom, you definitely have luck on your side." She turned and walked off without saying goodbye.

"This news calls for something sweet," Luna said. "Everyone to the bakery. Uncle Albert's been experimenting with white chocolate and pecan crumble tarts. They're amazing. And I need an energy boost as I process all of this."

I was going to protest again, but a sharp look from Indigo and Odessa kept me quiet. When my friends ganged up on me, there was little I could do but fall into line and accept their help. But it rubbed the wrong way. I'd always seen myself as the group protector. This was the opposite of protecting them. I'd just shoved them in the direct line of the cursed skull's fire. If any of them got hurt, I'd never forgive myself.

I didn't speak until we got to the temporary bakery Albert was using while his old bakery was being rebuilt after a fire destroyed it.

Luna ushered us to a table and served herself behind the counter, clattering mugs onto a tray and grabbing tongs to select treats.

Albert hurried out of the kitchen, staggering under the weight of a huge tray of chocolate brownies. He set them down and gave us a cheery wave. "Having a fun girls' day?"

"Something like that." Luna kissed his cheek. "Is Cole back there?"

"Coming right out, gorgeous." Cole Kellam emerged, carrying six trays of brownies in one hand. Typical showoff werewolf. He set them down, and Luna wrapped herself around him and gave him a big kiss.

I looked away. Not because I was unhappy seeing her content, but Luna had just demonstrated why I couldn't have my friends involved in this mystery. They had families, familiars, or loved ones to look out for. They had people who'd miss them if anything bad happened. Indigo had Olympus and her familiars, Luna had Cole, her uncle, and Tuffin, and Odessa had a blossoming relationship with Sol and all her scarecrows to look out for. All I had to worry about was a mangy hellhound, an annoying cat I couldn't get rid of, and the mold that refused to be scraped off the inside of my fridge. When I was dead, no one would miss me.

After Luna had extracted herself from Cole's arms, she hurried over with a tray loaded with white chocolate and pecan crumble cake and a cafetiere of coffee. She served us all and settled into a seat.

"Start from the beginning," Indigo said. "Leave nothing out. We'll know if you do."

With much reluctance, I filled in the blanks, telling them about the case I'd been forced to work on, the suspects, and how long I had left before the curse kicked in.

"What about the suspect you took to the Magic Council?" Indigo said. "Won't Rosina have a bone witch contact you can speak to?"

That's what I needed to find out, but I planned to do it on my own. "Rosina's a weird one. At first, she seemed like a typical bimbo mistress, only there for the money and parties. But she's more complicated and has her own agenda."

"Did you get to the bottom of why she was stealing from Delano? The things you told us she bought were unusual," Luna said. "Why was she at that discount place?"

"It'll come out in the questioning. And I didn't know about the bone witch connection until after I'd taken Rosina in. She could have more information for me."

Odessa shuddered. "If she'd gifted a bone to a witch for that skull, it would have been obvious. No one can hide that kind of injury."

"I haven't checked her toes. She could be missing one."

Everyone grimaced.

"Bone takes a while to grow back. Even the best doctor won't be able to click their fingers and create a whole new bone in an instant," Luna said.

"Maybe she sacrificed someone else," I said. "A relative or someone she loved."

"Are you sure Rosina is guilty?" Indigo said.

The more I looked into the skull and bone witch connection, the less certain I was Rosina was the guilty party. But if not her, I was back to square one and had barely any time left to figure out who the killer was and where they got that cursed skull.

As my friends talked options about the bone witch and my impending demise, I made my excuses and slipped to the restroom at the back of the bakery.

Fire Fang slunk behind me, not doing a great job of being discreet. When I tried to close the door on him, he barged his way in.

"What are you doing?" I leaned on the door, but he wouldn't move.

"I was going to ask you that question. You're sneaking off."

"I'm not. I need to use the restroom. You're not watching me go. We've had this talk before."

"You've been fidgeting in your seat for ages and looking around. You're after an escape. What are you planning to do, jump out the window?"

This annoying hellhound knew me too well. Even after my friends had scolded me for leaving them out of this mess, I was still determined to keep them safe. And the only way I could do that was by giving them the slip and figuring out the missing bone witch puzzle alone.

Fire Fang shoved his way in. "Storm, don't do it. They want to help. And they have connections. Use them."

"I'm not using my friends. And their connections will get them killed if they poke around in this mystery. I'm not taking that risk." I unlatched the window and shoved it open.

"Should you make that decision for them? They're free to help you if they want. And it's clear they do. You have amazing friends."

I looked out the window. We were at ground level, so it would be easy to get out.

"Ignoring me doesn't make this go away. Go back and talk to them. You can work out a solution together."

"I have a solution. They made me realize I need to check in on Rosina and see what Olympus has discovered. What if the wrong person got arrested?"

"Rosina isn't innocent."

"Maybe not of theft and deception, but triple murder? I'm not so certain she's guilty of that."

He growled and nipped at my ankle. "You're really going to do this, you headstrong crazy buttoned witch?"

I butt-hopped onto the ledge. "You can either stay here and hang out with my friends or join me. Whatever you do, make it quick and quiet."

"Stubborn witch. Of course I'm coming, too."

"I hope you're not too big to get through the window. If you are, I'm leaving you behind." I wriggled through and landed in the alleyway behind the bakery. I was surprised to see the stray cat waiting outside. I shook my head at her as I hurried past. "I'll deal with you another time."

It wouldn't be many minutes before my friends realized I'd made a run for it, so I jogged to Olympus's office, Fire Fang right behind me. I barged in without knocking, glad to see Olympus sitting at his desk.

"Storm! Everything okay?" Olympus glanced over my shoulder.

"Not really. What's the situation with Rosina? Has she confessed to the murders? Where did she get the screaming skull from?"

"Slow down. Take a seat."

"I don't have time to sit. I literally don't. If Rosina's confessed, I have to find out who she paid to get the skull."

His forehead puckered, but Olympus had been around me enough to know I cut straight to the point. "Why is this so important to you?"

I sucked in a breath. "It's a matter of death. My death. I got cursed by the skull."

"I... goddess above, Storm. I didn't know." He half-rose from his seat.

"Now you do. You see why I don't have time for a chit chat. Let me see Rosina."

"Slow down for a minute. You have that long, right?"

"Yes. A few days. No more."

"Sit. Please."

Fire Fang loped over to where Olympus's leopard familiar, Monty, was watching the conversation with wide eyes from his bed. He nudged him to one side and joined him.

I dropped into a chair. "What has Rosina told you?"

"She hasn't confessed and keeps protesting her innocence. And despite digging into her connections and her history, she has no link to the screaming skull."

"The skull was most likely created by a bone witch. Did you see anything in her past about bone witches? She must know one, or her family has a connection with them. Rosina isn't as straightforward as she looks."

Olympus waved a hand to silence me. "I know. But Rosina was honest when I questioned her. She told me about her fake relationship with Delano and her former connection with the Valenti witches. She also revealed she's taken money and magic from Delano."

"Which means she uses immoral means to get what she wants. It's only a few notches along before she's tangling with a bone witch and making deathly deals. And you need to do a full medical examination on her. She could be missing a bone."

"A... bone?"

"It was the price for the skull. Bone witches love a chunk of fresh bone for their magic. Is she injured?" In my haste to resolve this case, I could have overlooked something. It wasn't a fun thing to admit, but I wasn't always right.

"Rosina is missing no bones. She has no connection to a bone witch, and she knows nothing about the screaming skull. Yes, she was being dishonest about her relationship and her intentions with Delano, but that's as far as the betrayal goes."

I slammed a fist on his desk. "Then talk to the bone witches. They must know where this skull came from. Find the witch who created it and I can solve the mystery. You must keep tabs on them. The

Magic Council is always poking into other people's business."

His expression looked pained as he shifted in his seat. "You know this as well as I do, but those witches operate outside the law. And they never come in quietly when we ask them to. We... we have an arrangement with the bone witches."

"You're scared of them?" I threw up my hands. "I shouldn't be surprised to hear the Magic Council backing away from a fight. This killer will get away."

"You don't think it was Rosina?"

"I... Not anymore. Maybe I jumped to conclusions when I discovered her theft. It was a good motive. What about you? Anything she said made you doubt her?"

"I don't believe she's the killer. And I was about to call and let you know I was releasing her. Rosina will pay for her crimes, but it won't be a triple murder charge." He sat forward, his expression growing serious. "And Storm, I'd appreciate it if you'd keep me involved when you're working a case. The Magic Council has information about these murders. We need to be kept in the loop. You dumped Rosina on me and left."

I slouched in the seat. Only Fire Fang coming over and putting his comforting, warm head in my lap stopped me from pacing out my frustration. "I figured you had everything you needed to make a charge stick."

"You were lucky I was overseeing this case. Other members of the Magic Council wouldn't be so forgiving."

I shrugged. I solved more cases than the Magic Council. Olympus had nothing to complain about. "If it wasn't Rosina, it must be another member of the family. Have you talked to them about the skull and the bone witches?"

"I questioned all of them. Bone witches never came up."

"Go back and question them again. Someone is lying. Tell them the bone witches are angry. They want their skull back. Even a family with that much power will flinch under the threat."

"I'm sure that's true. But if any of them are connected to a bone witch, there's little we can do. They work to their own agenda and have their own way of enforcing laws. It's been like that for thousands of years. It's safer for everyone that way. Fewer fatalities."

"The Magic Council is powerless against them, then. Why am I wasting my time here?"

"Because we both want to see justice done."

"Your justice wheels creak too slowly for me. I need that skull now." I stood and marched to the door.

"Wait. We are working on it. But these things take time. With this new information, the case has to be re-examined."

"That's not good enough."

The door slammed open, almost whacking me in the face.

Chilton burst in. "I know Rosina is here. Set her free. I can prove she's innocent."

Chapter 19

I ushered a perspiring Chilton into the office. "Tell me why you think Rosina is innocent."

He swiped a hand through his hair once, twice, three times. "Because the night my father was cursed with that skull, Rosina was with me. We're dating. And it's serious."

"You told me you were alone that night."

"I had to. Rosina was my father's mistress. At least, that was what everyone was supposed to believe. He'd have destroyed me if I ruined the charade."

"You knew about their arrangement?"

"I knew their relationship was different from the other affairs my father had. I got curious and looked into it."

"You snooped on your dad and his mistress together?"

Chilton scowled at me. "You make it sound distasteful. But I realized their relationship wasn't genuine. And I've grown close to Rosina over the last few months. She's smart and funny. She's got big ideas and wants to change the world. Just like me. I developed feelings for her, but never dared to hope she'd feel the same. Not when she was with my father."

Olympus looked up from the file he'd been checking. "In your statements, you and Rosina informed me you were alone in your bedrooms that evening. It's a crime to falsify an alibi."

"We panicked. My mother doesn't know about us, and I knew she wouldn't approve."

"You can't blame her. Rosina stomped all over her marriage," I said. "Now, she's taking you."

"Which is exactly why we kept this quiet. We hoped things would get easier when whoever cursed my father was found, and we could reveal our relationship. Take it slowly, so people would get used to it."

"You still shouldn't have lied," I said. "I've wasted time pursuing suspects I needn't have bothered with." Time I needed to save my life.

"Sorry about that. But Lucian kept telling us you'd figure it out because he'd hired the best, so I had nothing to worry about. He looks after the family, so I believed him. Then you arrested Rosina."

"We should speak to Rosina," I said to Olympus. "See what she has to say."

"Let me see her," Chilton said. "When you arrested her, I was so shocked. I've been looking for her ever since. I even went to the Magic Council headquarters. They eventually told me she was being held here."

"You can't see her until we've questioned her again. Wait here. Fire Fang, Monty, don't let this guy out of your sights. If he moves wrong, you can bite him."

"No biting," Olympus muttered as we left the room.

We headed to the cells and discovered Rosina sitting on the floor, her back against the wall.

"Why did you lie about your alibi?" I said to her.

She blinked slowly, twice. "I didn't lie. I was alone."

"Try again. Chilton is here, and he's telling a different story."

Her gaze went to the door and worry crossed her face. "What's he told you?"

"You first. Were you really alone the evening Delano was cursed?"

"I want to see Chilton before I say anything."

"That's not how this works." I kneeled, so we were eye to eye. "Rosina, this is serious. You're on the verge of being charged with murdering three people. Unless you tell the truth, you're not getting out of this cell. You'll never see Chilton again."

She chewed on the side of one nail. "I don't want to get anyone in trouble. Enough people have been hurt by what's gone on in this family."

"You'll be hurt if you're put behind bars for something you didn't do," I said. "Jail isn't an easy ride. I need to find the person who used that skull. Not just to get justice for the Discord family, but to make sure I stay alive, too."

"Oh! Of course. You're cursed as well. I promise, I'm not holding out on you to be difficult. I want to help."

"So tell the truth and quickly."

She lowered her head for a few seconds and ran her thumb across her palm several times. "I'm in a relationship with Chilton. We've been dating for a few months. I liked the look of him as soon as I made my arrangement with Delano. But, of course, I couldn't be seen dating Delano and Chilton. We started out as friends, but things developed. Then Chilton told me how he felt. I tried to resist, but he's such a sweetheart."

"And the night Delano was cursed?"

"We were together in Chilton's room. He slipped away after dinner, and once I'd spent a little time with Delano, I made my excuses. He was so full of himself after making the announcement about spending his money that he didn't notice me leave. I made sure no one else was around then slipped into Chilton's room."

"I should charge you both with wasting our time," Olympus said.

Rosina's gaze cast down. "You have a right to, but I hope you don't. We had our reasons for keeping this quiet."

"Selfish reasons. Let's get you two together," I said. "I need to know everything."

"You're letting me go?" Rosina said.

I looked at Olympus, and he nodded as he unlocked the cell door.

"One question. Are you missing any bones?" I said.

Rosina's mouth dropped open. "Missing a bone? No."

"Take off your shoes. Show me your toes."

"My... toes?"

"Yes. Shoes. Now."

Rosina slipped off both heels. She wasn't missing a toe bone. She hadn't made a deal with a bone witch.

"This way." I gestured her out of the cell.

Olympus led Rosina to an interview room, while I collected Chilton and brought them together.

They hugged for an embarrassingly long time until Olympus cleared his throat. "There'll be time for a reunion later. Take a seat."

Chilton and Rosina sat next to each other, holding hands.

I took a seat next to Olympus. I didn't hold his hand.

"What do you need to know?" Rosina said.

"I'm so sorry about this, Storm," Chilton said. "I hated keeping secrets. But I love Rosina, and I'd do anything to keep her safe. After she was arrested, I realized the truth about our relationship had to come out if I was going to protect her. I'll have to accept my mother's disapproval. I'm not leaving Rosina."

Rosina smacked a kiss on his cheek, a grin on her face. "That's the first time you've told me you love me. I love you, too."

"That's adorable. But we're not here to fix your relationship. Were you also stealing from your father?" I said to Chilton.

"No, that was just me," Rosina said. "And the money I've made isn't for me or Chilton."

"What were you doing with it?" I said.

"When I got together with Delano, I hoped he'd use his power for good. And I saw potential in him. Before we made our arrangement, we discussed charitable giving and helping the less fortunate. He agreed to consider it."

"The less fortunate. Just like the charity Chilton set up to help magic users?" I said.

"Exactly that. But it became clear Delano had no interest in charitable giving. He used my desire to help others to sweet talk me into the deal. By then, I was in too deep and couldn't back out. I kept hoping he'd change. I thought he could be a better man when he saw the right path."

"It's a shame you didn't know my father as well as I did," Chilton said. "He's always been driven to make more money for himself. It was his only passion. He neglected everything in favor of that. Even his family."

Rosina squeezed Chilton's hand. "Delano had no social conscience, so I became it. All the money went to Chilton's shelter and the troubled magic users. I'd make a donation, or if they needed specific things, I'd bulk buy clothing and food. That's what you caught me doing."

"And I support everything Rosina does," Chilton said.

"You support her stealing?" Olympus said.

"My father had more than enough. He was hoarding, instead of giving back. And I know you don't think that highly of jinn, Storm, but I'm different. Rosina opened my eyes. She showed me how I can help others. We've supported hundreds of magic users to get back on their feet. And I plan to set up another shelter soon."

"Perhaps you cursed Delano together," I said. "You both wanted his money, so you got rid of him without getting your hands dirty. Are you missing any bones, Chilton?"

"Bones? Of course not. Why do you ask?"

"We'll get to that. Lift your shirt and take off your shoes," I said.

His gaze was confused as he obliged. There was nothing missing, and no recently healed scars.

"My father's assets would have made a huge difference to our charitable work." Chilton tucked in his shirt. "I tried to convince him about changing his focus or letting me ethically invest some of his money. He wasn't interested."

"So you killed him to achieve your goal?"

"No. We were together that night. We're not killers. We're philanthropists. We only want to do good, not harm," Rosina said.

"My father found out about my shelter and mocked me. It was then I realized, if Rosina and I didn't do something proactive, we'd never have the opportunity to make a big difference," Chilton said.

"Was that something murder?"

"No! And you can see for yourself where we've been investing the money. The charity is legit. We have accounts to prove it," Chilton said.

"I'll need to see those," Olympus said.

"I'll give you the details. Check whatever you like. We have nothing to hide." Chilton passed over the information to Olympus.

Olympus stood from his seat. "I'll look at your general financial records, too."

Chilton and Rosina handed over their information without complaint.

"All the money I got was funneled into the charity. None of it went to us," Rosina said.

"I'll run the checks now. It won't take long." Olympus left the room but returned a few seconds later. "Storm, I've just had a message and need to step out for a few minutes. The information is being checked at HQ. Are you good here?"

"Sure. Do what you need to do," I said.

Olympus hurried out and closed the door.

"You never wanted to be like your dad, did you?" I said to Chilton.

"Again, I'm sorry about lying when you questioned me. I only did it to protect Rosina. My life's been amazing since I found her. She made me realize my father wasted his assets and used them on material things. Pointless things that didn't make him happy."

"I once asked Delano if he spent all that money because he was looking for something to fill the void." Rosina huffed out a breath. "He laughed in my face and told me using my brain was dangerous, and I should stick to what I was good at. Looking pretty and keeping his friends entertained."

"He was a real piece of work," I said. "It's almost a surprise something like this hasn't happened to him sooner."

"Father had five assassination attempts on his life," Chilton said. "He hurt so many people to get what he wanted. And Rosina is right. He was a deeply unhappy man. He'd lost his way. He even stopped using his jinn wishes. He hated anyone in the family granting wishes, either. It's not natural to refuse to help others. That's a part of what we are. Jinns give people their heart's desire."

"He stopped you from making wishes, too?" I said. "When I spoke to Hattie, she showed me a storage unit full of jinn lamps."

"Mine's in there," Chilton said. "My father forbade any of us to go there, but I used to sneak my lamp out occasionally. The urge to grant wishes gets too strong. I'm sure that was a big part of Dad's problem. He suppressed his natural instincts, thinking he had to hoard more and more and never give back."

As Rosina and Chilton sat there, their hands clasped together, shooting each other shy smiles, I could see their love was genuine. They weren't lying. They also weren't missing any bones. I had the wrong suspects.

"What do you know about bone witches?" I said.

"Not much," Chilton said. "Of course, everyone's heard about them. I've never met one. I don't think I'd like to."

"What about you, Rosina?"

"I stay away from dark magic. It gives me the shivers. I just want to do good work." Her eyes widened a fraction. "Do you think that's where the cursed skull came from? A bone witch used it on Delano and the servants?"

"It's an avenue I'm investigating. What about other members of the family? Would they have any dealings with bone witches?"

They both shook their heads.

"You're not thinking of going after a bone witch, are you?" Rosina said. "They're dangerous. My dad told me tales about them when I misbehaved to scare me into being good when I was a child. It always worked."

"I may have no choice. There are only a couple of days left before the curse gets me."

Rosina's hand went to her mouth. "I'm so sorry about that. Lucian was wrong to trick you into helping us. But he'd do anything for Delano. They were always together. Always looking out for each other."

"They loved to compete and try to be the best and have the most. It was gross," Chilton said. "They'd egg each other on and try to outdo each other. It must have been exhausting."

"Delano must always have won," I said. "He had more resources than Lucian."

"Materially, sure. But Lucian is a smooth customer. And he never married, so he could always outdo my father with the ladies. That used to rub Dad the wrong way. I have a feeling that's why he chose Rosina. He saw something in her that the other women he'd dated lacked. She's the complete package."

"That sweet of you to say," Rosina said. "Your father was not without his charm, though. I fell for his smooth lines about our partnership. Once he got me where he wanted, he went back on his word."

"I'd never do that to you," Chilton said.

"You don't have to tell me. Your incredible actions with the shelter prove how dedicated you are to helping those less fortunate. You're an amazing man. Even though I had to endure Delano to find you, it was worth it."

They simpered over each other for a few seconds.

"Since we're innocent," Chilton said, "can we go? I've barely spent any time with Rosina recently. We have a lot of catching up to do."

"You need to wait until Olympus has checked your information."

"We don't have to stay in the cells, do we?" Rosina said.

"You can wait in the office, so long as you don't make a run for it. If you do, Fire Fang and Monty will stop you."

"We won't be running anywhere. As long as I'm with Rosina, that's all I care about."

I led the happy couple back to the office. It was stifling in there, so I yanked open the door.

Sitting on the step was the screaming skull. And the second I saw it, it let out an ear-piercing shriek.

My gaze shot to Rosina and Chilton. They were also staring at the skull. I grabbed it, as the edges of my vision darkened, and blasted out the most powerful restraining spell I could.

The skull quivered in place, as if trying to move.

Fire Fang bounded out of the kitchen and clamped his huge teeth around the skull just as the scream faded. The skull stopped moving and started to smoke.

I was sweating as I used every ounce of my power to control the skull. The dark energy leaching out of it was fighting my magic. And it felt like it was winning.

"What do we do? What do we do?" Rosina's face was drained of color as she stared at the skull. "That's what killed Delano and the servants. Now we're cursed, too."

"At least this proves your innocence," I said through gritted teeth. "You wouldn't curse yourselves."

"We can't be cursed. We have too much to do. All our good work will have been for nothing. Storm, help us," Rosina said.

"That's what I've been trying to do, although I wasn't helped by you both lying to me and the Magic Council."

Rosina clamped one hand over her ear and thumped, as if trying to dislodge the cursed scream. "We never hurt anybody. All we wanted to do was help others. Chilton, what should we do?"

He looked as equally shaken as Rosina, but had dropped into silence as he peered at the skull.

Rosina shook him. "Do something."

"One of you go see if Olympus has any ghost jars in storage. The holding magic in the jar should keep this thing from vanishing." I needed to make sure this skull went nowhere. I could use this. It would help me find the source of its power.

Neither of them moved.

I growled. "Go find a ghost jar. Now." I didn't want Fire Fang touching that thing any longer than he had to.

Chilton shook himself and hurried away. He returned a moment later with three jars. "Will any of these do?"

"Put them down and test each one. Choose whichever is the strongest. Hurry!"

With shaking hands, Chilton inspected each ghost jar. "This one is the best." He pulled off the lid of a battered brown jar.

"Fire Fang, drop the skull in there." I kept the restraining spell on the skull but was shaking with the effort.

Fire Fang dragged the skull along the floor, seeming unable to lift his head. With a grumbling roar, he dumped the skull into the ghost jar.

I slammed the lid in place and wound my restraining spell around the jar several times to give it an extra layer of protection. When I pulled back my magic, sweat trickled down my face, and my stomach rolled over. I shook off the feeling. I had to concentrate on the skull. I now had a huge piece of the missing puzzle, and I wasn't letting it get away.

"We have to do something." Rosina sounded almost hysterical as she gripped Chilton's arm.

"We will. At least, Storm will. She'll deal with this." There was a hopeful, desperate look in his eyes.

I stared at the ghost jar.

"Storm. You do know what to do with that skull, right?" Chilton said.

"Yes. I should be able to find out who created it." But I needed to see straight first and stop wanting to pass out. "I'll need to extract some of the magic from it. Every magic user has a signature trail. Get that, and we've got the bone witch who made it."

"We won't be able to do it quickly enough. We're going to die. I already feel bad. The curse is taking me," Rosina said. "Chilton, fix this."

He stared at me helplessly.

"Fire Fang, calm down Rosina." I could afford no distractions, and a squeaking, panicky witch was a distraction too far.

Fire Fang loped over and nudged her back to the seats. She tried to shoo him away, but he kept nudging, and when she didn't oblige, he knocked her to the floor and sat on her.

Chilton hurried over to help her up, but a growl from Fire Fang made him back off.

"Rosina will be fine under Fire Fang. Once she's calmed down, he'll stop using her as a cushion." I swiped the sweat from my forehead.

"You'll fix this, though?" Chilton's voice shook with emotion. "We won't die?"

"That's the plan." My concentration wasn't helped by how dreadful I felt. I was sick to my stomach, had a pounding headache, and my vision kept blurring. Was this a side effect of being exposed to the skull for a second time?

"Who would want us dead?" Chilton said.

It was a good question, and I'd been so focused on capturing the skull, I hadn't considered who'd left it outside. "It has to be someone from your family. They knew Rosina had been arrested."

"This attack was meant for Rosina?" Chilton kneeled and grabbed her hand.

"Whoever planted that skull wouldn't have known you were here," I said. "You've been looking for Rosina at different Magic Council locations. And why would they think you'd come after her? Unless they knew about your secret relationship."

"No one does."

"You don't think it was Augusta, do you?" Rosina squeaked out from beneath Fire Fang. "She really thought I was Delano's mistress. She could have left the skull here to get rid of me."

"Mother wouldn't do that. She hated you, but she's no killer. And why kill you now my dad is dead?"

"Revenge? Because Augusta thought you rubbed her nose in the affair you were having with Delano." I shook my head, then wished I hadn't as everything spun. "Although Augusta had every reason for wanting you dead, she doesn't have the power to control a screaming skull."

"I agree. She didn't do this," Chilton said.

"Other members of your family have more power, though. They've taken a big risk to get rid of Rosina. They could have been seen planting the skull outside."

"Uncle Erik has no problem with Rosina," Chilton said. "He likes her."

"And I like him. He's a sweet guy, although he drinks too much."

"From everything I've learned about Erik, he's not much for forward planning," I said. "He wouldn't have had the energy or inclination to sneak to this office and plant the skull. What about Hattie?"

"Auntie Hattie wouldn't hurt Rosina, either," Chilton said. "She's making plans for her future. She's finally happy. I've even seen her smiling when she thinks no one is watching."

"What's Hattie planning to do?" I said.

"A magical detox to begin with. She's entering a convent for magic users who want a new path. She's considering becoming a mortal."

We all shuddered at that hideous idea.

"Auntie Hattie wouldn't jeopardize her chance of freedom to get rid of Rosina," Chilton said. "She finally has something positive to look forward to."

"And we barely speak," Rosina said. "Hattie kept out of my way. I tried to make friends, but she made it clear she wasn't interested and didn't approve of my involvement with Delano. I understood her values, so I left her alone. She had no quarrel with me."

"If it wasn't Augusta, or Hattie, or Erik, that leaves us with Lucian," I said.

Chilton shook his head. "He's the family protector. He's always looked out for us. Whenever any of us got in trouble, he was there. He's been like a second father to me at times. My dad used to get so caught up in work he'd forget important things. Lucian never did. He got me gifts for my birthday and was around on the holidays. Lucian gains nothing by cursing Rosina."

"And Lucian saw me as the latest in a long line of Delano's girlfriends. I was an irrelevance. He tolerated me being around because Delano wanted me, but he barely paid me any attention. And he was immune to my flirting. Much like Hattie, he left me alone."

The ghost jar rocked from side to side. I grabbed it and sat on it. I wasn't sure how long I'd be able to contain the skull, or if being exposed to it for any length of time would make me even sicker, but I had to figure out who planted that skull outside.

"Can Fire Fang get off me now?" Rosina said. "I'm sorry I panicked, but I was shocked when I saw the skull. It feels like everything has fallen apart, just when we were able to get on with our lives. I lost control of myself. It won't happen again."

"So long as you stop squeaking," I said. "My head can't take it."

Rosina looked shamefaced. "I promise, no more squeaking."

Fire Fang released Rosina. He walked over to me and sniffed the ghost jar. "We need to get this thing somewhere secure before it blows."

"Agreed. Maybe the safe in the office?"

The door opened and Olympus walked in. He looked at the chaotic scene before his gaze settled on the ghost jar. "Did we have an unwelcome haunting?"

"Not quite. We had an unwelcome cursed skull," I said. "I opened the door to get some air, and the skull was there. It screamed at us. I've shut it in here."

"Did anyone get cursed?" His gaze went to Rosina and Chilton.

"We both did," Chilton said. "And Storm took another hit."

"Monty, are you okay?" Olympus looked around for his familiar.

Monty poked his head out from under the desk. "I'm proudly cowering. I didn't see the skull when it screamed."

I nudged Fire Fang. "Are you good?"

He nudged me back. "I'm fine. No sour slug skull is getting me."

"We were just figuring out why someone would leave the skull outside your office," I said.

"Was Rosina the target?" Olympus walked to his desk, skirting around the ghost jar.

I massaged my aching forehead. "Most likely."

"I got a call from HQ on my way in. Everything Rosina and Chilton told us was true. They volunteer for several charities and make regular donations. Rosina has barely any money, so there's no stash she's been hoarding. Same with Chilton."

"I told you we were doing good," Rosina said, sounding only slightly less squeaky.

"What's your next move, Storm?" Olympus said.

"Nothing too life changing. Just find the bone witch who created the skull, figure out how to undo the curse, and save us all."

Chapter 20

I tasted dirt. I inched open my eyes to find I was on the ground. It was dark, and I was sweating, even though I felt a chilly wind drift across my face, followed by a plop of rain on my forehead.

Something heavy and warm was on my chest, and with effort and a groan, I lifted my head to see the stray black cat curled on my stomach.

"What's going on?" The words croaked out of me. I felt like I'd aged a hundred years.

The cat lifted her head and looked at me. She stood, walked to my face, and licked my nose.

I didn't have the strength to stop the hot, rough tongue from scratching my skin. My arms and legs were too heavy to move.

The cat licked me again and gave a soft meow, huffing her breath over my face. For once, I was happy to see her.

"Where am I?" I turned my head slowly, but all I saw were trees. There were no houses or people around. "Fire Fang?"

There was a rustle close by, and Fire Fang appeared from under a bush.

"You're awake." He crawled a couple of inches toward me and collapsed on his belly, letting out a pained wheeze. "I feel like a slimy cod piece."

"Me, too. What happened? And where are we?"

The cat had stopped licking my nose but stared at me intently, looking like she was trying to convey a message through the intensity of her glare.

"You don't remember?" Fire Fang said.

"The last thing I remember was talking to Olympus, Chilton, and Rosina. We were in Olympus's office, and I was figuring out how to contact a bone witch."

"I don't remember much more than that, but you said you wanted to visit Silvaria again now you had the skull. You figured she'd recognize the magic signature."

A vague memory of that conversation hit me. "I... I did. But then what?"

"I'm not sure. We must have left Olympus's office. I think we're in the cemetery in Witch Haven."

"How? Why? And why didn't you get help?"

"I can't move. I'm ill. I've never felt like this before."

"What's wrong with you?"

Fire Fang didn't speak for a few seconds, making my stomach lurch worse than it already was.

"Fire Fang, did you look at the skull when it was screaming? I thought you'd gotten away with it. You didn't say anything."

He huffed out another breath. "I'm cursed, too. And the curse has slammed into me like an ogre's war cry. I wasn't feeling good when we were with Olympus, and it only got worse. I keep blacking out.

And I'm overheating, even though there's frost on the ground."

I closed my eyes for a few seconds. Fire Fang had been cursed because he was with me. I had to get on my feet and deal with this skull once and for all.

"You still with me?" he said.

"Just thinking and trying not to be ill. Why is the cat here?"

"She showed up just when I woke. She checked on me then sat on you. I reckon she's looking out for us."

The cat slow-blinked at me, then settled back on my stomach. Even though I was a sweaty mess, her weight and warmth were a comfort.

"We must have been here for hours. It wasn't even dinnertime when we were speaking to Olympus," I said.

"I can't be certain, but I think we've been here a whole goblin nobble day and night."

"A day! I've lost a day!"

"I tried to stay awake and track the time, but I kept blacking out. We've been here a while."

"And no one found us?"

"I tried calling and howling, but my fuzz bucket voice keeps disappearing. I sounded like a scolded pup when I howled. It was embarrassing. And these trees are muffling the sound."

"If we're in Silvaria's cemetery, she should have heard us." How had we gotten here? Had the skull brought us here? If so, why?

"I tried to find someone, but I can barely move," Fire Fang said. "Every muscle hurts, and my bones feel like turkey gobble jelly. Maybe the curse affects hellhounds worse than other magic users."

"Maybe it does." It hadn't made me feel great the second time around. "But you'll still have seven days. That gives us plenty of time to fix this."

Silence followed. I may have passed out again.

"Storm, what if you've been double cursed?"

My eyes flicked open. "That's not a thing, is it?"

The cat hissed softly and returned to licking my nose.

"You blacked out after the skull screamed at you again and lost time. A second blast of curse can't be good for anyone. Even a strong witch."

"What does that do to my time left? I had days. Now I have..." No clue if I was about to drop dead any second.

"We have to find out which goblin meat jockey pie cursed that skull. Someone is controlling it. They're messing with us."

My head was too full of chaotic thoughts to think straight.

The cat leaped off my chest and let out a howling wail. She sounded in distress, but there didn't seem to be anything wrong with her. She almost sounded like the screaming skull.

My head jerked up. "The skull! Where is it?"

"It came with us," Fire Fang said. "It's over there." He pointed with his nose to some bushes.

"Is it still in the jar? We can't let it get free. Show me where it is."

Fire Fang crawled on his belly while I dragged myself along on my hands and knees.

I spotted the brown jar on its side. The lid was still on. When I gave it a gentle shake, the skull rattled inside. But the jar was smoking, and there were cracks on the outside. It wouldn't hold the skull for much longer.

The cat had followed us and stood a short distance away. This cat had been a pain in my behind since she'd shown up at my apartment, but she was my only option. "If you understand me, go find Silvaria. She looks after the cemetery. She has a place right at the back, tucked behind some trees."

The cat didn't move.

"She's not going anywhere. She's looking out for you," Fire Fang said. "I'm glad someone is. My gooseberry bush vision is going dark."

"We need to keep moving. We have to get to Silvaria. We have the skull, so she can help us figure out which bone witch created it."

"Then let's crawl," he said. "You ready?"

"If I pass out, drag me along." I fitted the ghost jar under my arm. It wasn't comfortable, but it was the only way I could carry it.

We'd been successfully slow-crawling for ten minutes before the ground beneath me vanished, and I plunged into a deep hole. I hit impacted dirt, and the air was knocked out of my lungs.

I opened my eyes, grateful not to find a body peering back at me. I flipped over, emitting the groan of a witch doubly cursed and stuck in an open grave. Fire Fang and the cat were peering into the hole.

I spat out dirt and checked the ghost jar was still intact. "Someone should cover these things up. This is an accident waiting to happen."

"It already happened. There's a ladder beside it. I'll lower it down. Nothing's broken, is it?"

"Just my spirit. And my ego."

Fire Fang chuckled, then tossed the ladder over the side.

It took a few tries and plenty of curses, but I hauled myself out of the grave. I was covered in mud, sweating, and my head beat out a bongo drum rhythm so fast it had me dizzy.

"Do you need a break?" Fire Fang said.

"No. I just need to watch out for the holes." I managed a few steps before sinking to my knees and accepting hands and knees crawling was the only way to go.

Half an hour later, and with the stray cat now riding on my back like I was her servant, we'd made it to the overgrown path leading to Silvaria's home.

I'd just shuffled onto the path, not looking forward to having to cross gravel on my knees, when magic blasted in front of me, spattering stone chips into my face.

"Corpses aren't permitted any closer. You know the rules. Go back to the hole you crawled out of."

"Silvaria. It's Storm. And I'm not dead. At least, not yet."

A light flashed on overhead, and Silvaria marched over. "You look ghastly. I thought you were one of my recently dead paying me a visit. And what's wrong with him?" She thrust a pointed stick at Fire Fang.

"He got cursed. And I got cursed again by the same skull. But we've got it. The skull is in this ghost jar." The smoking jar was still tucked under my arm.

Silvaria's head jerked back, and she crouched to stare at the ghost jar. "Not for much longer. Is magic containing it?"

"Yes. But the jar is cracking. If I black out again, the skull will escape. Whoever has control of it wants it back."

"I'm sure they do. With this skull in your possession, you'll figure out who created the curse."

"That's why we're here. You gave me that list of names, but I didn't get through them. I was hoping you could look at the skull and—"

"No, I won't do that." Silvaria stood and backed away. "You shouldn't be here."

"You understand this magic."

"I'm not a bone witch. I'm a cemetery guardian. Different thing. I protect the dead. Those witches, they exploit them."

"You have a connection to the dead. You must have crossed paths with bone witches. You may have dealt with this magic before and can recognize its signature."

Her gaze flashed from me to Fire Fang, and she shook her head. She glanced at the cat, who was still on my back, but said nothing.

"Silvaria, I'm not the only one cursed. Other people were there when the skull screamed."

"Then I'd better dig more graves, hadn't I?"

She could be mean, but surely she wasn't that mean. Silvaria wouldn't let me, Fire Fang, Chilton, and Rosina die, would she?

"How about I pay for your dance lessons for the next year?"

Silvaria turned on her heel and settled her stick on the ground. "Is that all your life is worth, a year of dance lessons? If that's the case, you're better off dead."

"Two years."

"Ten years, and you pay for me to go on an all-inclusive, month long dance cruise around South America."

"You want to go on a cruise? I can't imagine you in a bikini, getting a tan by the pool."

"And neither can I. But there's a Latin American cruise I've had my eye on. I've been saving."

"Fine. Dance lessons and the cruise. Just help me figure this out."

"Silvaria, you shouldn't manipulate a dying witch in her hour of need." The deep female voice slid from the darkness.

She glanced over her shoulder, her scowl deepening. "People never give out of kindness. You have to take your chances when you can. Storm needs my help, and I need that cruise."

I squinted through the darkness to see the other woman, but she remained in the shadows. There was something about her energy that made me hot and cold and eager not to linger.

Silvaria looked down at me and shook her head. "Crawl inside. The hellhound, too. Let's see if we can figure this out. But I'm promising nothing."

By the time I'd crawled into Silvaria's home, the other woman had vanished, but I could sense her presence. "Who's your guest?"

"Someone you need to meet, although you shouldn't if you value your life." Silvaria set the ghost jar on a rickety wooden table. She pulled out a vial of green potion from a cabinet in the kitchen and doused the jar with it. "That'll hold it for a while."

"Do you recognize the magic signature?" I didn't have the strength to get into a chair, and Silvaria hadn't offered me a hand, so I leaned against the wall, letting the cat jump off first, then slid to the floor.

Fire Fang dropped his head into my lap and closed his eyes.

Silvaria walked around, pulling out mugs. She filled them with a steaming, pungent liquid. She walked over and shoved one into my hand. "Drink that. It'll help with the pain."

It smelled like bog water, but the second I took a sip, the throbbing ache in my bones eased.

"Not about to die, are you?" Silvaria peered down at me.

"Almost."

She grunted and sat in a seat away from the skull.

"Why shouldn't I meet your friend?" I said.

Silvaria looked at the shadows in her hallway. "Some magic you never need to get involved with."

"That's not an endearing thing to say." A shadow stepped forward, revealing a willowy witch of an indeterminate age with silky black hair. She was dressed head to toe in black with a lace collar and lace gloves. She drew nearer to me, and my eyes rolled back in my head.

"Enough of your games, Onyx. Storm's already been injured by your trickery. And she's no good to you. Keep away from her." Silvaria's words came out sharply.

"I'm curious to meet a witch who remains alive after being doubly cursed by one of my skulls. She must have power." An icy scratch slid across my arm.

I forced my eyes open, although they refused to focus. "You created the screaming skull?"

Onyx stood in front of me, bent at the waist, her black eyes devoid of emotion. "My ancestors did. My mother passed it to me before she died. It's powerful, isn't it? Just like you."

"It's killing people. Three so far. And four more have been cursed."

She reached out and ran a strand of my sweat dampened hair through her fingers. "There is little time left on your sand clock. It's running through grain by grain, and it's almost empty. Such a pity. I sense your energy. You control the elements."

"Right now, I'm just controlling my ability to see straight." I flicked a glance at Silvaria. Her lips were pressed together as she watched Onyx. Then she caught my eye, grabbed a magazine, and looked away.

Onyx moved her hand away from my face, and I noticed a ring with a white circle and a black slash across it past my face.

The pain faded as a puzzle piece clicked into place. "Why are you wearing the same ring as Lucian Barkridge?"

Chapter 21

"Lucian Barkridge? I don't know him." Onyx backed away, hiding her face behind her hair.

"Is that how you control the skull? Whoever wears one of those rings has power over it?" My heart beat out an erratic rhythm. It felt like it was going to stop at any second. But I was on to something, and I'd keep fighting until I got the truth.

"I picked up this ring from a local store. This person you speak of must have done the same." Her hand was behind her back, hiding the ring.

"I don't believe you."

Silvaria hissed out air. "You shouldn't question a bone witch if you value your life."

Onyx chuckled, although there was no humor in the sound, more like a veiled threat to watch my step. But I had no time left. I had to step where I needed.

"How much did Lucian pay you so he could use the skull to kill people?" I said.

"Nothing," Onyx spat out. "This is not your business."

"Since I've been doubly cursed by your screaming skull, it is my business. I need answers to stop more people from dying."

Tension radiated off Onyx as she paced the room.

Silvaria sat at the table, leafing through a cruise brochure, not concerned about what we were talking about. Although I caught her glance my way and sensed she wasn't as calm as she appeared.

I focused on Onyx, even though the floor felt like it tilted and my heart pitter-pattered a death rattle in my chest. "If Lucian didn't pay to use the skull, then he has something over you. Is he blackmailing you?"

"Blackmail! He'd be a fool to try. I'd destroy him. I still might."

"Then what is it? Why would a powerful bone witch give a sleaze like Lucian something so potent? You must have known what he had planned."

Silvaria glanced up from her cruise brochure. "Onyx, Storm isn't the worst witch I've ever dealt with. And she has connections that could be useful to you in the future. Remember why you're here."

Onyx glared at me. She rubbed the ring on her finger. "Quiet, cemetery guardian. Let me think a moment."

"Lucian has something you need?" I said.

Her black gaze shifted my way. She snarled, before drawing in a breath. "He has information about my daughter. She was involved in some mildly illegal activity not so long ago."

"And Lucian found out. He's got evidence showing your daughter's crime?"

Onyx gnashed her teeth together. "He does. What did you call him... a sleaze? It's a perfect description. He's a slippery eel, full of fake words and pleasantries, while he seeks your soft underbelly to stab. He found mine and struck a blow. He came to me and said he'd reveal everything to the Magic Council if I didn't do his bidding."

"Lucian forced you to hand over the cursed skull. Did you know what he wanted it for?"

"The only time anyone wants a cursed skull is to commit a dark deed. I didn't want the details. I gave him the skull, told him how to control it using the ring, and sent him on his way. He's an evil man. A dead man walking when I get my chance to strike."

I shook my head, struggling to focus. "All this time, he's been claiming to be Delano's best friend. Yet he murdered him and two servants. But why?"

"The man is suspicious of everything. I told him how to use the skull, but he insisted on testing it first." Onyx stopped by the window. "People believe dark rumors about bone witches, but we don't waste life. Those servants died for nothing. Their bodies weren't even used for magic. Such a waste of resources."

I wrinkled my nose but kept quiet.

"When I approached Lucian after the first death occurred and asked for the skull back, he said he wasn't finished. He was only testing its power to make sure I hadn't tricked him and said I could have it back when he was done with it." Her snarl reappeared, making her look more animal than witch.

"Did Lucian tell you why he wanted Delano Discord dead?"

"He didn't tell, and I didn't ask. I wanted nothing to do with it." Onyx strode to the ghost jar and placed a hand on the top. "Now I have the skull back, but until Lucian returns the ring, he still has some control."

"You took his bone? Was it from his leg? He hides it well, but he doesn't like stairs and has a slight limp." Lucian must have been in agony concealing that gruesome payment from everyone.

"Yes. Part of a leg bone. It was needed to meld the magical energies together. I made sure he felt it when I extracted my payment." A shark-like smile hit her face.

That wouldn't have been fun, but it was no less than Lucian deserved. "So we find him and force him to give you back the ring. His control will be over."

"He still has the evidence on my daughter. The deal was he'd return the skull and hand over the evidence at the same time."

"You were going to let him get away with that?" I said. "If it was me—"

"Oh, no. I have plans for Lucian Barkridge. He may think he can control a bone witch, and for a short time, I accepted his dominance, but he underestimated me. The bone witches lurk in the shadows for good reasons. Once I take Lucian into our shadow world, he'll never come out. He'll never be seen again. People will wonder what happened to the heartless man who murdered so many innocent people. Justice will be done, but it'll be done using our methods. He will never share the information he has on my daughter." Onyx cracked each knuckle while speaking.

Silvaria grumbled under her breath and cast a worried look in my direction.

"Now you have the skull, you can undo the curse I'm under?" I said.

A flicker of what might have been sympathy passed across Onyx's face before the blank indifference resurfaced. "With a double blast of the curse, you don't have long left. And it seems the skull magic has become unstable through misuse. I suspect that idiot tinkered with it."

"You can't save me?"

Onyx shook her head. "I'll make sure your bones are put to good use once you're dead."

"Don't touch her," Silvaria growled out. "This one is not for you."

They embarked on a glaring contest.

"Save Fire Fang. He's only had a single dose of the curse." I tapped Fire Fang to rouse him.

"I can try. You don't get many creatures cursed by the skull, though. I assume the reversal process will operate using the same method. Either that, or it'll kill him."

Fire Fang grumbled, but he was barely conscious, so he couldn't fight the decision I'd made.

Onyx crouched in front of him. A glow of hazy gray magic formed between her hands, and she ran them from the tip of his nose down to his tail several times.

She pulled back the magic and tilted her head. "He is just a hellhound?"

"Sure. Well, he's crossed with something else, but I've no idea what. Does that matter?"

Onyx tried again. "It's not having an effect. The magic is being pulled in two directions. It's trying to remove the curse from two entities. But that's not possible. What is this beast?"

I rested a hand on Fire Fang's head. "He's unique. And he's suffering worse than anyone else who's been cursed."

"It must be because of the instability of the magic. I'm losing control of it. I feel it seeping through this place."

"Shouldn't you be asking why?" Silvaria said.

My eyes had closed, and I'd blacked out for a few seconds before I jerked awake. "What was that?"

Silvaria huffed out a breath. "Why did Lucian curse everyone?"

I didn't have an answer. Lucian had no motive for killing Delano. His future was now as unstable as the magic in the skull now Delano was dead.

"I need to figure that out," I said. "But I also need to destroy the skull. Onyx, will destroying the skull erase the curse?"

Her lips pursed as she moved to the ghost jar. "Yes."

"Then what are you waiting for? Blast it into dust."

She raised a hand. "Only one thing can destroy it, and I have none of that to give."

"What is it?"

"The only thing stronger than the hatred poured into it."

"There's nothing stronger than hatred," I said.

Onyx moved closer and ran an icy, bony finger down my face. "There is. Love. And lots of it. I hope you have an abundance of love in your life, or this curse isn't going away."

I gulped down my panic. I wasn't in love, I had no family, and Fire Fang just about tolerated me most days. Where would I find such strong love?

"Would killing Lucian destroy the curse?" I said.

"Sadly not, or I'd have done it immediately. But it would still be fun to try, wouldn't it?" Onyx said.

The stray cat, who'd been sitting in the doorway watching us, turned and raced out of the room.

I groaned as my heart thumped too fast. The end felt terrifyingly near, but I wasn't ready to die. I had too many unfinished things in my life.

"Drink more tea and take this potion." Silvaria shoved a vial in my hand and topped up my mug. "This is healing magic. It won't cure you, but it'll hold off the worst of the symptoms."

I downed the bog smelling liquid and potion and was finally strong enough to get to my feet, even though my legs shook. "Thanks. And some for Fire Fang."

"He's a hellhound. They're almost impossible to kill," Silvaria said.

"We kill them," Onyx said. "Bone witches hunt them for fun."

I bared my teeth at her. "Stay away from my hellhound."

"I have no interest in this sad specimen. He's hardly good sport, since he can barely keep his eyes open. Although his mix of power is a curiosity I'd enjoy exploring."

I blocked Onyx's route to Fire Fang, even though a puff of wind would knock me over. "Silvaria, I need him. And he needs your magic."

"Waste of a good spell," she grumbled as she poured tea into a bowl and passed it to me.

I crouched beside Fire Fang and encouraged him to drink. After he'd lapped up the contents of the bowl, his eyes opened.

He staggered to his feet and shook out his fur. "What in the name of Satan's pom-poms is going on?"

"No time to talk. I've figured out Lucian has control over the screaming skull. He's the murderer."

Fire Fang growled deeply. "I never liked that guy. Who's this?" He looked at Onyx.

"Someone you don't want to know." I nodded a thanks at Silvaria. "I need to take the skull."

Onyx opened her mouth to protest, but a look from Silvaria kept her quiet. There was an interesting dynamic going on between these two.

Silvaria shoved the ghost jar at me. "Get it out of my home."

I grabbed the jar, pausing when I got to the door. "Onyx, it wasn't a coincidence you were here, was it? Were you looking for your skull, or did Silvaria send for you?"

She tutted. "A cemetery guardian never sends for a bone witch. They don't have that kind of power."

Silvaria grunted again. "Onyx owed me a favor, so I called it in. I figured if she wasn't involved, she'd know the bone witch who was."

Silvaria had just earned her cruise. And I'd toss in free champagne as well, if I survived. "I appreciate that."

"Get out of here. You witches always bring trouble to my door. Shoo, before I set my corpses on you."

I flashed Silvaria a grin, then dashed out on shaky legs.

"What's the plan?" Fire Fang was staggering on his paws, but kept up as we hurried away.

"It's time to dig into Lucian's past and see what he's been up to in his present. We need to find out why he wanted Delano dead."

I'd been researching on my laptop while sitting in the car outside the Discord house, staking out Lucian for three hours. His limo was parked out the front, and a peek through a window confirmed he was inside.

I had a dozen tabs open on my computer, all linked to Lucian and his rise through the ranks. He'd amassed an impressive fortune over the years, which was mainly invested in property.

Fire Fang was snoozing on the back seat, and I was happy to let him sleep. That curse had done a number on him, and although he hadn't complained once, I wasn't sure he had seven days left or if his clock was running down too fast, like mine.

As for the screaming skull, I'd locked that beast in the trunk.

"This is interesting." I was reading through a list of Lucian's investments after hacking the firewall on his business bank account.

Fire Fang grumbled. "If you're still looking at his financials, it won't be interesting."

"In the last three years, Delano made large deposits into this bank account. At least, it looks like Delano did it. But what if Lucian stole the money? They were like brothers, so Delano could have trusted him enough to give him access to his accounts. Then Lucian could have transferred whatever he liked."

"You think Delano found out, and Lucian killed him because of it?"

"It's one motive. Almost a million has been deposited into Lucian's account over the years. Delano was a wealthy guy, but if he studied his outgoings, he'd realize something was off."

"Why use the screaming skull as the murder weapon?"

"Because Lucian wanted Delano to suffer? As we're experiencing, being cursed isn't pleasant. Maybe Lucian had a score to settle with Delano. No one has said anything good about Delano other than Lucian. He could be lying, and the best friend act is a front."

Fire Fang tilted his head and his ears pricked. "There's a car coming."

We were tucked out of sight behind a row of trees, so it was easy to watch the large, sleek black limousine arrive.

Lucian came out of the front door of the house. He opened the car door, extended his hand, and

Augusta appeared. She grasped his hand and slid out.

Lucian didn't let go of her as they stood beside the car and talked.

"That looks cozy," Fire Fang said.

"It does. Lucian is making himself at home."

"Could Augusta be another reason Delano got cursed? Lucian and Augusta were having an affair and got found out."

"We need to confront him. We know the truth from Onyx, we have the skull, and Lucian's still wearing that ring. It could be enough to get him to confess."

"Since he has that ring, it means the skull is still dangerous to us. We should leave it in the car," Fire Fang said.

"We need it. The way I'm feeling, my magic won't do us much good. That skull is our only weapon."

"I have a few weapons." Fire Fang gnashed his teeth together.

"And they're fine weapons. But you're also cursed and struggling to stay awake."

"It's nothing I can't shake off."

"The skull comes with us. We'll bluff and claim we can control it, too." I sucked in a few breaths, waited until my vision cleared, slid out of the car, and collected the skull. "Let's move."

Lucian and Augusta were heading inside the house as we approached. They turned as they heard us.

"Storm! Have you got news?" Augusta's gaze went to the ghost jar.

"Yes. We know who killed Delano and your servants." My gaze was on Lucian as I spoke.

"That's excellent news," he said calmly. "Come inside and we'll talk." He'd also noticed the ghost jar and wasn't looking pleased. He must have guessed what was inside. Or maybe the skull called to him, like all powerful, dark magic.

"We could. Or you could just confess," I said.

"What does Lucian have to confess?" Augusta said.

The skull rocked inside the ghost jar.

"Storm, you look unwell," Lucian said. "Maybe I overestimated your ability to solve this mystery. You should take a break if you're finding this too stressful."

"Storm knows who the killer is. We need to know what she's discovered," Augusta said. "Although Lucian is right. You don't look well. Would you like to—"

"You go inside. I'll deal with this," Lucian said.

Augusta pursed her lips. "My husband was killed, as were two valuable members of the household team. I deserve to know what's going on."

The ghost jar rocked again, and although my ears had been buzzing since I'd been doubly cursed, I heard it make a little shriek. Was Lucian playing with fire and activating the skull with his ring? Or maybe he was testing me to see how I'd react if the skull kicked off again.

Since I was most likely sucking in my last few breaths, I had little to lose by seeing if either theory was correct. "You shouldn't have messed with me, Lucian. A dying witch is a dangerous witch."

Lucian's tongue flashed across his bottom lip. "Go home, Storm. Your services are no longer required."

"Before I do, I need to do this." I yanked the lid off the ghost jar, grabbed the skull, and pulled it out.

The second it was released, it screamed. And Lucian and Augusta were staring right at it.

Chapter 22

"Admit this is your work, Lucian, or we're all dead." The skull shifted in my grip, but I wasn't letting go. My brain felt like it was boiling. So this was what being triple cursed felt like. My hands were clammy, and I rocked back and forth on my heels, but I wasn't losing the skull. It would have to gnaw my hand off at the wrist before I dropped it.

Augusta was pale as she stared at the skull. "Lucian! What is Storm talking about? What's going on?"

"Do you have something you need to confess?" I said to Lucian.

Augusta clasped his arm. "Say something. Are you involved with this? Do you know about the skull?"

Before Lucian answered, a car pulled up behind us. Hattie and Chilton climbed out.

"Stay back," Augusta warned them. "The skull just screamed at us. We've been cursed."

Hattie and Chilton hurried over, despite Augusta's warning.

"You have control of that skull?" Chilton said to me.

"I don't control it. But I found the bone witch who inherited the skull, and she told me who she gave it to." I arched an eyebrow at Lucian.

He still didn't respond, although he wasn't looking as composed as usual.

I answered the question everyone wanted to know. "The bone witch, Onyx, gave the skull to Lucian. The ring he's wearing means he has power over it. He murdered Delano, Sam, and Suzanne."

Lucian placed his hand in his pocket so no one could see the ring. "Storm, you're unwell. And you're making no sense. These are all delusions. Why would I murder my best friend?"

"And two servants," I said.

He dismissed the comment with a hand wave.

"Lucian, if you had anything to do with this, you must make it stop." Augusta tried to get him to look at her, but he seemed reluctant to make eye contact. That was a sure sign of a guilty conscience.

The front door crashed open, making us jump, and Erik staggered out. His eyes were bleary and his clothes disheveled. "I heard a scream."

"Go inside. You won't be able to help," Lucian said coldly.

"You should all stay," I said. "Lucian has something you need to hear."

"In case the message wasn't clear, you're no longer employed to investigate this mystery. You're incompetent and sick. And it was irresponsible of you to bring that skull here. Augusta is now cursed because of you."

One look at Augusta revealed her doubts about Lucian's honesty. Her face was white and her lips pressed together as she continued to glare at him.

Her gaze met mine. "Storm, how do you know Lucian is involved with this bone witch?"

"I'm not! Don't let this messed up excuse for a witch get to you," Lucian said. "Augusta, trust me. I've only ever had your best interests at heart. The whole family means so much to me."

"I met the witch who gave the skull to Lucian. The only reason she handed it over was because he has damning evidence against her daughter. Evidence he planned to leak to the Magic Council if she didn't do what he told her to do. Which, by the way, is one of the dumbest moves I've ever heard. If you cross a bone witch, your life is over. Just like everyone who's been cursed, Lucian has a ticking clock against his name."

"I'm not worried about some twisted witch with a morbid bone obsession." The sweat on Lucian's forehead suggested otherwise.

"You have met her though?" Augusta said.

He didn't respond.

"Lucian, for whatever reason you did this, it has to stop. If for no other reason than..." Augusta looked at the assembled group, "you love me."

Chilton's head shot up and he stared at his mother. "Lucian is in love with you? What about Dad?"

Hattie shook her head. "You were as bad as each other, carrying on with other people."

Augusta's cheeks flushed, and she lowered her gaze. "I'm sorry you all had to find out this way, but we've been seeing each other for months. We kept it a secret because your father would have terminated the alliance. I couldn't risk my family."

"Are you serious?" Erik roared with laughter. "That'll teach Delano a lesson. Oh, wait. He's already dead. Well, serves him right. Dirty old dog. How does he like it?"

"Be quiet," Augusta and Lucian said at the same time.

Erik wobbled on unsteady knees but kept his mouth shut.

"And that piece of news gives you even more motive for using the skull," I said to Lucian. "You coveted Augusta."

"That's not how it is," Lucian said.

"Now I have your motive, I can message Onyx. Oh, in case you didn't know, she's in Witch Haven. She's looking for you and wants her skull back. She'll tell the truth about what's going on."

Lucian's gaze flicked to the densest patch of shadows. "She's here? That wasn't our arrangement."

"Arrangement! It was you." Augusta staggered back, putting distance between them.

"Onyx is close by, waiting for her chance to strike. You tried to destroy her family, so she's here to return the favor. Tell the truth, and you may get out the other side alive."

"Lucian! Fix this. Deal with this bone witch. You've taken things too far," Augusta said.

For the first time since meeting him, I saw a flash of panic in Lucian's eyes, but it swiftly vanished. "Let her come. I'm loyal to this family."

"Show them the ring you're hiding," I said. "It was made by Onyx. It's how you control the skull."

"If that were true, why did I let the skull scream and curse Augusta?" Lucian said.

"Because you're not in full control. Onyx is close, and that skull belongs to her. She also wears a ring just like yours. And the magic in the skull is unstable, because you've been misusing it. Onyx knows, and she's angry. You'd better pack your bags and run. Oh, wait. You can't. Missing part of a leg bone would make running impossible."

Lucian shifted his weight and shot a worried look at Augusta. "This is all nonsense."

"You limp when you walk, although you've gotten good at hiding it. And when you came to my apartment, it took you ages to get up the stairs. Is that because you're growing back a missing bone? Your payment to Onyx."

"Is this true?" Augusta said. "You told me you injured your leg playing hockey."

"It's nothing. The witch has lost her mind."

"Show me this ring," Augusta said.

"The ring is irrelevant."

"He only started wearing it recently," Chilton said. "I commented on it because it's unusual. Does it really control that skull?"

I looked over my shoulder. "It does. And I can't be certain, but I just heard Onyx cracking her knuckles in the shadows. She'll be here any minute to take you out. What will it be? Take your chances with the bone witch or hand yourself over to the Magic Council? At least with them, you'll get a fair hearing.

The bone witches will boil you up and fight over the fragments."

"Do it for us. Save the family you care about so much. Save me." Augusta grabbed his arm.

Lucian shoved Augusta away. "I never loved you."

Her eyes narrowed. "Say that again."

"I wanted everything Delano had. His house, his money, his wife. I took it all because I could. Because I deserved it."

"You told me you loved me. You said you'd always protect us." Horror was written across Augusta's face, along with a dose of rage. "And you said you'd make Delano see sense. Neither of us were happy, and we wanted our freedom. Then he died, and..." She waved a hand in the air.

"Or rather, Lucian murdered him," I said.

Lucian smirked at Augusta. "Foolish woman. You were so desperate to escape, you'd have believed anything I told you. We had our fun, and I had satisfaction in taking you from Delano, but I'm bored. And Storm has handed me a golden opportunity. She activated the curse and gave you seven days left to live. Then I'll be free of you."

Augusta shrieked and kicked Lucian's injured leg.

He howled and staggered to the side, just as Erik threw himself at Lucian and landed a clumsy punch on his jaw.

Lucian rubbed his leg, glaring at Erik as Hattie pulled him away. "You should think twice about coming for me. I control the skull. I could curse you and your spinster aunt with a snap of my fingers."

"I don't know why you're so smug. You were here when the skull screamed. You're cursed just like me and Augusta." I leaned heavily on Fire Fang as the curse bit through me. There was a coldness in my bones I'd never felt before, and my limbs shook with the effort of remaining conscious.

Lucian held up his hand with the ring on, and another smirk marred his face. "Wearing this ring means I'm protected from the curse. And there's nothing you can do about it."

Fire Fang pounced at Lucian. His mouth clamped over the finger wearing the ring.

Lucian yelped as he fell back, Fire Fang on top of him.

There was a sickening crunch, and Fire Fang bounced away, staggering on his paws.

When I looked back at Lucian, he was clutching his hand. "He bit me!"

Fire Fang paced toward me, his head down and his chest heaving. His nose was wrinkled in a look of disgust.

"Ooooh! You didn't? You bit off Lucian's finger to get the ring?"

He nodded, his mouth full.

I petted his head. "You're such a good boy. Now, let's see what we can do about this skull. There must be a spell that'll destroy it." I tossed the skull on the ground and slammed a devastation spell into it. The spell was illegal, but it had power.

The skull wobbled but didn't break.

"Come on, I have to do this." My magic was sliding around inside me like a first-time ice skater.

Fire Fang mumbled something around the finger, but I couldn't make it out over the intense pounding in my head and ringing in my ears.

"There must be something to neutralize it." I slashed my hands through the air, summoning lightning, but other than a brief rumble of thunder, nothing happened. My magic was dying, along with me.

Fire Fang mumbled again and nudged me with his enormous head, gesturing with his nose to something behind me.

I turned around, not believing what I was seeing. Racing along the driveway was the stray black cat, and right behind her were Luna, Indigo, and Odessa.

"Get out of here," I said. "I've got the cursed skull."

My friends exchanged glances, none of them happy ones.

Fire Fang spat out the finger and stomped a paw on it. "Remember what Onyx said. The only thing that'll destroy the skull is love. And it's right here."

I sank to my knees, my vision blurry. "It's too dangerous to involve them."

"Quit talking like that." Indigo marched over. "And once this is over, we're having a serious talk about what real friendship means."

"You shouldn't be here." My heart pounded as my vision darkened. It was too late for me, but I had to keep trying. My friends couldn't die.

"I've been talking to Olympus," Indigo said. "I know what's going on. This is the screaming skull?"

I nodded. "Please leave."

"Not happening," Luna said. "What's the situation?"

"We've got a ring that controls the skull," Fire Fang said.

"We know what to do," Odessa said. "I've been reading up on cursed skulls ever since it showed up outside your apartment. You didn't fool us with the line about kids leaving it. Everyone form a circle. On your feet, Storm. You join in too, Fire Fang. Even though Storm doesn't admit it, she has a soft spot for you. She might even love you, and we need every drop we can squeeze out of this mess if this is going to work."

I was too weak to fight them. "Don't let Lucian get away. He did this." I pointed him out.

"He's not going anywhere," Luna said. "Why is his hand bleeding so badly?"

"Fire Fang bit off his finger." I leaned on Indigo and Odessa to get upright. It hurt to inhale, so I held my breath.

"Gross. Let's do this," Odessa said. "Feel the love we have for each other. No protesting, Storm. You never say it, but we know how much you care for us. You're always looking out for us."

"Even when you should let us help you," Indigo said. "You wouldn't be in this mess if you did that more often."

I gritted my teeth, focusing on staying alive.

We stood in a circle for several minutes, pulsing out magic across the skull. Although it smoked and shook, it remained intact. The curse wouldn't break.

"Sacrifice," I mumbled. "Bone magic needs sacrifice. The witches take bones to make magic. They must also use it to destroy."

Indigo grimaced. "Does anyone want to give up a bone so we can break the curse?"

"We already have one," Fire Fang said. "Lucian's finger. Let's toss that in the mix, along with the ring." He poked the bloody finger inside one of the skull's eye sockets and stepped back to reform the circle.

It only took a few seconds before the skull wobbled and exploded into dust.

I collapsed into Odessa's arms, exhausted, drained, and covered in bone dust. As I clung to her, I spotted the stray black cat racing off. If I ever saw that furball again, I owed her big time. She'd just saved my life.

⁂

"I'd hate to be in Lucian's shoes." Odessa collected the empty pizza boxes off the table in my living room as I lounged on the couch.

After a day left to recover in bed with Fire Fang passed out beside me, I felt much better. So much so, I'd invited the girls around that evening.

Order had been restored now the mystery of the screaming skull was solved. Although I could still feel bone dust in my hair.

"Same here." Luna was stretched out in a chair beside me, one hand on the pizza food baby in her belly. "He's being fought over by the bone witches and the Magic Council. He's in for a rough ride."

"And he has no one but himself to blame," I said.

"I'm just glad everyone is safe," Indigo said, "and the skull is gone."

"Blasted apart by our everlasting love for each other." Odessa returned with a plate of chocolate and pumpkin spiced cookies and set them on the table. "Even though Storm never admits she loves us, she just proved she does."

I shrugged and stroked my fingers through Fire Fang's fur. I wasn't big on talking about my emotions, but I showed them the best way I could. My friends knew that. They understood I could be prickly and difficult, but that didn't mean I loved them any less.

"Thanks for helping," I finally said.

"We shouldn't be speaking to you," Indigo said. "You kept us in the dark about this case. You almost died because of your stubbornness."

"It was a safety issue. I didn't want any of you getting cursed. Believe me, after having several doses of that curse whack me, it was no walk in the park."

"You don't have to tackle every problem alone. Not when you don't have to," Odessa said. "We're here, and we want to help."

"If that stray cat hadn't terrified us into following her," Luna said, "you wouldn't even be here."

"I might."

They glared at me.

"Fine! I'm aware of that. I owe that cat my life."

"She hissed and spat and snarled until we had no choice but to see what she wanted," Odessa said. "She even took out two scarecrows to reach my farmhouse."

"Does that mean you're moving her in?" Fire Fang said. "I don't mind having a tiny furry turkey gobbler here."

I didn't want to be responsible for another body, even a small furry one, but I'd figure out a way to make things up to that cat. Maybe find her the perfect family to move in with. Something to make her happy.

"I'll think about it," I said.

"That's a no," Luna said. "The cat likes you. You can fit her into your life."

My phone buzzed with a message from Tulip. I bolted upright as I read it.

Take a look at this. I think I found Eden.

My finger trembled as I clicked the picture she'd sent. Although it was blurry, it was Eden.

I was on my feet and heading into the bedroom to grab a bag before I stopped myself. I looked back at my friends, who were staring at me in surprise. Even Fire Fang looked startled by my sudden movement.

"I think... I think I've found Eden." I held up the phone, my hand shaking.

They gathered around me and stared at the picture.

"It could be her," Odessa said. "But I'm not sure."

"I have to be certain. I was sent a lead a few days ago and sent Tulip to investigate because I was involved in this dumb case. I should have gone myself. If I had, I'd have Eden back."

Indigo gripped my arm and squeezed. "Take your time. Don't rush. This isn't the first time you've been sent pictures that look like your sister."

I let out a slow breath, but all I could think about was getting there and checking for myself. "I have to go. I know you all understand."

"Of course we do." Odessa hugged me. "Go. When you get back, you can tell us everything."

"Keep an eye on Fire Fang for me," I said.

"I'm not going with you?" He grumbled out his unhappiness.

"I won't be long. I don't want anything to scare Eden. And you..." I gestured at him. It took a few minutes to get over being terrified when meeting Fire Fang for the first time.

"Turkey basting goblin nobble." Fire Fang stalked away.

I dashed into the bedroom, grabbed a few essentials, and was about to cast a translocation spell to the address Tulip had sent me when my phone rang.

I almost dismissed the call, but it was from the vet, and I'd been waiting to hear about the results on Fire Fang's blood tests.

"Make this quick. I'm about to disappear for a few days," I said.

"Storm, this is Doctor Hooper. Sorry we keep missing each other."

"No problem. You have Fire Fang's results?" I poked my head out the bedroom door. Fire Fang was on the couch, grabbing leftover pieces of pizza crust and cookie.

"I wanted to talk to you rather than send a summary." She drew in a breath. "There's something strange about the results."

"Strange as in an illness?"

"No. Fire Fang is healthy. But I ran the tests three times to be sure what I was seeing. At first, I thought it was an anomaly."

"Go on. I need to be leaving, not talking."

She was silent for a heartbeat. "Fire Fang isn't a hellhound."

"He looks like one. What is he?"

There was another pause. "His test results show he's mortal."

You know what's coming? More books featuring Storm and Fire Fang!

The Case of the Poisoned Pumpkin is waiting for you.

When a drowning turns out to be a poisoning and a hellhound turns out to be a mortal, you know there's trouble ahead...

I survived the screaming skull. Just. But now I have another case getting in the way of finding my missing sister. If only people would leave me alone... but I never let my friends down.

Gaian Grimm died from a misfiring spell. At least, that's what it initially looks like.

Micky Cox is the prime suspect, but then his body is dragged from Serpent Lake, and his accomplice is found on his knees with a fireball about to snuff him out.

What should be a simple investigation turns into a coiled curl of confusion. Why do people keep dying? Is there a connection? And who are the masked magic users who keep following me?

Throw in a poisoned pie, a long-hidden secret that'll blow apart the magic community, and the issues with my hellhound, and I doubt I'll get much sleep any time soon.

THE CASE OF THE SCREAMING SKULL

***

Welcome back to the magical world of Witch Haven for your next adventure with Storm Winter, our jaded witch. She's determined never to give up looking for her missing sister, even if a poisoned pie and a brush with powerful royals get in her way

About Author

K.E. O'Connor (Karen) is a mystery author living in the beautiful British countryside. She loves all things mystery, animals, and cake.

If you want to be part of the Witch Haven crew, practice spells, solve a few murders, spend time with amazing witches and their talking familiars, and get a **free** book, join her weekly newsletter.

Sign up today.

Newsletter:
https://BookHip.com/QKGDWJW
Website:
www.keoconnor.com/writing
Facebook:
www.facebook.com/keoconnorauthor

Also By

Spells and Spooks
Hexes and Haunts
Curses and Corpses
Muffins and Moonlight
Cupcakes and Cauldrons
Pancakes and Potions
Hauntings and High Jinx
Hauntings and Havoc
Hauntings and Hoaxes
The Case of the Screaming Skull
The Case of the Poisoned Pumpkin
The Case of the Cursed Candy
Fire Fang
Silvaria